CARPE DIEM

AUTUMN CORNWELL

SQUARE
FISH

FEIWEL AND FRIENDS

NEW YORK

SQUARE
FISH

An Imprint of Macmillan

Library of Congress Cataloging-in-Publication Data
Cornwell, Autumn.
  Carpe diem / Autumn Cornwell.
    p. cm.
  Summary: Sixteen-year-old Vassar Spore's detailed plans for the next twenty years of
her life are derailed when her bohemian grandmother insists that she join her in
Southeast Asia for the summer, but as she writes a novel about her experiences, Vassar
discovers new possibilities.
  ISBN: 978-0-312-56129-1
  [1. Adventure and adventurers—Fiction. 2. Grandmothers—Fiction. 3. Artists—
Fiction. 4. Authorship—Fiction. 5. Secrets—Fiction. 6. Life skills—Fiction.
7. Southeast Asia—Fiction.] I. Title.
  PZ7.C8164512Car 2007
  [Fic]—dc22

                                        2006032054

Originally published in the United States by Feiwel and Friends
Square Fish logo designed by Filomena Tuosto
First Square Fish Edition: 2009
10 9 8 7 6 5 4 3 2 1
www.squarefishbooks.com

For J.C., my husband and fellow adventurer

Prologue

"July 27: I'm freezing. My head itches. I can't remember the last time I had a shower or anything to eat besides sticky rice. This is not how I planned to spend my summer—or end my life. If only we hadn't answered the door that rainy night in May . . ."

(Scribbled on water-stained, college-ruled
notebook paper with a red felt-tip pen.)

PART ONE

Stateside

CHAPTER ONE
You Can Plan Your Life

THE PACKAGE CAME DURING THE HOUR OF REFLECTION, that sacred time after dinner when we peruse goals accomplished during the day and set goals for the day to come. ("If it worked for Benjamin Franklin, it can work for us," as Mom would say.)

We were sitting in our living room, my favorite room in the house, with its stone fireplace and floor-to-ceiling books—all in Dewey decimal system order. And no TV—because that's "living vicariously through other people." Dad was editing the proofs of his latest book, *How to Increase Your Personal Productivity in 2,000 Easy Steps;* Mom was writing in her *Journal of Excellence;* and I was tackling my Life Goals. This is what I had so far:

VASSAR SPORE'S LIFE GOALS

1. Graduate valedictorian from the Seattle Academy of Academic Excellence (with a minimum of 5.3 GPA).

2. Graduate with honors from Vassar (and receive an honorary certificate because of the whole same name thing) then get PhD in (TBD) from an Ivy League school (TBD).

3. Marry a 6'5" blond surgeon (or judge) for love by age 25; have three children by age 35 (two girls, one boy).

4. Publish the definitive book on (TBD) by age 37.

5. Receive Pulitzer prize.

The particular goal consuming me that evening was #2. Graduate school was only six years away, so I couldn't afford to waste a single minute.

See, I'm not the odds-on favorite to be class valedictorian because I'm extra gifted or super smart. Oh, no. It's because I do the Big P: Plan. ("Chance favors the prepared mind." Louis Pasteur.) My rival at the Seattle Academy of Academic Excellence, Wendy Stupacker, never plans—she procrastinates, then crams. Lucky for her she has a photographic memory. We're tied for valedictorian—for *now*.

Of course I had other personal life goals—just not for my parents' eyes. Like planning my first boyfriend. I had him already picked out: John Pepper. It wasn't that Mom and Dad necessarily wouldn't approve of John Pepper. He was one of the first guys admitted to the Seattle Academy of Academic Excellence once it stopped being girls only. He was tall, blond, dressed in primary colors, aimed to be a neurosurgeon, had only minor acne, and no longer wore thick glasses thanks to laser surgery. He totally fit my prototype. Not that he even knew I was a carbon-based life-form who attended his school. However, once I plan something, it's as good as done. Even if my parents claim I don't have time for serious relationships if I want to get my doctorate at an Ivy League school.

"Boyfriends are like water—endlessly available," Mom told me. "Attending an A-list school is a once in a lifetime opportunity."

I'd refrained from correcting her that water is endlessly available unless you happen to be tented in the Sahara Desert.

"How's this?" I handed my list to Mom, who skimmed, then returned it.

"After the Pulitzer, then what? Think *big*, Vassar."

I thought a moment, then added Life Goal #6: *"Create the Dr. Vassar Spore Betterment Foundation to train the less fortunate around the world how to plan their lives like I did"* and handed it back. Two could play this game.

She laughed. "Excellent! Now that's what I call thinking big. Wasn't that a fun exercise? As W. Clement Stone says, 'Aim for the moon. If you miss, you may hit a star.' Goals give you targets to shoot for. Too many teens today have no idea where they're going. They're lost, they're drifting. Lilith's daughter hasn't even applied to colleges yet—and she's a senior! No wonder she's on the verge of a nervous breakdown." She patted my hand. "Not all parents are lucky enough to have daughters like you, Vassar."

Mom used to be a life coach. Once I was born, she gave up her career. Or, as she puts it: "I switched careers: from life coach to Vassar's coach."

A full-time job these days.

But I actually don't mind the nightly recaps—or visioning for the future. Sure, it borders on geekdom and isn't exactly my first choice how to spend my evenings, but it keeps me organized. And since I'm aiming for the Ivy League, I need all the help I can get. In fact, once a month, Amber—one of my three best friends (and fellow academes)—comes over during our Hour of Reflection so Mom can oversee her daily, weekly, and monthly goal lists. Amber also needs all the help she can get since her parents are sports fanatics and only care about her three older brothers' collegiate football and basketball achievements. Academia holds absolutely no interest for them. Without our support and Mom's guidance, she'd have been kicked out of the National Honor Society months ago.

I'd just finished the pros and cons of a PhD in Physics and was starting on the pros and cons of Archaeology when Amber text-messaged my cell phone: *Have U asked yet?*

I cleared my throat. "Uh, I was wondering, could I skip my Calculus Tutoring Session on Friday night so I can go to the dance?" Not that any guys ever asked us to dance—we all danced in the "four-girl molecule cluster." As if that's how we wanted it. No boys needed here, thank you very much. Better to pretend you don't care—don't care that Wendy Stupacker is always every guy's first choice. *Always.*

Dad looked up from his manuscript. He's an efficiency expert and consultant. Corporations and factories hire him to discover where they are wasting time, money, and manpower—and then to remedy it. In his spare time he writes. This is his second book. The first was coauthored with Mom: *Plan Is Not a Four-Letter Word*.

"Did you say something?" Dad asked, clicking his mechanical pencil.

Mom laid down her pen and asked, "And where is this dance?"

This is where it got tricky. "At the public high school." Before she could respond, I hurriedly used my best ammunition: "Amber's, Laurel's, and Denise's parents are letting them go." In Denise's case, they were forcing her to go. They felt she lacked social intelligence and needed practice in the necessary male-female interaction skills.

"You know how we feel about functions at the public high school. It's not the idea of recreation that concerns us. Of anyone, you certainly deserve downtime activities."

"But you can trust me—"

"Of course we can trust *you*, Vassar. It's the public school crowd we can't."

Stalemate.

"However, as you know, we're not going to tell you what to do," said Mom. "Your father and I reared you to make the right decision. Isn't that right, Leon? Leon?"

Realizing he'd missed his cue, Dad affirmed quickly: "Right, right. The choice is completely up to you."

I hate it when they do that. That's the problem with having parents like mine: You're genetically programmed not to let them down.

"I'll think about it," I said. But we all knew what my "choice" would be. I couldn't bear the looks of disappointment on their faces.

As Mom and Dad went back to their journal and book respectively, I text-messaged Amber: *They said NO. Told U.*

The doorbell rang.

"We aren't expecting anyone, are we?" Mom asked with mild irritation.

Dad and I shook our heads. Visitors during the Hour of Reflection were strictly verboten.

"I'll take care of it." Mom rose regally from the overstuffed chair that threatened to swallow her up.

Although a pint-sized five feet two, Mom carried herself as if she were six feet tall with a crown on her blond bob. Birdlike—but a bird of *steel*. Nothing delicate about her. Dad was only a few inches taller than her, with unruly, reddish-blond hair cropped short, pale blue eyes, freckles, and a compact body in perfect shape for his age—thanks to his daily five-mile run and aversion to beer. Where I got my five feet ten lanky build and dark brown hair and eyes was one for the geneticists.

Mom placed a beige envelope with a mosaic of foreign stamps on the coffee table, next to the tea things.

"UPS. For you, Vassar."

For me? I wasn't expecting anything. I'd already received my Jumbo Wall Calendar for the next school year. What else had I ordered from www.planyourlife.com?

Mom poured boiling water over our tea bags. Herbal.

No caffeine in the Spore household. ("We get our energy from the thrill of a job well done," Mom would say.)

"Who's it from, Althea?" asked Dad, not lifting his eyes from *How to Increase Your Personal Productivity in 2,000 Easy Steps*.

"Your mother," said Mom in a flat tone, showing him the return address: Gertrude Spore.

How to Increase Your Personal Productivity in 2,000 Easy Steps dropped to the floor and a handful of pastel Tums popped into Dad's mouth. Tums were always within easy reach in his breast pocket, since emotions of any sort triggered heartburn. Especially emotions about Grandma Gerd. Dad claimed it was acid reflux, but Mom said it was psychosomatic.

"What does she want? Tell me she's not coming to visit." He chewed rapidly, calcium gathering in the corners of his mouth.

I wiped off the raindrops and examined the cancellation marks. "It's from Malaysia." It was postmarked April 1— my sixteenth birthday, a month and a half earlier.

Dad burped softly.

I sliced open the envelope with a butter knife and removed a plain white envelope and a card made of tree pulp decorated with grains of brown rice in a starburst pattern. I opened the card and read aloud:

"Happy Birthday, kiddo! Can you believe it? I'm sorta on time for once! But, hey, turning sixteen is a BIG DEAL. Open the white envelope."

It was a round-trip plane ticket. To Singapore.

"Ta-da! One all-expense-paid summer vacation backpacking through Malaysia, Cambodia, and Laos—with ME! Southeast Asia won't know what hit it! Toss some drip-dries into a backpack, apply for a passport, and get ready for the adventure of a lifetime. . . ." I trailed off, stunned.

"It's obviously Gertrude's idea of a joke." Mom picked up her *Journal of Excellence* and resumed writing with her fountain pen. (It's her sole inefficiency.)

"But the ticket looks genuine," I said.

"Oh, she's up to something. I can feel it," said Dad, massaging his stomach.

Poor Dad. Not only was he adopted, Grandpa died when he was six years old and Grandma Gerd had flipped out—turned bohemian. She'd disappear for days, carousing with the seedy artists who lived in the seedy areas of Seattle. So Dad was forced to become a man. He wore a little blue suit and hired and fired his own babysitters, shopped, cleaned the house, and even managed the checking account. Mom said it was the "Only Child with the Impractical Parent Syndrome": When no adult seems to be taking responsibility, the child by default *must,* in order to maintain some semblance of a normal life. When Dad met Mom, he was finally able to relax and leave life's more assertive duties to a woman even more type A than him. An efficiency expert and life coach—it was a match made in heaven. (Or, to be more precise: in an office supply store. They simultaneously grabbed for the same Post-it notes.)

"We'll simply thank her and refuse the offer," Mom said, setting her teacup in its saucer with a decisive *clink*. She smiled at me, showing her dimples. "Gertrude just doesn't understand the responsibilities of the gifted student." Mom insisted upon calling me gifted, even though she knew perfectly well my academic record was the product of good planning.

The thing was, I'd never even met Grandma Gerd. Or seen any photos of her—Dad said he "misplaced them." (Highly suspicious, coming from a man who filed his socks. By color.) All I knew was that she was a nomadic artist of sorts. But I always got a birthday present from her, even if it was usually five months late. A Vietnamese mollusk hat on my eighth. A pair of mustard-yellow, pointy-toed Moroccan slippers for my tenth. An oversized leather wombat on my twelfth. And the "collage" made out of a rubber ball and fifteen swizzle sticks on my fifteenth. Then there were all the long-distance calls from Third World countries, with the fuzzy background noise and hollow clicks.

"Strange," I said as I put the ticket back in the envelope. "I wonder what made her send—"

The phone rang.

CHAPTER TWO
Grandmas Don't Blackmail

*I*T WAS GRANDMA GERD. CALLING COLLECT FROM MELAKA, Malaysia. For an artist, she sure had a good sense of timing. Dad chewed yet more Tums as she insisted on being put on speakerphone. Her exuberant voice boomed up at us from the coffee table. Grandma never talked when she could bellow.

"Let me guess: It's your Hour of Refraction. How's my Leonardo?"

Dad hates his flowery given name and insists on being called Leon. Not that Grandma Gerd ever does.

"Reflection," he said in a compressed voice.

A series of throaty chuckles, then:

"Happy Birthday, kiddo! How does it feel to be sweet sixteen?" Then, without waiting for my answer: "So, did ya get kissed?"

"She'll have more than enough time for boys after college, Gertrude," Mom said, in a tone civilized yet squelching.

"Shame. Sweet Sixteen, Never Been Kissed. So how did you celebrate? Tell me you at least had a big party?"

Mom said: "Vassar had an intimate gathering after the Latin Triathlon. Some very nice girls from her—"

"Girls, bah."

Mom opened her mouth, then closed it.

"So, kiddo? What do you think of my gift?"

But before I could respond, Mom said with a plastic smile, her dimples now two craters:

"It was very thoughtful of you, Gertrude. Only a month and a half late instead of your usual five. Unfortunately, it's not on The List."

"The List? What list?"

"Vassar's summer has been planned out far in advance. The List includes AP English, Advanced Latin Camp, a Sub-Molecular Theory course—"

"And? What she misses this summer she can make up the next."

Earth to Grandma! I had the next two summers meticulously planned—all advanced placement courses and extra-curricular activities.

"If I don't keep up with those courses, I won't make a 5.3 GPA—which happens to be the new 4.0," I said. "And then Wendy Stupacker will get valedictorian—"

"Whoa, whoa, whoa. Have you ever floated down the Mekong on a rice boat, lulled to sleep by the rustling bamboo?"

The three of us exchanged long-suffering looks.

"Have you ever climbed the ruins of Phnom Bakheng in

Angkor to experience the most mind-blowing, Technicolor sunset of your entire life?"

I mentally squared my shoulders. Grandma Gerd can be a bit unnerving.

"Valedictorian and a 5.3 GPA are *very* big deals. In case you weren't aware, they mean entry into Vassar and Ivy League grad schools like—"

"Would civilization end as we know it if you went to a state school?"

A collective intake of three breaths. A state school!?!

"Come on, kiddo, don't you want to live, feel, explore, experience—"

"Gertrude, even *you* know this is impossible on such short notice," Dad interrupted. He never called Grandma Gerd "mother." Ever.

"Balls. She'll have two weeks to plan. That's more than enough time."

"Technically, it's one week and six days," he replied.

Mom gave Dad a nudging look. She often has to do this because he's a "conflict avoider." If someone cuts in front of him in line at the DMV—he'll pretend he didn't notice. If a waitress accidentally adds an extra crème brûlée to his bill— he'll pay it. Anything to sidestep confrontation. Reluctantly, Dad cleared his throat and said, "Although it's a very kind offer, Gertrude, it's . . . it's absolutely out of the question."

"*Kopi dua*—thanks." We could hear the clinking of glasses and some static, then: "Well, Leonardo, you're forcing me to bring *it* up. In mixed company, no less . . ."

It?

Mom clutched my arm, her clear-polished nails digging into my skin. "Vassar, would you fill up the car." It was a command, not a request. Her dimples had completely disappeared.

"Don't go to Gus's Gas—his tanks aren't calibrated correctly," said Dad automatically. "And take Franklin Avenue. It's two minutes faster than Main."

Usually there's nothing I like better than to drive the Volvo anywhere, now that I've got my driver's license. But I wanted to witness Grandma Gerd's failed attempts to coerce my parents.

Grandma Gerd's voice again broke the silence. "Hello? Anybody there? Leonardo, it's time she knew the truth about—"

But Mom and Dad simultaneously grabbed for the phone before she could finish.

Truth about what? Well, I'd know soon enough. Mom and Dad never kept secrets from me.

As I carefully navigated the Volvo wagon out of our cul-de-sac toward the nearby gas station–convenience store–coffee shop (not Gus's), I took offense at what Grandma Gerd seemed to be hinting about my life: that just because I hadn't left the continent or backpacked through Europe, I wasn't well-rounded. Could I help the fact that Dad is deathly afraid of flying? Or that Mom's abhorrence of the outdoors ("too many variables") prevented camping from ever being on the agenda? So I hadn't traveled. Who cared? How could that omission remotely affect my life? Or, more important: my academic record? After all, just how many museums, galleries, symphonies, and plays had I gone to? Just how many books had I read? If I wasn't cultured, who on earth was?

And her insinuation that I was somehow abnormal because I hadn't yet been kissed infuriated me. None of my friends had boyfriends yet. The only girl at the Seattle Academy of Academic Excellence with any dating experience was Wendy Stupacker, who'd discovered boys in sixth grade—which certainly hadn't helped her procrastination any. Photographic memory and photogenic looks—tough life.

I returned as swiftly as the speed limit allowed. After parking with precision, I took care to slip through the front door noiselessly. Good. They were still on the phone, so wrapped up in their debate they didn't hear the car. I tried to eavesdrop, but could only make out a random word here and there: "Bubble . . . birth . . . too young . . . rubber ball . . . dying . . . egg . . ."

Then Mom hissed: "Gertrude! It's blackmail, and you know it!"

The words "dying" and "blackmail" especially intrigued me—that is, until Mom said, "Is she back yet?"

"I'll check," said Dad—anything to get out of a Grandma Gerd–Althea Confab.

I darted back into the kitchen and yanked open the refrigerator just as Dad appeared in the doorway. Beads of sweat dotted his freckled forehead, and inkblots of perspiration stained his gray polo shirt. "Vassar? Come in here, please."

"Sure," I said with faux nonchalance as I popped open a can of apple juice.

I followed Dad back through the kitchen into the living room. Mom wouldn't meet my gaze. She concentrated on doodling in her *Journal of Excellence*. I'd never seen her doodle before. This was a rough drawing of a pear. When she noticed I noticed, she quickly turned the page. Dad blotted his face with a paper napkin, leaving a tiny shred of blue stuck just above his eyebrow.

I bent over the speakerphone.

"Hello, Grandma Gerd. I'm back—"

"She hung up," said Mom, her voice shaking. "Leon, why don't you tell Vassar what we've decided."

They made room between them on the couch, so I squeezed in. With a quivering hand, Mom tucked an errant strand of hair back into my ponytail. Dad patted my knee, then ran his hand through his red hair, patted my knee, smoothed his hair, patted, smoothed, patted, smoothed. I'd never seen them so agitated, so awkward, so un-Spore-like. Not even last year, when Wendy Stupacker beat me in the regional spelling bee with "ektexine" and went on to place fourth at the nationals in D.C.

"Yes, well, Vassar, we've decided that a trip with Grandma Gerd through Southeast Asia . . . that such a trip would be invaluable . . . perhaps help you formulate . . . would heighten . . ." Dad stumbled on and on in a highly inefficient manner. What he said was of no consequence. What was important was that they wanted me to abandon my scholastic endeavors for a mere vacation! As soon as Dad brought his babble to a halt, I said as much.

They carefully replied that they thought it would be good for me to go, that I should go, that I *must go*.

What? Were these the same parents who'd previously said the words "Grandma Gerd" with the same note of horror they said "unsystematic" or "waste of time" or "un-planned"? Who were *now* authorizing her to take me—their *only* child—into the intrepid jungles of Southeast Asia? When they'd just dissuaded me from attending a public school dance a mere six blocks away?

"But what made you change your minds? You *never* change your mind."

Dad dug in his breast pocket—empty. He moaned.

Still not quite meeting my eyes, Mom said, "Think how much it would mean to Grandma Gerd to spend some quality time with her only . . . grandchild." I could tell it pained her to say it.

It just didn't make sense. Having a daughter named Vassar *not* get into Vassar would be *sacrilege*. Not to mention embarrassing. And it would disprove Mom's theory: If an applicant to Vassar, the elite women's college, was named Vassar in addition to having a stellar academic record, how could they possibly refuse her? All her advanced planning would be for nothing—and I'd be known as "that loser Vassar Spore who goes to State."

One of Mom's biggest regrets was not getting accepted to Vassar College. She felt life would have been just *that much* better if her dream had been fulfilled. She vowed if she had a daughter, she'd guarantee she got in. "And whether she chose to attend or not would be entirely up to her. But she'd have the option I never had."

But now suddenly that wasn't a priority?

What on earth could Grandma Gerd possibly blackmail my parents about? It was time to be direct:

"Is she blackmailing you? Is 'egg' a code word?"

Mom froze, teacup halfway to her mouth. "Eavesdropping is an odious habit, Vassar! I'm ashamed, *ashamed* of you."

"Odious," echoed Dad weakly. His face was so white, his freckles looked like chocolate sprinkles floating on a latté.

"So," I processed as I went along. "What you're saying is that I *have* to go on this trip at the sacrifice of my academic record."

Mom's face crumpled. She let out a little wheeze. The next thing I knew, she was racing upstairs to their bedroom and slamming the door.

"Excuse me, Vassar." Dad unsteadily got to his feet, then slowly climbed the stairs, keeping a tight grip on the banister.

The *American Heritage Dictionary* defines a nervous breakdown as *A severe or incapacitating emotional disorder, especially when occurring suddenly and marked by depression.* Mom had never broken down before, as far as I could remember.

She'd been firmly in one piece with never so much as a chip missing.

Dad closed and locked the door to their bedroom, but I could still hear uncontrollable sobbing—this from a woman who'd never shed a tear in my presence. (Not even the faintest appearance of moisture when Dad had read *The Yearling* aloud.) I could barely make out Dad's low, consoling murmuring.

Then Mom's voice escalated: "She'll find out—you *know* she'll find out! Gertrude will tell—"

Dad's gentle but firm voice interrupted: "No, she won't. Even Gertrude wouldn't stoop . . ." Then it became muffled and indistinguishable.

After half an hour, Dad abruptly hurried out of the bedroom (carefully closing the door behind him) and drove off in the Volvo. He squealed into the driveway twenty minutes later and dashed into the house clutching a white paper bag in one hand and a traffic ticket in the other. Back into the bedroom, locking the door behind him. Fourteen minutes, thirty-six seconds later—the crying stopped.

I was tempted to call or text-message Amber, Denise, and Laurel. But I dreaded imparting the information that the Spore household was not what it seemed. My friends had always looked up to my parents, wished they were their parents.

"With parents like yours, who needs willpower?" they'd say.

(Wendy Stupacker hadn't been as complimentary. She

said my parents were "weirdos" and that Mom was "over-compensating for hidden inadequacies" and that Dad was "uxorious." But I knew she was just jealous because both her parents were major players in the finance industry and never had time for her.)

I sat motionless on the couch. What on earth could transform my normally cucumber-esque mother into a character from a Tennessee Williams play? And my normally law-abiding father into a lawbreaker?

The Big Secret. That's what.

I felt as if I'd returned from school and accidentally walked into the wrong house.

I felt out of context.

I felt numb.

CHAPTER THREE

The Advanced Latin Study Group
Gals—Minus One

AMBER LEANED FORWARD, HER HUSKY VOICE AN OCTAVE lower than normal: "Listen to this: Sam Westman from study hall said that Tony Keeler who lives next door to John Pepper said that John plans to restore a boat this summer and sail it to Crescent Island for camp-outs. AND that there's a certain girl he'd like to have along—who just *happens* to be in the Advanced Latin Study Group."

She flipped her fire-engine-red pageboy expectantly and ate a thick steak fry off the tray that Laurel was balancing in her right hand—an effort for pint-sized Laurel since she barely reached Amber's shoulders and had wrists like twigs.

"Hearsay," said Denise, not looking up from her Latin textbook as she leaned against the rain-splattered window.

We were riding the 7:04 a.m. ferry crossing the Puget Sound to the Seattle Academy of Academic Excellence. The sky was overcast with streaks of gray, tufts of white, and shards of sun. Drizzling. All our fellow students who lived in Port Ann made the hour ferry ride to and from

Seattle every day. We didn't mind—it gave us two hours a day to do our advanced placement homework, practice our Latin, and eat fries. Once aboard, we'd rush to secure a booth in the concession area—the most desirable section on the boat. Or we'd hover until one became available.

That's what we were doing now: hovering.

Impatient at my lack of response, Amber said with her mouth full of fry:

"Stop being obtuse. Who else could he mean but you, Vassar? The girl he stares at during Latin when he's supposed to be conjugating verbs."

I felt my cheeks get warm.

"Perhaps his laser surgery left him with faulty depth perception," said Denise, flipping a page.

Amber and Laurel ignored her.

There's a chance John Pepper knows I exist? My plan had turned into reality—far faster than I'd expected. I allowed myself to daydream: wind tousling his sun-bleached hair (tousle, tousle, tousle), sunlight glinting off his gleaming teeth, sharing a laugh as together we tug on various ropes to hoist the mainsail. His minor acne disguised by a tan. Wearing his white rolled-up jeans and deck shoes. I grab his muscular arm to steady myself. He puts an arm around my waist and draws me close to his rock-solid— why, oh why, must I be banished to the Malaria Zone *now*!?!

"Vassar? Earth to Vassar, come in, Vassar."

I was back on Earth. Back to reality.

"Soooo . . . what do you think?"

Before I could reply:

"Booth!" Amber shouted, and raced ahead of a forty-ish businessman who was also making a beeline for the just vacated booth. She'd learned something about competition, growing up with those three older brothers. We snatched our backpacks and elbowed past him. He stood there stunned, clutching a croissant and *Wall Street Journal* to his chest as we swiftly slipped past him into the booth one by one: big-hipped, Doc Martens–wearing Amber; delicate Laurel in Laura Ashley and lavender-framed glasses; and sturdy Denise with her round, flat face, blond Dutch-boy bob, and penchant for surf shirts. And me.

Laurel deposited the tray of fries in the center of the table and rubbed her wrists.

"Join us, sir," Amber said sweetly, fluttering her fake eyelashes and coyly tossing her hair. "There's more than enough room."

Miffed, he strode down the aisle.

"Too bad. He was cute," Amber said, shoving another fry in her mouth.

"For a balding, middle-aged, boring person," said Denise.

Amber sighed. No one would ever take her for the Seattle Academy of Academic Excellence's reigning chess champion. She looked like an extra from *Pretty in Pink*. And she was forever having crushes—sometimes three going at once. Or four, if she'd just been to the gym. "He could have taught me the mysteries of the stock market . . . the romance of capital gains—"

"Vassar, what's wrong?" asked Laurel abruptly in her wispy voice, peering at me through her glasses.

"Yeah. You don't look happy that John Pepper *may* like you," said Amber.

Denise looked up from her Latin book.

I took a deep breath. "I have some bad news."

After I finished telling them, there was complete silence. Not even so much as the chewing of a fry. Then:

"An all-expense-paid trip to Southeast Asia! I wish my grandparents gave presents like that. But no, I get a Dr. Scholl's Foot Bath," said Amber.

"You know, it seems so out of the blue. She's never even visited you before," said Laurel. She delicately dipped her fry in ranch dressing.

Denise's face was mauve. "Don't you guys get it? Cannot you comprehend what this means? Now that Medusa-Cyclops-Hydra from Hades-Slag of Slurry will take vale-dictorian! Once again I maintain: There is no God!"

"Ssshhh, Denise," I said, gesturing toward the senior citizens in the booth next to us craning their necks.

"Oh, right—*Wendy Stupacker.*" The normally refined Laurel practically spit the name.

"It's not enough she's rich, drives a convertible with alloy rims, and runway-models part-time in the summer—now she gets val!" Amber's howl was almost as loud as Denise's.

They were taking it harder than I expected. They'd always been indignant on my behalf at the way Wendy had treated me: Wendy and I had been best friends in elementary school and junior high. *The Future Val and Sal,* we used to write in our yearbooks, not caring who got what. But once we hit high school, suddenly I wasn't best friend material anymore. One day Wendy simply stopped returning my calls, replying to my emails, acknowledging me in the hallways, or sitting next to me at lunch. So what used to be good-natured competition turned into a full-blown academic rivalry.

"You were our only hope. And there's no way Denise can surpass her," said Laurel.

Denise had contracted mono (Irony: the kissing disease with no fun to show for it) her freshman year, which put her slightly behind in AP classes. So although she was a certified genius with a 150 IQ, she was in second place behind Wendy and me.

"I can't believe your grandma is doing this to us," said Laurel, shaking her head.

"Why are your parents even letting you go? Have they joined a cult? Been experimenting with mind-altering substances?" asked Amber half-seriously.

Denise fixed me with her protuberant blue eyes—known to disarm many an opponent during forensics tournaments or mathalete competitions. "Why don't I talk to them, reason with them. Stress the detrimental effect this will have not only on your academic career but on the entire Seattle Academy of Academic Excellence. The reverberations will be deadly. Not to mention what it'll do to Wendy's monumental ego. All of Seattle won't be able to contain it."

"Actually, they had no choice—"

Denise cut me off. "Come on, Vassar, it's worth a try. Anything to prevent us having to watch that smug piece of tripe give the valedictorian speech. Anything. Including selling myself as a specimen for science experiments or joining the cheerleading squad—no sacrifice would be too great."

The vision of no-nonsense Denise in a swirly skirt and hoisting pom-poms, performing a routine with mathematical precision momentarily distracted us.

"It's not *that* funny," said Denise.

When we finally stopped laughing, I scanned the booths around me, then lowered my voice. "Actually, my parents were forced into it. Under extreme duress."

The ferry lurched, and we all reached out to stop the plate of fries from sliding off the table.

With their eyes glued to mine, I whispered:

"Blackmail."

"Blackmail!?" they said in unison, their eyes lighting up like the Bunsen burners in our Advanced Chemistry Lab. Denise snapped her Latin book shut. They all leaned toward me.

"Divulge!"

"Spill!"

"Extrapolate!"

The four of us met last year in the Advanced Latin Study Group. We were all able to bypass the regular Latin Study

Group since we'd studied Latin in elementary school and junior high. There were four guys—including John Pepper—and one other girl: Wendy Stupacker.

At that point, I was sick of brown bagging it alone while Wendy lunched with the Seattle Academy of Academic Excellence elite. I complained to Mom. She said I needed to "empower myself" and to be "more intentional" about whom I selected as my next best friend and that I should go about it in an organized, scientific manner—"as if you were doing it for the Science Fair or Advanced Placement Biology."

She was right.

So I created this:

Vassar Spore's Potential Best Friend (PBF) Search

GOAL: *To select a new best friend.*

CANDIDATES: *Denise, Laurel, and Amber from Advanced Latin Study Group*

Denise

BACKGROUND: *Product of college professors—one with a PhD in Physics and the other a PhD in Kinetics. Lives in a condo overlooking the Puget Sound. Her older sister, Fran, failed to inherit the family genes and dropped out of college to sing backup in a garage band.*

EXTRACURRICULAR HIGHLIGHTS: *Head of Forensics Team; Vice President of National Honor Society; fluent in Spanish and German; gaining proficiency in Japanese; Science*

Fair winner; MVP of mathaletes; plays French horn in the marching band.

GPA: *4.8*

COLLEGE OF CHOICE: *Harvard*

LIFE GOAL: *To go into medical research and discover the cure for allergies, cavities, or male-pattern baldness. ("One of those problems that aren't a matter of life and death, yet no one has been able to solve.")*

CONS: *Can be intimidating—impatient with the less intelligent around her. Doesn't know how to have fun.*

MISC: *Although she'll deny it publicly, she collects hippos: figurines, pictures, stuffed animals. Has hundreds of them. Adamant atheist. Her sole nonacademic goal: learn how to surf.*

PBF RATING: *Good*

LAUREL

BACKGROUND: *Lives in a restored 1920s apartment above her mom's shop—the kind that sells bunches of dried roses, handtooled leather journals, and vials of pheromone oil. Single mom who's also petite and flowery—so when Laurel helps out in the shop, the customers always mistake them for sisters. Unlike me, she hates being an only child. ("Then take one of my brothers," Amber told her. "Please!")*

EXTRACURRICULAR HIGHLIGHTS: *President of Etymology Club (three members to date); Secretary of National Honor Society; Captain of Flag Corps; nine years of piano lessons; fluent in Scandinavian languages; volunteers on Wednesdays as a tutor for inner-city kids.*

GPA: *4.0*

COLLEGE OF CHOICE: *Dartmouth*

LIFE GOALS: *Trying to decide between Pediatrician, Child Therapist & Counselor, and Principal of a Private School for Underprivileged Children. Loves—no, LOOOOVES—kids. Wants to adopt ten children of various ethnicities from around the world.*

CONS: *Her mom sews all her clothes. Although not a con per se, too much flora can be tiring on the eyes. . . .*

MISC: *Is the only one of us who's been asked out. (But she's waiting for one guy in particular to get up the nerve to ask: Garrett, who assists our school librarian. Preppy and nice—bordering on so nice, he seems simple. But he's not. He's just . . . <u>nice</u>.)*

PBF RATING: *Very Good*

AMBER

(At first I thought she'd wandered into the Advanced Latin Study Group by mistake, on her way to drama auditions.)

BACKGROUND: *Lives in the suburbs—complete with boat, camper trailer, and three motocross bikes. Her parents work in boring management jobs and live for the weekends. They wish Amber were in better shape to compete athletically like her three older brothers. ("Amber, the last time a big pear won a volleyball scholarship was <u>never</u>.")*

EXTRACURRICULAR HIGHLIGHTS: *Seattle Academy of Academic Excellence chess champion; member of National Honor Society (by the skin of her teeth); does makeup for Drama Club productions.*

GPA: *3.5*

COLLEGE OF CHOICE: *None yet—TBD.*
CONS: *Thinking <u>after</u> speaking. Sneaking cloves on the deck of the ferry. Has no clue what she wants to do when she grows up— no Life Goal (much less what to major in, in college).*
MISC: *Works at a thrift shop on weekends—and spends all of her salary on 1980s clothes. Collects ska albums.*
PBF RATING: *Good—with minor reservations.*

However, it turned out that I didn't have to pick just one PBF. The four of us immediately bonded over our immense dislike of Wendy Stupacker.

By our sixth Advanced Latin Study Group meeting, we were all best friends.

And I didn't miss Wendy one . . . little . . . bit.

Laurel, Denise, and Amber consumed a second course of fries and Diet Cokes as they stared at the words neatly written in blue ink in my notebook.

Bubble. Birth. Too young. Rubber ball. Dying. Egg.

"Dying as in eggs or dying as in dead? Egg as in scrambled?"

"Come on, use your cerebrum, Amber . . . how could that be a blackmail-able offense?" Denise shook her head.

"Hey, we're cerebrum-storming here. You're not allowed to nix any idea. At least until the hypothesis has been proven not—"

"Vassar, sure you didn't actually hear 'leg'?" asked Laurel.

"No, I'm positive it was 'egg.'"

"Maybe it's an Easter-themed secret." Amber slurped the last of her soda.

Rubber ball.

Denise chewed a fry rhythmically as she looked off into space. "The rubber ball is especially intriguing. So innocuous. So seemingly unimportant—but perhaps holding the clue to the entire thing."

"That must refer to the birthday collage she sent me last year."

"Seemingly irrelevant—hence, probably highly relevant," Denise went on.

Too young.

"There are *lots* of things Vassar's too young for. . . ." Amber snorted.

Denise raised an eyebrow. "Thank you, Amber. Your perception is staggering."

Birth.

"Birthday? Rebirth?"

"Afterbirth?" Laurel said, then immediately clapped a hand over her mouth.

"E*www*!" we all said.

Bubble.

"Bubble, ball, and egg are all round."

"Once again, Amber, your ability to state the obvious never ceases to amaze—"

"Ohhh!" Laurel practically levitated in her seat.

Denise whirled toward her: "What? You've discerned a pattern?"

"Aren't they just adorable?" She waved at a class of kindergartners in uniforms wobbling by.

We exchanged looks.

Denise focused stern eyes on Laurel. "Let's stay on task here."

"Oh, sorry, sorry," said Laurel in her fluttery way.

After a few more minutes of brainstorming, Denise finally turned to me and said, "There's no way to figure this out until you get to Southeast Asia. Too many variables, as your mom would say. We need more material to work with."

"Man, Vassar. This sucks. I mean, the trip could be so cool . . . but obviously not at the expense of valedictorian, Vassar, the Ivy League, and all your goals. Talk about having your entire life turned upside down," said Amber.

The ferry lurched again. No, wait. This time it was my stomach.

CHAPTER FOUR

Last Rites

Amicus certus in re incerta cernitur.
A true friend is discerned during an uncertain matter.

DURING LUNCH WE HELD A FUNERAL.
For my valedictorian.

Amber said it would be cathartic—for *all* of us. We buried my hopes in the corner of the soccer field. Denise presided over the last rites. We wore black armbands Laurel made out of construction paper. And we each scooped dirt over a copy of my academic record. Afterwards, we sat in a little circle around the grave and attempted to eat our bag lunches. But no one was hungry. Except for Amber, who was never *not* hungry.

We chose to ignore the stares and snickers of our fellow students.

"Philistines," Denise muttered under her breath as a pack of freshmen boys walked by, pelting us with M&M's.

But Laurel was oblivious to the chocolate rainfall. Picking at her spinach salad topped with sunflower seeds and jicama, she asked: "Why couldn't your grandma take you to Oxford or London? Think of the scholarship, the great thinkers who came from there. Not to mention Stratford-on-Avon."

"Or even Italy. The Sistine Chapel, the Vatican, *David* . . . *David* . . . the oh-so-divine *David* . . . ," said Amber with a cheesy grin. Cheesy because cheddar from her sandwich was stuck in her braces. She subtly picked up two M&M's that landed in the grass next to her . . . and ate them when she thought we weren't looking.

"Angkor Wat in Cambodia is said to be one of the great wonders of the world. Supposedly it surpasses even the Great Wall of China," said Denise. Then, to Amber: "You've got mayonnaise on your chin."

Amber wiped her chin and pointed to Laurel. "Well, she's got spinach between her teeth."

Laurel delicately removed the shred of leaf, then said to me, "I hope you like rice, because that's going to be your primary staple from now on. Mrs. Kawasaki, my piano teacher, says she eats rice for *every* meal. Even breakfast."

We all sat and pondered a life of perpetual rice.

"Malaysia, Cambodia, and Laos. Why couldn't she have started you someplace easier—like Japan?" Amber said. "And where is Laos, anyway?"

Denise took out the mini atlas she always carried in her backpack. "Let's see . . . Laos. Here we are. It borders Thailand and Vietnam. The latitude and longitude of Vientiane, the capital city: 17° 58' N, 102° 36' E."

"Laos. Hope you don't get any lice!"

"The proper pronunciation is 'Lao' like 'Dow,' as in 'Jones,'" said Laurel to Amber.

Then there was a glum pause. All of us trying to think of something positive to say. And failing. The only sound was the crackle of Amber trying to open a bag of honey-mustard pretzels.

Denise slammed her atlas shut. "Come on! The three of us have a collective IQ of well over four hundred. I should think that we could brainstorm a solution to Vassar's Valedictorian Problem. Am I right or am I right?"

"You're right!" said Amber and Laurel.

"Then time for Idea Procreation! We'll give ourselves ten minutes to brainstorm a solution to the problem of Vassar's threatened academic record. Get out your pen and paper. Take it seriously—pretend it's going to count for ninety percent of your SAT score. Operation Damage Control—go!"

Denise's eyes gleamed as she scribbled across the college-ruled paper. There was nothing she liked more than a challenge. She thrived under pressure. The only time I ever saw Denise flustered was around boys. She just didn't know what to say to them. Not that I was any expert—but at least I didn't break out in hives when I got assigned a male Chemistry Lab partner.

Amber's lower lip protruded—signaling an extra-intense level of concentration. When I thought of how she got no attention at home, it infuriated me. Her parents had never gone to even one of her chess tournaments. "If there isn't a ball, there isn't a point," her dad would say. Talk about Philistines.

Laurel's hand fluttered as she wrote her own special short-hand. Her ultrafemininity was deceiving. Though there were German shepherds bigger than Laurel, nothing stopped her when she wanted something. The way she was subtly manip-ulating Garrett so that he'd think asking her out was *his* idea was nothing short of genius.

And here they were, all three of them, collectively com-ing to my rescue.

Who else had such wonderful, loyal friends? Before I could stop them, tears ran down my nose.

"Watch it—you're blurring my ideas," said Amber, mov-ing her paper with its red felt-tip-pen ink away from me.

Ten minutes later, they had it:

I'd simply push Advanced Latin Camp to next summer and take the Sub-Molecular Theory class at the junior col-lege during Christmas vacation. And I would convince Prin-cipal Ledbetter to allow me to write a novel as a substitute for not only the entire class grade in AP English—but also in AAP English: Advanced *Advanced* Placement English.

"But what would my novel be about?" I asked.

Denise gave me an incredulous look. "Your trip, of course. Don't reinvent the wheel. Just write everything that happens to you as fiction. Change the names and there you go."

"If necessary, embellish," said Laurel.

"Or just make stuff up," said Amber, her mouth full of pretzels.

"The plot would be the main character trying to figure out The Big Secret. Like a detective story," said Denise.

"But what if I never find out?"

"Then that'll be your ending,"

"What if it's really boring? Do you think I'd still get credit?"

Denise shrugged. "Why not? Look how many boring novels get published every year in the name of literature."

"And actually win prizes for being so boring," said Laurel.

"Yeah, being boring must be some sort of prerequisite," said Amber.

It was worth a shot.

I blew my nose. My parents may have let me down, but my friends sure didn't.

"Besides, colleges are very hip on the whole intercultural/cross-cultural experience," Laurel said.

Denise added: "And I guarantee you, a novel about your travels in Southeast Asia will definitely increase your odds of getting into Vassar, *Vassar.*"

"And the best part: It would put you ahead of Wendy!" Laurel could hardly contain her excitement.

"So? What do you think?" asked Amber.

One by one, I looked at each expectant face. Then said: "Wendy will make a fine salutatorian."

They all jumped up and cheered in Latin:

"Euge!"

A green M&M sailed through the air and bounced off Denise's forehead.

After all, how hard could it be to write a novel about *me*?

CHAPTER FIVE

Never Mind

*I*COULDN'T WAIT TO TELL MY PARENTS THE BRILLIANT Plan. I especially hoped it would make Mom feel better— that not all was lost in my academic career. I was determined to produce the best novel ever written by a sixteen-year-old. My plans didn't stop with valedictorian. Oh, no. I would publish this book and become a teenage personality. With sales in the millions. Interviews. Book tours. Magazine covers. My own fan club.

Wendy Stupacker would be reduced to a mere gnat in the scheme of things.

And John Pepper would have the excuse he needed to ask me out.

Every Ivy League college would be asking—no, *begging*— me to grace their campus with my presence.

Normally, when Dad came home from work he'd immediately change into his yellow jogging suit with the green stripes for his run. Then he'd clock in his time on the chart stuck to the refrigerator, next to my daily schedule. And after school, I'd help Mom in the garden. For someone usually so immaculate, she sure loved mucking around in the dirt and adding decaying vegetables to her compost heap. If it was raining, we'd play Boggle or Scrabble until Dad finished his run—he ran rain or shine. Then Dad and I'd prepare dinner while listening to NPR.

But not tonight.

Tonight, Mom "hermitted" in her room, and Dad slumped at the kitchen table. His normally crisp button-down shirt was rumpled, and a thin line of missed hairs glinted along his left jaw.

"Hi, Dad."

He jumped. "Vassar!" He stared at me as if our next-door neighbor's basset hound had walked into the kitchen on two legs and addressed him by name. Then he snapped out of it. "How was school?" But before I could answer: "You'll certainly be missed around here this summer. If only your mom and I could have—" He stopped short.

"Could have what?"

"Never mind. Never mind. You know your dad's just an old softy." He stood up and poured himself a glass of water.

I hugged him. "I wouldn't trade you for any other dad in the world."

That choked him up. He gave me a tight squeeze back, sloshing water onto the floor.

Then before I could stop myself, I asked, "Dad—what's The Big Secret?"

He froze—then backed away from me, spilling more water down the front of his shirt. He actually looked . . . *scared*.

"Come on, you can tell me. I promise I won't tell Mom."

He just stood there, mute. As if not trusting himself to say anything without her there to chaperone.

Then he turned and tore precisely one square off the paper towel roll and wiped up the floor. "I'm sorry, Vassar. I can't . . . I can't talk about it." He wouldn't meet my gaze.

To prevent any other questions, he quickly removed precut vegetables and meat from the refrigerator and busied himself with dinner. He and Mom always set aside Sunday evenings to plan and prep meals for the week ahead, so each day of the week had its own plastic container. *Tuesday's Dinner:* stir-fry. ("If only people would realize that plan equals freedom. Once you plan, you don't have to waste time every day rethinking the same issues, remaking the same decisions," Dad would say. Often.)

Forcing a jovial tone, he said, "An exotic meal for you tonight, Vassar: mushrooms, sprouts, onions, sliced rib eye— over rice. Stir-fry. This'll help prepare your taste buds for Southeast Asian cuisine." He opened the refrigerator. "Let's see. Where's the ketchup?"

I knew I wasn't going to get anywhere with him. So, while I set the table, I told him The Brilliant Plan. He was just as impressed as I was.

"We can always use another author in the family. Why don't you go on up and tell your mom? She needs to hear this. It'll perk her right up." He looked at his watch. "Dinner will be ready in eight minutes and fifteen seconds."

As I headed up the stairs, the phone rang. Dad answered.

"Oh, hello, Amber. . . . Late for what? . . . Tonight? . . . Unfortunately, Althea will have to reschedule. There will be no Hour of Reflection in the Spore household to-night. . . ."

As I entered their bedroom, Mom quickly slipped a book under the mint-green duvet. But not before I saw the cover: a buxom maiden kissing a muscular farm lad who seemed to have misplaced his shirt.

I sighed. My numerous attempts to steer Mom toward works more literary had failed. There sat *Don Quixote, Tristram Shandy,* and *The Portrait of a Lady* in a patient row—untouched—on her bedroom bookshelf. For a woman who was highbrow in every other area of her life—including a fondness for Puccini—she certainly sank low in the fiction department.

Mom looked strangely fragile and vulnerable without makeup, wearing bifocals and a beige cotton nightgown. I'd never noticed the deep lines between her eyes, or how far the corners of her mouth drooped when she was fatigued. Moss-green walls combined with the mint duvet created the illusion she was drowning in a vat of split-pea soup.

She struggled to sit up, adjusting the pillow behind her back.

"Sorry about last night. I wasn't—it must have been something I ate. But I'm feeling much better now."

Since when did beef Stroganoff upset anyone's stomach?

I noticed a bottle of pills on her nightstand.

Great: Grandma Gerd is driving Mom to self-medicate.

"Up for a rousing game of Boggle?" I shook the plastic box of dice enticingly. "Come on, you know you are. We have eight minutes until dinner. And you owe me a chance to even the score."

She managed a weak smile. "Maybe later."

I set the game down on her nightstand. Then, in as peppy a tone as I could muster: "I have some news that'll cheer you up."

But The Brilliant Plan didn't seem to make a difference. Her eyes still held an expression of foreboding. The lines were still there. Her mouth still drooped. Apparently, my odds of making or not making valedictorian were secondary to The Big Secret.

She stared at me a moment, then asked, "Vassar, are you happy?" As soon as she said it, I could tell she wished she hadn't.

"Happy? What do you mean?"

"Oh, you know . . ." She forced a light tone. "Has your life so far been a happy one?"

I'd never really thought about it. "Why wouldn't it be?"

She considered for a moment, then lightly shook her head. "Never mind. Is that stir-fry I smell?"

"Want me to bring you some?"

"No!" The very idea seemed to turn her stomach. "You eat with Dad. I'll just have . . . toast and broth. Afterward we can start on your packing list. After all, it's only twelve more days until . . . until . . ." Her voice cracked as she reached for a Kleenex.

And I slipped out the door.

CHAPTER SIX

You Can't Over-Prepare

YOU CAN'T SIMPLY UP AND GO TO SOUTHEAST ASIA. ESPE-
cially into the Malaria Zone. Oh, no. You need shots,
malaria pills, a passport, and a whole drugstore of "just in
case" medicine.

Luckily, over the years my forward-thinking parents had
instructed our family physician to give me every vaccina-
tion on the market: "Never know what you can pick up
these days on the streets of Seattle—or in homeroom," said
Mom. And all three of us had our passports—"In case we
should ever need to leave the country at a moment's notice," said Dad. Not that we'd ever used them. So, the fact I
only had thirteen days to prepare turned out to be less the
logistical nightmare it should have been.

However. Since I was leaving the weekend after school
let out, I had no time to research Malaysia, Cambodia, and
Laos. No time to *plan*. This made me itchy. But I figured
Grandma Gerd had some sort of itinerary for the summer.
And I'd just have to catch up on my research on the
plane—after all, I had twenty some hours in the sky to read
all my guidebooks and reference materials.

In the thirteen days before my departure, my moods fluc-
tuated. One minute my heart thump-thumped in anticipa-
tion of the exotic adventure before me, and the next minute
I was slammed with a wave of intense homesickness—
though I hadn't so much as set one foot on the plane.

And then there were the conversations between Mom
and Dad that came to a halt the second I entered the room.
And the way they still couldn't quite look me in the eye.
Mom wasn't writing in her *Journal of Excellence*. Her garden
was left to fend for itself. Even her best friend, Lilith,
couldn't snap her out of it with long, gossipy phone chats,
brunches on the waterfront, or her all-time favorite warm-
weather perk: Puccini in the Park. It was as if she was in
limbo—waiting for something. Something not good. Her
normally optimistic outlook on life was replaced with
shadowy uncertainty. She sighed. A lot.

Dad worked, ran, and proofed his book. Although he
kept up his routines, he was on autopilot . . . enveloped in a
mental fog. At dinnertime, he couldn't seem to finish his
meals. He actually left half of his favorite entrée (broiled
salmon with mango chutney and okra) on the plate.

But Laurel, Denise, and Amber were enjoying themselves immensely. They strode down the school hallways,
three abreast, with mysterious looks on their faces as if
they were all part of a conspiracy (which I guess they
were . . .). And would break into laughter for no reason.
When Wendy Stupacker passed by, they'd whisper under
their breaths: "Checkmate, Stupacker!" (Amber). *"De inimico*

non loquaris sed cogites!" ("Don't wish ill for your enemy; <u>plan it</u>!") (Denise). Laurel was too ladylike to utter threats. Instead, she'd narrow her eyes and purse her lips in an attempt to look menacing—and succeed only in looking constipated.

They planned out their summer: AP classes, college seminars, and daily meetings at a local coffee shop to work on homework, email me, and edit my manuscript pages.

I realized I'd give anything to switch places with them.

Not that I'd ever admit it.

They were counting on me.

"Postcard labels?"

"Check."

"PTP?"

"Check."

"Ticket, passport, ATM card, extra cash?"

"Check, check, check, and check."

"Laptop with accoutrements?"

"Check."

"The Traveler's Friend–brand travel accessories in their entirety?"

"Check."

"All three *Genteel Traveler's Guides* and three *Savvy Sojourner's Guidebooks*?"

"Check."

"Water purifier?"

"Nice try, Dad. You know very well that's covered under the subcategory of Traveler's Friend–brand travel accessories."

"One hundred and fifty-three items. Looks like you've thought of everything," said Dad, handing me the itemized Packing List and pink highlighter.

"*Numquam non paratus*—never unprepared."

He gave me a wan smile. "I'll go put on my back brace so I can load up the cars." Then he headed up the stairs.

With a grunt, I snapped the last of the locks on my ten pieces of black luggage, which filled the entire living room—the reason we had to take both Volvos. I carefully tucked the keys into the flesh-colored money belt hiding under my Traveler's Friend Linen Blouse and zipped it shut. Denise, Laurel, and Amber all watched solemnly, sandwiched between my suitcases. This was a portentous occasion. The farthest Laurel and her mom had traveled was to the Grand Canyon. Amber's family skied Vail in the winter and jet skied Newport Beach in the summer. Denise's family had been as far north as Banff and as far south as Cancún. And no Spore had ever left the state.

Until now.

Oomp pa pa! Oomp pa pa! I checked my PTP—Portable Travel Planner. A going-away gift from my parents. A matchbox-size Dayplanner Organizer/watch/mini-computer/cell phone/compass/atlas/encyclopedia all in one, conveniently located where my watch would be.

"My PTP has just informed me that I have four hours before my plane takes off. So we'll be departing for the airport in exactly thirty minutes."

"What song was that? Sounded like our school's marching band," said Amber, unwrapping some Red Vines.

"John Philip Sousa. Dad programmed it."

Laurel daintily blew her nose, then tucked the Kleenex into her periwinkle skirt pocket. "Vassar, you won't forget my spoons, will you?" She'd given me $100 to buy a silverplated sugar spoon from each city I visited. It was a habit she'd picked up from her grandma—who happened to be one of the more traditional variety. "I want to add to my collection." ("Collection" in her case meaning two: the Grand Canyon and Yosemite.)

"Well, it's on my To Do List, and if it's on my To Do List—"

"It's as good as done," said Amber, Laurel, and Denise together.

Laurel handed me a bundle of little white envelopes. "Open one a day for a quote that should in some way pertain to your trip."

"They're in Latin," said Amber.

"To keep you mentally supple," said Denise.

I opened the first envelope, labeled "Day of Embarkation," and read:

"*Da mihi sis crustum Etruscum cum omnibus in eo . . .*"

Amber and Laurel laughed uproariously.

"I don't get it—"

"Substitute *'pizza'* for *'crustum,'* and you'll die laughing," said Denise drily.

" 'I'll have a pizza with everything on it.' Ah, yes, that'll sure come in handy in the jungle."

I read another one: "Are you in *omnia paratus*?" I smiled. "Yes, as a matter of fact, I *am* 'ready for anything.'" I gestured at my mountain of luggage. "Everything I could possibly need is in here. Even a collapsible plastic shower."

Dad walked by wearing his black back brace. "Ladies, you have six minutes, forty seconds to say good-bye to Vassar." He headed outside. I heard the beeps of the Volvo alarms.

Denise got down to business:

"So, the plan is that you'll email us each chapter via hookup or Internet café—apparently there are tons of them all over Southeast Asia. Especially in places where the backpackers loiter. We'll proofread them and let you know if something isn't clear. By the end of the summer, you should have a completed first draft ready to turn in."

"That'll give you two weeks to edit before turning it in to Principal Ledbetter," said Amber.

Good ol' Principal Ledbetter. After much persuasion, she'd agreed to let me write the novel for AP/AAP English credit, but with one stipulation: "It must be turned in on the first day of school, to count. Is that clear, Vassar? There will be no extensions or exceptions." It would be a tight squeeze—but well worth it.

I sniffed. I'd succumbed to emotion more times in the

last two weeks than the rest of my life combined. "You guys . . ."

"Vassar, you'd do the same thing for us," Laurel said, blowing her nose again. By now, her skirt pockets were bulging with used tissues.

"And don't waste time emailing us personal messages or travel details," said Denise.

"Or buying us souvenirs," said Amber.

"Except for my spoons," said Laurel.

"Spend your energy writing those chapters," said Denise.

Then Amber pulled a small box out of her backpack. "It's from all of us. Bon voyage!"

"*Bona fortuna!*" said Laurel.

Good luck. I sure needed that.

I opened it. A necklace with an inscribed silver medallion: *Nulla dies sine linea.*

" 'Not a day without a line,'" translated Denise. "A simple yet constant reminder of what you're there for."

"It's real silver," said Laurel.

"Oh, you guys!" I snatched one of Laurel's Kleenex.

"Watch out—you'll tarnish it," said Amber.

"If John Pepper asks about you, we'll give him your email address," said Laurel.

"But *only* if he asks," I said firmly.

Amber nodded. "Yep. Hard to get. That's the way to play it."

Denise rolled her eyes. "Such wisdom, O experienced one."

"Time's up, ladies," Dad called.

We visibly deflated.

I hung the necklace around my neck and hugged Laurel, Amber, and Denise good-bye.

"Oh, wait. Can you give this to your mom?" Amber shoved a wrinkled piece of paper into my hand. "My Summer Goal List. I was supposed to turn it in at the last Hour of Reflection, but—"

"Why is it so sticky?" I distastefully held it by a corner.

She licked her fingers. "Honey-mustard dressing?"

Then, as the three of them walked out the door, Denise added:

"By the way, I've been pondering those words you overheard. You should focus on cracking the term 'egg'—no pun intended. My sixth sense tells me it's the key to the whole thing. Perhaps it concerns a poultry-related tragedy. Diseased hens laying tainted eggs—from hen to egg to dying. See the trajectory?"

"Thanks, Denise. I'll definitely keep that in mind."

Then they were out the door.

I polished my medallion.

I missed them already.

CHAPTER SEVEN
No Matter What

WHEN WE CHECKED IN WITH SINGAPORE AIRLINES AT the Seattle-Tacoma International Airport, Dad had to pay a fee for my extra pounds of luggage. While he was taking care of it, Mom tugged my arm—the familiar cue that she wanted to whisper in my ear—and I bent my head down to her level. She gave me the usual Spore Family Pep Talk Suitable for Any Auspicious Occasion and ended with:

"Oh, and Grandma Gerd may tell you some strange stories, but don't believe a word of them. Especially if she's been drinking—"

Before she could finish, Dad reappeared with my claim tickets. She coughed, then said, "And that's why hydration is absolutely vital in humid climates."

If Dad was suspicious, he didn't let on.

"A couple hundred dollars is a small price to pay to ensure you'll be prepared for every emergency," Dad said as— *zip zip!*—I tucked the claim tickets into the money belt under my blouse.

Then Dad handed me a rectangular wrapped gift. "For the plane."

As I unwrapped it, Dad whispered to me, "Please send only positive emails and postcards. I don't think Althea could handle even the faintest hint that you're not happy. Of course, if there's an emergency—God forbid—that's another story."

During the last two weeks, Mom and Dad had experienced a complete role reversal. He was now taking charge, and she was happy to let him. It unsettled me.

"*The Efficient Teen—Special Annotated Edition.* Thanks, Dad." Actually, the book could prove a liability since I was supposed to stay awake as long as possible on the flight to prevent jet lag.

All too soon we were at Gate 24. I secured the locks on my carry-on bag and my laptop case-slash-briefcase combo, then double-checked that my money belt was zipped.

Mom tucked something into my hand. "International calling card. Because your PTP cell phone may not work over there. Call us if anything—*anything*—happens. Promise?"

"Promise."

"Nervous?" asked Dad, his pale blue eyes starting to water.

I kissed his freckled cheek. "I'm prepared. As you've always said, preparation eliminates anxiety. Why would I be nervous?" But inside, my stomach whirled like his motorized tie rack.

Dad popped a couple Tums. Mom gulped down one of her new pills when she thought I wasn't looking.

"Singapore Airlines Flight 273 to Singapore now boarding. . . ."

Group hug. I kissed the top of Mom's blond bob and Dad's red fuzz—then broke away quickly. Time to get it over with. Couldn't let Mom see me get emotional.

I handed the flight attendant my boarding pass and refused to look back as I walked down the gangplank to the plane. Their sad, pensive faces were too much to take.

Their voices echoed after me:

"Remember to do those isometric exercises in your seat!"

"Apply sunscreen at least fifteen minutes before sun exposure!"

"Take your vitamin C packets hourly!"

"Don't forget you're a Spore!"

They were just being parent-y. Showing me they were "fine."

"Mask!"

Ah, yes. The white surgical face mask to cover my nose and mouth. "You can't take chances with your health, especially on planes, those virtual war zones of airborne germs," Mom had said. And had instructed me to wear it the *entire* time on the plane. "You'll have the last laugh when you arrive in Singapore flu-free."

Oh, there'd be laughs, all right—mocking laughs from the flight attendants and fellow passengers. The face mask was buried deep in my carry-on. And there it would stay. What Mom didn't know wouldn't hurt her.

Just as I walked through the airplane door, Mom's last words pierced the air:

"We love you—*no matter what!*"

I sat next to a goateed businessman wearing a brick-red tie and a blue button-down shirt with MCT embroidered on the pocket. He was drinking a beer and reading a newspaper—which he folded up the second I fastened my safety belt.

"Hi! First time to Singapore? My seventeenth. Ah, yes, the privilege (or is it a curse? Ha-ha!) of the field service engineer in the global semiconductor industry. Heard of semiconductors? No? Well, you should. There's a semiconductor in that laptop of yours. See this?" He pointed to his tie tack, which was a shiny metal-and-copper square. "This little beauty here is what makes all your electrical components work. . . ."

He proceeded to regale me with the entire history of semiconductors until three beers later he mercifully fell asleep.

I noticed everyone around me was sleeping, so I risked putting on the white face mask. After all, better safe than sorry. Then I blew up a neck pillow, stuck in orange earplugs, set up a portable folding footstool, and took out my laptop.

Not a day without a line!

I typed: *A Novel by Vassar Spore.*

Then stopped. The Big Secret beckoned me. I typed the words I'd overheard barely two weeks ago:

Bubble. Birth. Too young. Rubber ball. Dying. Egg.

All together they added up to something capable of sending Dad for Tums and Mom for Valium.

But before I could brainstorm any further—I fell asleep.

PART TWO

Malaysia

CHAPTER ONE

The Malaysian Cowboy

WHERE WAS BAG #8? BAGS #1 THROUGH #10 WERE all accounted for, with the sole exception of Bag #8. They stood in a row like soldiers, each black piece affixed with a giant chrome VS. ("Much more efficient once you're in baggage claim. Saves you at least thirty seconds per bag identification," Dad had said. He was so right: Not one other passenger had giant chrome monograms.)

I moved closer to the baggage claim conveyor belt to scrutinize every suitcase chugging by.

Ahh! There was the tardy Bag #8 finally sliding down the chute, easily identifiable from all the other black suitcases. With the help of two kindly businessmen, I loaded Bags #1 through #10 onto four luggage carts.

"Starting your own import-export business?" asked the heavy one, winking at the thin one as he plopped the last bag on the pile.

"No, simply prepared," I said.

The rest of my flight had been uneventful—except when I lined up for the bathroom forgetting I had my face mask on. Highly embarrassing. Especially when I made a toddler cry.

I consulted my PTP and scrolled through the To Do List Upon Arrival: *#1: Arrive safely, disembark at 3:05 p.m. (don't forget anything!), and get luggage. (Check!) #2: Meet Grandma Gerd in airport lobby. #3: Drive from Singapore to Melaka, Malaysia (time frame approximately three hours).*

It took a bit of maneuvering to propel all four carts into the lobby—that and help from various middle-aged men who just could not stand by and watch as I inched my way across Singapore International Airport. As I guarded my ten pieces of VS luggage, I searched the milling Asians, twenty-something U.S. and Canadian backpackers, and business-men and businesswomen. Over in a corner, a pack of international engineers gathered under a royal blue banner that read: MODERN COMPONENT TECHNOLOGIES ANNUAL SEMICONDUCTOR CONFERENCE! They all wore white polos or button-down blue shirts with royal blue MCT logos whether they hailed from America, Africa, or Asia.

But I saw no one who looked grandmotherly. Not that I was worried. After all, my flight had been early. Grandma Gerd still had exactly nine minutes and twenty-four sec-onds to meet her granddaughter.

"Hey, little lady. You dropped your money belt," said a husky male voice with a slight twang.

An Asian guy a couple inches shorter and a couple years older than me pointed at a flesh-colored money belt at my feet. He wore a straw cowboy hat, a button-down Western shirt, jeans, boots—and thick black sideburns shaved to points on either side of his mouth. He sucked on a Chupa sucker, the white stick shifting side to side. I involuntarily backed away.

"Oh, no. Mine's around my . . ." But before I could say "waist," he picked up the money belt, unzipped it, pulled out the passport, flipped it open, and read, "Vassar Spore—what, no middle name? Born 19—"

I snatched the passport out of his hand and, in doing so, managed to drop my leather briefcase—sending all six travel guides whizzing across the airport floor, narrowly grazing the feet of two passing Thai flight attendants.

"Good aim," he drawled. "Somebody bowls."

I scrambled to retrieve the guides and briefcase. He followed me, his boots making loud staccatos on the tile floor.

"Mis-sus Vas-sar Spore. What's it like bein' saddled with a name like that?"

Since *ignoring* wasn't working, I tried *dismissive*: "Thank you for my money belt and passport. Good-bye." I couldn't believe my money belt had slipped right off me! It must have been all that physical exertion with Bags #1 through #10. In the future, I'd have to cinch my money belt extra tight. Thank goodness it had happened in a relatively safe environment. I pushed the record button on my PTP:

"Note to self: Buy safety pin for money belt cinching."

As I turned away, a warm hand gripped my arm.

"What's your hurry, little lady? Hanks Lee," he said, and held out his hand. "Hanks plural, not singular."

I hesitated, wondering whether it was advisable to shake

hands with a strange guy, especially one with unfortunate facial hair channeling John Wayne—or was it Elvis?

"Hanks, the van's here," my seatmate, the American engineer with the goatee, called over to him, motioning for him to join the rest of the Modern Component Technology group.

While "Hanks" was thus distracted, I backed away, leaving him standing there with his hand extended. I painstakingly pushed all four luggage carts towards the front entrance—which was easier said than done, especially with one hand guarding my waist. *Are all Southeast Asians this forward?* From the movies I'd seen, I expected gracious, polite, retiring types. And I would never have taken that "cowboy" for an engineer! What a strange world this was.

As I slowly made my way through the glass doors of the airport (inching each cart forward ten feet at a time), humidity enveloped me like a warm, damp towel. My skin—used to the mild Pacific Northwest—didn't know what to make of such a climate. Each pore independently opened and secreted moisture.

Bodies surged forward, waving papers printed with RAFFLES, THE LAMBERTS, STEPHEN CHO, MR. JOHAANSON, TURTLEDOVE HOSTEL, and ANNE MILKY written on them—but no Vassar Spore.

"Whoa there, don't go runnin' away now. Aren't you the same Vassar Spore who needs a ride to Melaka?" There he was again. He pulled a folded-up piece of paper out of his back pocket.

So after sneaking a look at my passport he thinks he can lure me away to who knows where?

I decided to nip this in the bud. "Thank you for your concern, but I don't need your help."

Without missing a beat, he refolded the piece of paper and returned it to his back pocket.

"Someone's awful cocky for a non-traveler."

How did he know I was a non-traveler?

"I'm not a non-traveler. I know exactly what I'm doing."

"All righty, then," Hanks said, backing away, his arms in surrender position, his boots clicking.

I checked my PTP: one minute, seventeen seconds left. My first time in a foreign country and no Grandma Gerd to pick me up. Why was I not surprised? I should have *planned* on her deserting me. Maybe she honestly forgot I was arriving today. I started perspiring even more. Mild panic set in. *Breathe in, breathe out.* Head between my knees, my ponytail grazing the floor, I gulped air as I tried to focus.

Upside down, I saw *him* watching me from the MCT group, not at all hiding the fact he was laughing at me. He said something to the engineers, and they laughed with him. Then they all migrated toward a line of silver vans, each one with the Modern Component Technology logo on the side.

Should I hire a taxi? After all, I knew the name of the guesthouse in Melaka: The Golden Lotus.

I tried my PTP cell phone. No reception.

International calling card to the rescue!

Although they must have been sleeping, Mom picked up on the first ring, her voice completely alert.

"What is it? What's happened? Are you hurt? Stranded? Sick? In prison? Abducted?"

I had to remain calm for her mental well-being. "The good news is, I've arrived safely—other than being bored to death by the businessman sitting next to me who may have had the beginnings of a cold. But fear not, I wore my mask. The bad news is—" Careful, Vassar! "Uh, not so much bad as *unfortunate* . . . Grandma Gerd isn't here to pick me up—"

"What!?!"

Uh-oh.

I could hear Dad's sleepy yet concerned voice in the background, "Give me the phone, Althea. I'll take care of this. Come now, let go of the—"

"Mom, don't worry, I'll be fine," I said in as cheerful a tone as I could muster. "I'll just get a taxi—"

"By yourself!? Alone!? Stop it, Leon, I'm talking to Vassar!"

There were rustling sounds, then Dad got on the line. "Vassar, what's going on?"

"Sorry, about this, Dad. It's just that—"

"Vassar Spore?"

I wasn't forgotten after all! I whirled around to behold a fifty-year-old Asian man wearing the crispest of crisp white MCT polo shirts and a mild frown. He had a slight stoop, a comb-over, and silver-rimmed bifocals.

"Yes, I'm Vassar Spore. Are you—"

"This luggage cannot all be yours," he said in an emotionless, abrupt tone.

"Well, yes, it is—"

"It was my understanding you were only staying the summer. Obviously, I was misinformed."

"Actually, I am—"

"Henry Lee, Sr.," he said, holding out his hand. "I sent my son to find you. However, he cannot accomplish even the simplest of tasks."

"Oh, so that was your—"

"Gertrude is waiting for you in Melaka. She was not able to meet your plane. Fortunately, we were coming here to pick up the engineers for the conference."

I felt oddly depleted. Henry Lee, Sr. was the type who sucked all the energy out of the room even before he'd stepped through the door.

"Dad? Grandma didn't forget after all. Tell Mom everything's fine. I'll email you later."

After hanging up the phone, I followed Mr. Lee over to the last remaining MCT van. I should have known. He slid the side door open to reveal six travel-creased engineers—and Hanks smirking in the backseat. He unfolded his piece of paper to reveal VASSAR SPORE written on it in black marker.

Mr. Lee frowned at him. "Junior, she was standing right over there. How could you have missed her?"

"Hard to see anything behind all that luggage—"

"This is my son, Henry Lee, Jr.," said Henry Lee, Sr. with little enthusiasm.

"Hi, *Junior*," I said.

"Hi, *Spore.*"

Although there was an empty seat next to Hanks, I chose the seat next to my former seatmate, the goateed engineer, who was already snoring, mouth wide open, head against the window.

"You have too many bags. We must send them in a separate car," said Henry Lee, Sr.

"But—but—" I got out in time to see the rest of my luggage—Bags #2 through #10—shoved into a black-and-pale-blue taxi.

"Are you sure Bags #2 through #10 won't get lost?" I asked Mr. Lee. "They contain the majority of my outerwear and essential emergency supplies—"

"The taxi will follow directly behind us," he said, sitting in the front passenger seat. As soon as I sat back down, we drove out of the airport and onto the main street.

Singapore looked just like Seattle—except bigger skyscrapers, more greenery, and a whole lot cleaner. I failed to spot even one piece of trash somewhere, anywhere. However, the humidity was still the biggest shocker. I was relieved when the driver cranked up the AC.

I darted a look behind me. Hanks reclined across the empty seat beside him, his cowboy hat covering his eyes. He wasn't like any of the boys I knew at the Seattle Academy of Academic Excellence, that's for sure.

"How do you know my grandma?" I asked Henry Lee, Sr. But he was already asleep. I looked around: The entire van was sleeping.

How can they sleep when they're in an exotic foreign country!?

Once we left the pristine metropolis of Singapore and entered Malaysia, it finally sunk in: I was in Southeast Asia. And a comprehensive first impression would be crucial for my novel! I took out my laptop and typed:

Rickety buses crammed full of people. Monkeys in palm trees. Smoke from rubbish fires in fields. Roadside stands selling mounds of prickly skinned red fruit.

Such descriptions would add verisimilitude to my story. But what should I call myself in the book? How about . . . Sarah Lawrence.

By now the whole van was a symphony of deep breathing, wheezes, and snores.

I snuck another look at Hanks—but this time his dark brown eyes were wide open. He gave me a wink. Embarrassed, I turned back around.

Upon arrival at the Singapore airport, Sarah was accosted by an oddity dressed as if he'd just finished a day's roping. His name was Wayne. . . .

CHAPTER TWO

The Golden Lotus

OVER THREE HOURS LATER, THE MCT VAN PULLED UP IN front of a hotel, a marble modern wonder with neatly uniformed doormen flanking the glass doors. The engineers awoke and unfolded themselves. One by one, they grabbed their sole piece of compact luggage and entered the luxurious lobby.

"The Golden Lotus looks like a Ritz-Carlton," I said, pleasantly surprised. I'd been a touch wary about my bohemian relative's choice of accommodations. But this would do just fine.

"It *is* a Ritz-Carlton. The Golden Lotus is the next stop," said Henry Lee, Sr., as he assisted an elderly Korean engineer out of the van and steered him toward the entrance. Hanks followed him, carrying the engineer's suitcase.

"Whatcha writing?" he asked as he passed by.

I closed my laptop with a snap. "Nothing."

Once the engineers had checked into their sumptuous home away from home, Mr. Lee and Hanks got back into the van.

I removed my *Genteel Traveler's Guide to Malaysia* and

Savvy Sojourner's Malaysian Guidebook to help me interpret the sights.

We cut down a side street, passing the trishaws (bicycle rickshaws) and bicyclists riding alongside the narrow river that curled through town. Traditional *kampongs* (village houses) were sandwiched between *kedais* (food stalls).

Now we were twisting through a Chinatown lined with shops and antique stores. Black Chinese characters on red signs. Some in English: FASHION FINERY, HOTEL SUPERB INN, MOST FORTUNATE BAR. I noticed many of what my guidebooks called "spirit houses"—basically miniature temples on platforms outside houses and shops. Each one had offerings of joss sticks, fruit, cakes, and even the odd bottle of Orange Fanta complete with striped straw.

Then we careened down another side street, and another, and another—

Was that an A&W Root Beer restaurant, complete with life-size dancing bear?

A couple more turns, then we abruptly stopped—our shadowing taxi barely avoided rear-ending us.

"We are here," said Mr. Lee in his unemotional tone.

The Golden Lotus Guesthouse was a colonial mansion with peeling white paint and fading gold trim that had seen better decades. Battered rattan chairs with faded honeycomb patterned cushions and side tables covered with brown coffee rings were scattered around the lobby. Worst of all: no air-conditioning. Only a lackluster ceiling fan wobbling overhead.

My clothes felt like I'd put them on straight out of the washer.

"Selamat malam," said the jovial Malay owner, *salaaming* me—her hands pressed together at chest level. Her permed black hair was pulled back in a purple headband that matched her purple blouse, purple eye shadow, and purple nails. She waved her hand with a purple flourish. "Good evening and welcome to The Golden Lotus. Have a seat, please. You must be *Cik* Vassar, correct? I am *Paun* Azizah. My son will bring you some refreshment shortly."

I momentarily perked up, recognizing that *Paun* meant "Mrs.," *Cik* meant "Miss," and *selamat malam* meant "good night." Look how fast I was picking up the culture!

The drivers and Hanks carried in Bags #1 through #10. Henry Lee, Sr. finished a halting and confusing conversation with Azizah, then turned to me and shrugged.

"You must wait for your grandmother—she has taken the only key. Paun Azizah gave her the original after she lost the spare. But she expects her back very soon."

"Yes, your grandmamma, she is so very forgetful," said Azizah, shaking her head merrily. She held up an embroidered wallet. "Again this morning she leave wallet on my counter. Last night she forget this." She held up a dried starfish. "Artists." She laughed.

On his way out, Hanks paused in front of me, a quizzical expression in his dark eyes. "You gonna be all right?"

"Of course," I lied. "Thanks for carrying all my—"

"No problem. Nighty night." Hanks tipped his hat at me and followed his dad back to the van.

I sat down on the lumpy rattan couch and checked my PTP: 6:16 p.m. Where was Grandma Gerd? What was going on?

The metal fan, creaking as it ineptly wafted warm air through the humidity, made me even more irritable. Azizah flipped on the black-and-white TV behind the counter and settled back to enjoy a turgid Malaysian soap opera. Two scrawny amber cats ambled in and flopped onto the cement floor.

A barefoot boy in red shorts and a Spider-Man shirt presented me with thick black coffee with a lot of sugar and condensed milk—Malaysian *kopi*. Slowly and precisely I read from my guidebook's page of Useful Malay Phrases: *"Terima kasih."* He slowly and precisely replied: "You're welcome" as if I were simple.

I did not like Malaysian coffee. It was too thick and too sweet and made me sweat even more. And the shrill voices from the melodrama were giving me a headache.

I wanted a shower. I wanted food. I wanted quiet. And I wanted Grandma Gerd here. Now.

I opened my Latin Quote for the day: *"Non calor sed umor est qui nobis incommodat."*

It's not the heat, it's the humidity.

They got that right, I thought, as I fanned my face with my guidebook.

To pass the time, I scanned the room for details to put in my novel. Something hanging on the wall behind the counter caught my eye: a piece of cardboard with five slices of glazed white bread nailed on it—and five cherry cough drops glued on each slice.

Azizah smiled. "Nice, yes? Your grandmamma call it: *Bread Coughs.*"

I choked and spit *kopi* all down the front of my Traveler's Friend Linen Blouse.

CHAPTER THREE
Grandma Gerd

*F*SSSHTTT!

    "Fantastic!"

I awoke to find a woman taking a Polaroid photo of my chest.

"Where did you get this stain? Look at the bilious brownish-yellow tones—fantastic! In the shape of a platypus—fantastic! Look, there's his bill and his webbed feet. Fan-ta-stic . . . Azizah, is this or is this not the most fantastic stain you've ever seen?"

"You're the artist," sang Azizah.

"Fantastic!"

Make that an artist in need of a thesaurus, I thought.

A tanned, lanky woman approximately sixty, about my height, loomed over me. I scanned her from top to bottom:

A shaggy mop of silver-grey hair. Her thick bangs higher on one side than the other. (Did she trim it herself? With hedge clippers?)

Tortoiseshell glasses with green polarized lenses. One of

the tortoiseshell arms had been replaced with a mismatched black one.

A carved ivory dragon necklace.

Baggy brown pants.

Worn leather sandals.

Toe rings.

She returned her Polaroid camera to her oversize, woven-fabric-made-from-a-loom bag, then attempted to tousle my hair. But since it was wet and stuck to my head, the most she could do was squish it. "Hello, kiddo. So, whatcha think of Malaysia?"

"Grandma Gerd?" Not quite what I pictured, but I'd recognize that bombastic voice anywhere.

"They said you were gifted." She smiled and blinked rapidly several times. Then she turned away and pulled a large red bandanna out of her pants' pocket and blew her nose. Thoroughly.

After shoving her bandanna back in her pocket, she peered at my chin. "That's a really big dimple you have there."

I covered my chin with my hand. I'm sensitive about it, even if Dad calls it "cute" and Mom says it gives my face a "piquant quality." If I had to have a dimple, why couldn't it be a cheek dimple like Mom's?

She leaned closer: "And that really is a fantastic stain."

Was the musty odor emanating from her sandalwood or patchouli? I never could tell the difference when I'd pass by the grungy musicians loitering in Pike Place Market.

I smoothed my hair back into place, pried myself off the couch, and rolled my head to relieve the crick in my neck. She shook the Polaroid and watched my bewildered pasty face come into focus—along with the now infamous bilious stain. Her fingers were covered with silver rings and her wrists clinked with silver bracelets.

She turned and I noticed:

A silver nose stud.

Denise, Amber, and Laurel would never believe that this apparition was my grandma—much less the person who was blackmailing my parents.

"What are those?" she asked in an odd voice as she pointed to my beige walking shoes.

"What?" I said, distracted by her nasal adornment. "Oh. They're Spring-Zs. Instead of normal heels, they have special extra-large coiled springs that provide cushioning and support. Mom says they're ideal for excess walking and varicose vein prevention."

She contorted her mouth, trying to hide a smile. What was so funny?

"So, did you have to wait long?"

I made a show of consulting my PTP. "Four hours and eleven minutes."

"Whew, that's a relief. Hungry?"

I was surprised how painfully hungry I was. "Yes."

"Then follow me!"

"What? We're going out? Now? At ten p.m.?"

❧ ❧ ❧ ❧ ❧ ❧ ❧

I followed Grandma Gerd down the uneven cement pavement past endless colonial architecture; many buildings had been painstakingly restored and painted bright colors. The upstairs were used as residences. Laundry hung over the balconies, the louvered windows and shutters closed for privacy. The downstairs were used as shops—everything from tailors to fortune-tellers.

I was not only in a foreign country, but in a completely different world. Every sight, sound, and smell was unfamiliar. I felt muffled. Was it culture shock? Or just jet lag? And nothing had prepared me for all the stares. At 5 feet 10, Grandma Gerd and I towered over every Malaysian—woman or man—who jostled past us.

We finally arrived at what Grandma Gerd called the "food stalls" for my first official meal in Malaysia. *Kedais* selling wooden sticks of chicken satay with peanut sauce. Pickled cucumber. Juice made out of papaya, pineapple, orange, and the aptly named star fruit. The hawkers poured the juice into plastic bags with straws for customers to take away.

There was quite a crowd eating late—even kids.

"Malaysia wakes up once the sun goes down. This place really gets hopping at two a.m."

I sure hoped she didn't expect me to witness it firsthand.

I followed Grandma Gerd over to a stall selling bowls of steaming curry *mee* (noodles) and she bought two bowls. I was about to say I'd prefer the Peking duck sold at a different stall—until I saw the man chop up the entire bird, bones and all, and dump it on a plate.

She dug around in her oversize bag. "Now where did that wallet get to. . . ." Eventually, she managed to scrounge enough Malaysian *ringgit* to pay the man. Then she led me over to a plastic table with two chairs, a container of hot sauces and chilies, and a mangy dog sprawled underneath.

I fanned my face with my big white hat. My hair was completely soaked. As were my linen blouse and slacks. And we were eating steaming noodles.

Grandma Gerd dug into her bowl with zest.

But I first chewed a Pepto-Bismol tablet to coat my stomach (*"Cuts instances of traveler's tummy in half!"* exclaimed *The Genteel Traveler's Guide to Malaysia*), then thoroughly rubbed the metal spoon with antibacterial soap. Only then did I cautiously sample a spoonful of the curry broth: surprisingly tasty, though a touch on the spicy side. I looked up to see Grandma Gerd gazing at me incredulously.

"Face it: You'll get sick in Southeast Asia. Everyone does. No big deal, just your basic cramping and diarrhea that comes from bacteria in food. It's all part of the experience." She waved her hand, sending her bracelets into a clinking frenzy.

"My guidebooks say I won't get sick if I simply peel all fruit, make sure everything is piping hot, drink only bottled water, liberally apply antibacterial soap—"

"But there's no way you can oversee every single itty-bitty detail of your existence. For example: Who knows whether that glass you're drinking out of was really washed between uses?" I put it down automatically. "Or if a cook with the flu sneezed all over those noodles? Or if that money there was last used by a bank teller who didn't wash his hands after taking a dump?"

I stared at her.

Oh, why couldn't she be more like Denise's grandma, who wore floral housedresses, did thousand-piece puzzles, and gave us Circus Peanuts. And who spoke in well-modulated *quiet* tones.

I looked down at my noodles. Germs, bacteria, disease— all around me!

"Uh . . . I don't think I'm hungry after all."

Grandma Gerd pushed back her empty *mee* bowl and stood up. "Then if you're done, let's get going."

"Back to the guesthouse?" I asked hopefully.

"Unless you want to hit a couple bars. The night's still young."

Was she serious?

"I think I'd rather go back to the guesthouse, if that's okay."

"Suit yourself."

On the way, she stopped to buy something brown, oblong, and prickly at a fruit stall. As she swung the plastic bag she said, "You're gonna be my right-hand woman this summer."

I yawned. "What do you mean?"

"This summer just so happens to be one of the biggies for me: an art commission. A *big* art commission. Meaning I can live off it for three years. Beats ESL. I hate teaching ESL. Anyway, it's a mega-huge collage made completely of found art, materials, photos, and rubbings from Southeast Asia. I've got all the other countries covered. Cambodia and Laos are the only ones left."

"What do you need me to do?"

"Keep your eyes peeled for found art. Think of it as a global scavenger hunt—like this." She dropped to a squat and pulled something out of the dirt—ignoring the stares of the passersby. She held up her find triumphantly: a strip of yellowed linoleum. She wiped it off with an old rag from her pocket. "Perfect example. Circa 1930 or there-abouts. Can't you imagine it? The old days of the British Raj. The lady of the house modernizing her *kampong*. . . ." She carefully placed it in her bag. "Oh, and there's a feather." She pointed at something white at my feet. I handed it to her.

Why not just dump every bit of trash in the city into her bag?

I picked up an aluminum Coke can. "Here."

"What's that?"

"Found art."

"Uh, no. That's new, perfect, clichéd. Trash." And she kept walking.

Who was this person? I had a whole new empathy for Dad—I couldn't imagine her being anybody's mother.

Half-asleep, I stumbled after Grandma Gerd down the cracked sidewalk, taking care not to step into the open sewer holes. Then it occurred to me it was as good a time as any to accomplish item #6 on my To Do List Upon Arrival: *Ask Grandma Gerd what she's blackmailing Mom and Dad about.* And it didn't hurt to try the straightforward approach—who knew? Maybe it'd work. I took a deep breath:

"Grandma, what are you bl—"

"Will you look at that!"

Grandma Gerd stopped so abruptly that I smacked into her and two elderly Malaysian women carrying bags of vegetables smacked into me. While I helped the women gather up their scattered herbs, tomatoes, and lottery tickets, Grandma Gerd stared transfixed into one of the *kedais.* This one contained a little bit of everything: padlocks, shiny plastic purses, rope coils, toothbrushes, giant square cookie tins, bottles of fish sauce, and bags of rice. The object of Grandma Gerd's attention was an empty rice bag lying next to the full rice bags. It was pea green with a red rooster and Chinese characters across the bottom. She picked it up and smoothed out the wrinkles.

"Have you ever seen anything more sensational?"

"A rice bag?"

"Open your eyes. How fantastic is that green? Most rice bags are white or blue. And this exquisite red rooster? Very rare."

By this time, the short, squat shop owner had come forward, rubbing her elbow with the pungent menthol salve, Tiger Balm. Grandma Gerd bought the empty rice bag off her for the equivalent of twenty cents, but I could tell she would have paid twenty dollars. The woman didn't seem to think it strange that a Westerner wanted to buy her trash. But I did.

"But don't you see? *This* is a work of art." Grandma Gerd was euphoric.

Was this what was in store for me? Garbage collecting for three months? It sure wouldn't make for a riveting novel. I guess I'd be forced to embellish.

And as for my question, I decided to wait for a time with less "artistic" distractions.

Then finally, *finally*, we returned to The Golden Lotus.

CHAPTER FOUR

LIM

CAUTION! One never, ever brushes teeth with tap water in Southeast Asia. Even in a life-or-death situation, the alternative could well do you less bodily harm than the bacteria flowing out of the faucet.
—*The Savvy Sojourner's Malaysian Guidebook*

A T THE GOLDEN LOTUS, GRANDMA GERD COLLECTED her wallet ("So that's where it went!"), dried starfish ("And I thought I'd lost you!"), and a large yellow fabric-covered journal off the counter. It was so overstuffed that it required an extra-large blue rubber band to hold the whole thing together.

She bounded up the sagging stairs, her long legs taking them two at a time. I dragged myself up the stairs after her. Once we reached the fourth floor, I asked—or rather panted:

"What's that under your arm?"

"My Everything Book. I keep everything in here. And I mean *everything*. Sketches, letters, photos, thoughts, materials, found art—" She waved the Polaroid of me and my stain. "And now this!" Then she paused. "But don't you get any ideas. This book is for my eyes only. Got it?"

I was stunned she'd think me capable of snooping. I gave her a cold, "Of course."

The guesthouse bedroom was simple: teak wood floors, teak dressers, and mosquito-netting clouds above each teak twin bed. Grandma Gerd's art supplies were strewn around the room, and a collage-in-progress made out of shells, kelp, bottle caps, and blobs of chewed gum leaned against the wall—which had neither a discernable subject nor a pattern.

After the twenty-plus-hour plane trip, three-hour car ride, and four-hour wait in the lobby, and our hour excursion to buy food and pick up trash—I was exhausted. All I wanted was to sleep. But first, I had to unpack my toiletries and pajamas from Bag #3.

Grandma Gerd scooped up a mound of clothes and an empty wine bottle from one of the beds. "There. All yours."

Lovely.

After carefully putting her Everything Book away in the top drawer of her dresser, Grandma Gerd opened the plastic bag and removed the large, oblong fruit with the prickly, brownish skin. She began to cut it into sections with a Swiss Army knife.

A rancid, sweet, fetid smell filled the room.

There didn't seem like much space for my suitcases. "What about my luggage?"

"Here, taste." Before I could dodge her, Grandma Gerd

shoved a chunk of white into my mouth. The assault on my nostrils and the conflicting savory-sweet-onion-dip taste propelled me into the bathroom, where I deposited my mouthful into the toilet. When I emerged, Grandma Gerd was still chewing contentedly. Savoring.

"Not your cup o' tea, eh?"

"What was that!?"

"Durian. The most popular fruit in Malaysia. A delicacy. You just don't have the palate for it. *Yet.*"

I shuddered and scraped every last bit off my tongue with a Kleenex. She would be waiting a long time. I'd never encountered a worse flavor in my life—and that included the time when I was five and ate Dad's antiperspirant deodorant stick.

She sprawled across *my* bed, propped her toe-ringed feet up on the bamboo headboard, cramming durian wedges into her mouth. Why couldn't she do that on her own bed?

It took the clerk's son and his preteen brother half an hour to carry Bags #1 through #10 up the narrow flight of stairs. As my luggage filled the room, Grandma Gerd said, with her mouth full of durian:

"Did you think you were staying until menopause?"

I couldn't help but feel irritated. Of anyone, *she* should know the importance of proper preparation for Third World countries. "A good traveler anticipates every eventuality. Mom says—"

"Oh yeah, we sure know what Althea would say, don't we?"

Grandma Gerd pulled a rubber bag the size of a box of Junior Mints from one of my suitcases and unzipped it.

"I hate to break this to you but you won't be needing an inner tube."

"It's not an inner tube; it's a Traveler's Friend Hygienic Seat. Dad bought it for me."

"A what?"

I plucked it out of her hand and demonstrated its attributes. "First you unscrew this little nozzle; after it inflates, you place it on the toilet and use the facilities. Once you're finished, you simply push it back inside the special rubber bag and—this is the revolutionary part—it sanitizes itself! All ready for the next usage. *And* it doesn't waste paper like regular seat covers, so it's environmentally sound."

She looked away and coughed, then said, "Anyway, you've got to consolidate. You can't trek through the jungle with all this. I'm shocked the airline let you check it all."

Time to change the subject. "So," I said. "What's the plan?"

"Plan?"

"The comprehensive itinerary for the whole summer."

Grandma Gerd just stared at me and took another bite of durian.

"You mean," I said, my stomach constricting, "you really don't have a plan?"

"You want a plan, huh?" She rummaged around in her oversize woven bag and pulled out an envelope. I eagerly took it from her and opened it.

"But there's nothing in here."

"Exactly. We're adventurers, kiddo. And adventurers don't plan. They live. They experience. They *LIM*: Live in the Moment. That's what we're gonna be doing this summer—*LIMMING*."

She can't be serious. "Mom says that's just an excuse for people too lazy to plan."

"Althea can go—" She stopped herself. Then grinned. "Come on, adventure doesn't exist when every question is answered in advance. And I already told you, we'll be going to Cambodia and Laos in search of artistic inspiration and found art. That's all you need to know."

"You mean you don't have *anything* planned out? No reservations, no tickets—nothing at all?" My stomach constricted tighter and tighter. I gripped the headboard to steady myself.

"We're gonna LIM and love it!"

"You don't have an itemized list of ruins, monuments, or views to see for each country?"

"LIM!"

"Grandma," I said in the sternest tone I could manage. "I'd prefer a plan."

She got up and stretched. "Well, it's time for you to hit the sack and for me to get a glass of red. How's that for a plan?"

I felt dizzy. I'd never been without a plan before in my entire life. Every single day was precisely mapped out. Take my typical schedule posted on the refrigerator back at home:

VASSAR SPORE'S DAILY ROUTINE

5:45 a.m. Arise and exercise!

6:10 a.m. Shower and grooming and Attitude Check (It's not a zit, it's a blemish!)

6:39 a.m. Eat breakfast while perusing goals for the day

7:04 a.m. Take ferry to school

8:15 a.m.–3:15 p.m. High School classes—mostly Advanced Placement (5.3 is the new 4.0!)

3:15 p.m.–4:15 p.m. Extracurricular activities

4:32 p.m. Take ferry home

5:30–6:30 p.m. Garden or Boggle with Mom; listen to NPR while making dinner with Dad

6:30 p.m. Spore Family Dinner (Time to listen, time to share, let's show we care!)

7:00 p.m.–8:00 p.m. Hour of Reflection

8:00 p.m.–9:30 p.m. Homework

9:30 p.m.–10:00 p.m. Positive Visualization Exercises (I'm holding the Pulitzer in my hand as I step up to the podium. . . .)

10:00 p.m. Lights-out

And, come to think of it, her "Live in the Moment" shouldn't be LIM, but LITM—if you wanted to be perfectly accurate.

"Had you given me more advance notice," I said, "I could have researched online and come up with a travel itinerary—"

"Kiddo, relax. Get some sleep. You're stressing over nothing."

As she opened the door, I blurted out:

"What are you blackmailing my parents about?"

She froze. Then turned back around to face me. Her eyes examined my face. Cocking her head to the side like a pigeon, she said, "Run that by me again."

"I heard you on the phone."

"Eavesdropping? Not very Spore-like." But she seemed pleased.

"I know you're holding something over Mom's and Dad's heads—that was the only reason they let me come. Mom even had a nervous breakdown."

"She did?" She seemed surprised. "Althea?"

"Does it have something to do with why you haven't visited us in the last sixteen years?"

She smiled. "Maybe I'm allergic to the Pacific Northwest."

"Then what's The Big Secret?"

After a moment, she shrugged. "Sorry, kiddo. Don't know what you're talking about."

"Yes, you do," I persisted. "Even Mom and Dad admit there's a secret. They just won't tell me what it is."

"Well, if there is a secret, what makes you think I'd tell you?"

"So there *is* a Spore Family Secret that everyone's keeping from me?"

She deposited a half-eaten durian wedge on *my* nightstand and, after giving my shoulder a quick squeeze, she was gone.

I took that as a "yes." And as a challenge. I'd been up

against much tougher questions on my practice SATs. I'd figure it out. It was just a matter of time.

I sealed up the remains of the pungent durian in a plastic bag and deposited it out in the hallway trash.

Even though I could barely keep my eyes open, for the next hour I completely unpacked and organized. Then I headed into the spartan bathroom to wash off my travel smell. It was completely tiled from floor to ceiling, which was smart since the "shower" consisted of a nozzle on the wall, which drenched the entire bathroom with water. Then I got ready for bed—remembering to brush my teeth with bottled water.

After tucking my money belt under my pillow, removing my silver Latin medallion (I *have* written my lines for the day, Denise, thank you very much!), and inserting my retainer, I slipped between the wrinkled but relatively clean white sheets. In went my earplugs and on went my eye mask. Then I quickly sat up and clapped my white surgical face mask over my nose and mouth: Nothing would keep me from sleep tonight, not even the lingering stench of durian.

CHAPTER FIVE

Nibbling

What better way to show solidarity and affirmation for his delightful culture than to greet the fellow in his native language? Witness the grin on his face and the spring in his step at your cheerful *"Selamat pagi!"* or insightful *"Bolehkah anda berbicara bahasa Inggeris?"*
—*The Genteel Traveler's Guide to Malaysia*

I AWOKE SURPRISINGLY REFRESHED TEN HOURS LATER AND began my morning routine. Grandma Gerd was still sleeping—evident from her bed-shaking snores. Somebody clearly needed a nasal septum operation.

VASSAR SPORE'S SOUTHEAST ASIA MORNING ROUTINE
1. Remove sleeping attire and retainer.
2. Unlock luggage locks.
3. Shower.
4. Get dressed.
5. Insert gas-permeable contact lenses.
6. Brush teeth with bottled water—not tap!

7. Apply facial 45 SPF sunscreen.

8. Apply body 45 SPF sunscreen.

9. Put on lip gloss and foundation (with 45 SPF sunscreen).

10. Blow-dry hair.

11. Put on money belt—secure with safety pin.

12. Apply insect repellent.

13. Take multivitamins.

14. Take malaria pills.

15. Take charcoal stomach pills.

16. Pause for a much-needed rest.

17. Put *The Genteel Traveler's Guide to Malaysia, The Savvy Sojourner's Malaysian Guidebook,* and laptop into briefcase.

18. Add camera.

19. Add Melaka City Walking Map.

20. Add bottle of water.

21. Add another bottle of water.

22. Add Kleenex.

23. Add Traveler's Friend Hygienic Seat.

24. Put on buttpack containing a small amount of American dollars, emergency electrolyte packet, antibacterial soap, Handi Wipes, and more Kleenex.

25. Lock locks on each piece of luggage and secure all of them together via cable to bed frame.

26. Put on hat and sunglasses.

Total Prep Time: one hour, thirty-five minutes.

Total Weight of Briefcase: twenty-five pounds.

While Grandma Gerd showered and dressed, I went to the downstairs lobby to type up the first couple chapters of my novel on my laptop. Typing up each day or so as a separate chapter to email my friends meant maintaining strict discipline. Especially if I was going to finish the novel by the end of the trip. Since Grandma was taking forever, I easily completed chapter one.

Sarah realized she'd have to be especially patient with her eccentric aunt Aurora, who was unlike anyone she'd ever met. Quirky did not even *begin* to describe her....

Azizah lent me some *ringgit* to use at the Internet café across the street.

"Your grandmamma always lose wallet and borrow from Azizah."

The café was a tiny room with four computers, four chairs, and little else. Three stations were being used by Malaysian students checking their emails before going to school.

I already had emails in my account. From my friends:

Denise: *Nulla dies sine linea!*

Laurel: *We're charting your journey in Denise's atlas. That way, we can experience your summer vicariously, starting with Melaka (formerly spelled "Malacca," which I prefer. Much more romantic) to wherever you end up.*

Amber: *What's the food like? Guess who I saw at the 7-Eleven? Yep, John Pepper. Told him you were in Southeast Asia. He was impressed. :) Asked if you got malaria shots. I told him they're not shots, they're pills. (He bought a Snapple and a package of Cornnuts—Ranch Flavor.) Gave him your email—*grin*.*

Laurel: *Let us know the second he sends you anything!*

Denise: *Don't forget to include history in your backstory for added resonance. Like: "Melaka traded with China, India, and Indonesia. Later it was colonized by the Portuguese, then the Dutch, then finally by the British. You can see the influences from all six countries on the streets of Melaka." Let us know if you need research. . . .*

Laurel: *Did you know that the word "amok" as in "to run amok" is Malay?*

Denise: *Don't waste time emailing us messages—just email your chapters. We're here waiting to edit. NOW!*

And from my parents:

Mom: *I hope you can actually receive this over there in Malaysia. Are you okay? I keep visualizing you stranded on the side of the road somewhere. Has Gertrude shown up yet? You tell her she is supposed to maintain physical contact with you at all times. All times! And you let us know immediately if/when you feel uncomfortable or in danger. Call us anytime! Anytime! (There's no time like the present.)*

Dad: *Vassar, please email your mother ASAP. She hasn't slept*

since you called . . . and you know how testy she gets when
she's tired. And remember: You can't make your messages too
positive. Were all ten suitcases present and accounted for?

I emailed my friends the first chapter. Then I emailed
Mom and Dad to reassure them I was fine: *I'm doing great!*
Malaysia is great! The guesthouse is great! Grandma Gerd is
great! It was overkill, but I didn't want Mom's Breakdown
#2 on my conscience.

I returned to The Golden Lotus just as Grandma Gerd
came down the stairs.

"Time to hit the trail!"

I couldn't answer—incapable of speech. For she was
wearing the green rice bag as a skirt! She twirled around so
I could get the full effect.

"A real eye-catcher, eh? I hemmed it and sewed in a
waistband"—she lifted her shirt and snapped it against her
flat stomach—"and voilà!"

She looked absolutely ludicrous. A rice bag lady. "Are
you sure you really want to wear that . . . in *public*?" I
asked.

"Don't think I've forgotten about you, Vassar," said
Grandma Gerd. She handed me a plastic bag. Inside was a
rice bag skirt just like hers—only blue with white Chinese
characters and a pink lotus.

Mom and Dad brought me up to be polite to my elders.
"Thank you. It'll be great for . . . for special occasions."

If Grandma Gerd saw right through me, she just smiled.

As if I'd ever wear matching rice bag skirts!

"You like it, don't you, Azizah?" said Grandma as she posed in front of the counter.

"Your grandmamma, she is very artistic genius," said Azizah. As if she knew genius, she with today's orange headband-blouse-nails-eye shadow combination.

"You want one, too?" Grandma asked Azizah.

"Please, no. I am not the rice bag shape," she said, pointing to her ample hips.

Oblivious to my frozen horror, Grandma Gerd headed outside. The thick, woven material didn't give with the movement of her legs. Instead, it hung like a tube around her bottom half. Two Malaysian schoolgirls passed her, muffling their giggles. A Westerner in a rice sack! What a preposterous sight so early in the morning!

Mortification!

I reluctantly followed her. *How embarrassing, embarrassing!*

To top it off, she was wearing her Vietnamese mollusk-shaped hat. Did Grandma Gerd know just how strange she was? Don't odd people always think they're normal? Like how G. K. Chesterton said a madman always thinks he's sane. And how all madmen were missing a sense of humor. But that was just it: Grandma had a very developed sense of humor. I wouldn't call it *good* per se, but most definitely *there*. So she couldn't really be completely insane. Perhaps just a small thread of insanity wove through the rice bag fabric of her being.

I guess I should be thankful she at least shaved her legs.

After I changed some of my American dollars into Malaysian *ringgit* at the bank, Grandma took me to a shabby but clean *kedai* for breakfast. Without consulting me, she ordered two plates of *nasi lemak*—coconut rice, fried anchovies, peanuts, sliced egg, cucumber, chili, and curry. Not exactly the ideal way to start your day. I steered clear of the chilies and ordered a Pepsi.

As I dug in my leather briefcase for my Pepto-Bismol, Grandma asked, "Do you really have to lug that thing all around? Look at that red indentation you're already getting on your shoulder."

"I want to have my laptop handy for any chance moments of inspiration."

"Suit yourself. Well, kiddo, today you're on your own." She stood up.

I snorted Pepsi out my nose. "On my own?"

"To explore Melaka by yourself. Solo travel is a crucial part of the travel experience. Meet me at MCT at dinnertime."

"MCT?"

"Modern Component Technologies. Any trishaw driver knows where it is. See ya!"

"But, wait! I don't have plans! Or an itinerary!"

"Lucky you!" And with that, Grandma Gerd threw her woven bag over her shoulder, adjusted her rice bag skirt, and stepped out into the traffic.

The *kedai* proprietor gazed at me impassively as he tooth-picked his teeth. I gulped down the rest of my Pepsi—without ice—and shakily opened my guidebook. The print blurred before my eyes.

Focus, Vassar! Focus! This isn't a big deal! How hard could it really be? After all, you're a Latin scholar! You have a 5.3 GPA!

I thought of how apt today's Latin quote was: *Certe, Toto, sentio nos in Kansate non iam adesse.* Loosely translated: "You know, Toto, I have a feeling we're not in Kansas anymore."

I frantically flipped through the pages and paused at a glossy photo of a trishaw driver.

That's what I'd do: hire a trishaw guy to peddle me around Melaka. Trying to be subtle, I pulled up my shirt and burrowed into my flesh-colored money belt. Supposedly, these things helped you be discreet about the amounts of money you were carrying around. But so far they seemed more awkward and inconvenient. The proprietor watched me with mild interest as I scattered a hundred *ringgit* across the floor of his establishment. After picking it all up, I painstakingly counted out the exact amount for my *nasi lemak* and Pepsi.

"*Terima kasih,*" I said.

"You bet," he said.

There was no problem procuring a trishaw—a mass of them converged upon me as I exited. The faces loomed in at me:

"Trishaw, miss? Trishaw?"

"Uh, how much?"

"Cheap, very cheap! Where want to go?"

"For a drive around Melaka—a scenic drive," I said.

"Sure thing, jump in, miss!"

I chose the ancient specimen with arms and legs the size of broomsticks. I'd barely climbed onto the lumpy red vinyl seat when the old man sprang onto the rust-encrusted bike and away we went. His scrawny legs pumped like pistons. I removed my laptop to type some in-action descriptions—which was a touch precarious, thanks to all the potholes. But as Dad always said, typing was always more efficient than writing longhand.

Sarah bumped her way down dirt roads, passing pigs and chickens. Unpaved roads . . . evident lack of city planning . . . disorganization . . . no structure . . . but charm . . . occasional whiff of sewage. Houses on stilts. Mirrors nailed to outside windows, which served to scare away evil spirits. Did she just see a giant monitor lizard crawl out of a drain into the river?

Onward, the driver pumped parallel to the river. Past *kedai* after *kedai* made of rusty tin and clustered with locals and backpackers alike drinking *kopi* and bottles of Tiger Beer. A large house caught my eye. It was like any other traditional Malaysian *kampong*. But what captured my attention was the sign: MR. TEE-TEE'S VILLA: A LIVING MUSEUM, ENTRANCE FEE: YOUR GENEROUS DONATION! Another sign read: ALL OUR WELCOME!

I quickly thumbed through my guidebook to find the page of Useful Malay Phrases.

"Berhenti!"

My driver stopped short as if he'd been shot.

As he got off the bike and squatted next to the trishaw to smoke a cigarette, I searched *The Genteel Traveler's Guide to Malaysia*, then cross-referenced it with the *The Savvy Sojourner's Malaysian Guidebook*. Mr. Tee-Tee's Villa wasn't mentioned in either. Dare I risk it?

A grungy college-age backpacker with green hair and a Canadian flag on his pack wandered up to the entrance. So there was another tourist. I took a deep breath: *Come on, Vassar, be adventurous.*

A short yet dapper man, who couldn't be a day under seventy, waved at us both from the doorway.

I bid him good morning with a perky *"Selamat pagi!"*

"Malaysian good, very good!"

Look at how with just a little effort on my part, I can bond effortlessly with the locals, Sarah thought.

"Everyone here speaks some English," said the backpacker in a seen-it-all-done-it-all voice.

I ignored him.

"Welcome! Welcome to Mr. Tee-Tee's Villa! I am Mr. Tee-Tee! Please enter my home!" he croaked at us. What few teeth he had were gold. His brown slacks and brown button-down shirt with button-down pockets gave the impression he was on safari.

"Behold my humble home, which I have opened up for

the enlightenment of our most welcome foreign guests. Please remove all shoes. I thank you." His head barely came up to my shoulder.

The backpacker slipped off his sandals in seconds, leaving me struggling to untie my Spring-Zs. Each room opened off an open-air central patio. The floors were teak (surprise), and the decor was a hodgepodge of traditional Malay and 1920s furniture.

A sign read: PHOTOGRAPHY DISALLOWED.

As the backpacker examined the black-and-white vintage photos on the wall, Mr. Tee-Tee nudged me and hissed, "You stay after he go. I give you present."

A present? I was intrigued. Mr. Tee-Tee was a bit strange—but a gift from another land? What a nice souvenir that would make.

Mr. Tee-Tee gave us a detailed tour of his abode. The master bedroom was elaborately decked out in emerald green, camellia pink, and royal blue silks interwoven with gold thread. An enormous carved wooden bed with a canopy took up almost the entire room. Two ornate Malaysian gowns were spread across it, complete with gold slippers and ornate headdresses. Mr. Tee-Tee heard my soft intake of breath. He whispered, "Want to wear? You pretty-pretty in traditional Malaysian wedding gown. After he go, you wear gown, sit on bed, take photo!"

I backed away. "No, thank you."

Mr. Tee-Tee looked hurt. "Many lady wear gown, sit on bed, take photo. . . . So sad, so sad. Where you from?"

"Seattle."

"Ah, American. 'Raindrops Keep Following on My Head'!" he crooned, his gold teeth glinting at me. His breath smelled like limes.

The backpacker elbowed in front of me and addressed Mr. Tee-Tee. "I'm from Toronto, where a friend recommended your place to—"

Mr. Tee-Tee took the backpacker by the elbow and steered him smoothly out the front door, giving him just enough time to grab his sandals. "Bye-bye! Come again!"

"But—"

"Bye-bye! Come again!" The screen door closed firmly behind him. Without missing a beat, Mr. Tee-Tee took my elbow and steered me through a doorway.

"And now—bumpety, bumpety, bump!—the moment you waiting for! Present!" We entered a 1950s-era kitchen that seemed frozen in time. The baby blue linoleum was worn and the yellow countertop was peeling, but the effect was still the same. He gallantly waved me into one of the modern white plastic chairs wedged around a Formica table.

"Mango juice, yes?"

"Uh, no ice, please."

"Mr. Tee-Tee's ice very okay." He handed me a striped plastic Tupperware cup filled with a bright pink beverage. I sipped it gingerly. "Sugarcane make sweet," he said.

Mr. Tee-Tee hummed merrily as he puttered around his kitchen. Soon the smell of toast filled the room.

"What are you making?" I asked.

"Present!" He placed a red plastic plate on the table in front of me. It was a grilled cheese sandwich with a heart shape cut out of it—which the red of the plate turned into a perfect valentine. "For you steal Mr. Tee-Tee's heart!"

I was flattered. How cute was he? And now that I thought about it, I *was* hungry. I took a bite. Cheddar cheese and white bread. The familiar taste was comforting. What a sweet old gentleman with a romantic streak—I stiffened, mid-chew. Mr. Tee-Tee was *nibbling my ear!* My right ear! Ineptly, of course, because of his lack of teeth, but nibbling nonetheless! Was *this* the real present? Or was he mistaking me for a piece of toast? With a little shriek, I leaped to my feet and clamped a hand over my moist ear and shouted (a touch garbled by the bread and cheese):

"Berhenti!"

Mr. Tee-Tee seemed genuinely startled as I backed through the kitchen door into the foyer, where I snatched up my Spring-Zs. He followed me, his expression crest-fallen like a toddler deprived of his toy.

"So fast? But first wear gown, sit on bed, take photo—"

"No! I will not wear gown, sit on bed, take photo! I'm leaving."

"Maybe you have sister who wear gown, sit on bed—"

"No!"

"But you did not finish your present!"

I didn't even stop to put on my Spring-Zs as I escaped through the front screen door and into the street.

Sarah's mind whirled: Is this what's in store for me!? Gummy old men seducing me with cheese sandwiches, then drooling all over my ears? Wanting to segue into impromptu and inappropriate photo sessions? After this, I'm definitely sticking to my guidebooks!

I ran down the dirt road in my socks, sidestepping chickens and leaping over potholes, until I came to a busy street. Just as I started to cross—something whizzed over my head, pinned my arms to my body, and pulled me out of the line of a speeding taxi.

Roped!

"No need to thank me, little lady," came the carefully manufactured drawl of Hanks. "All in a day's work."

There he was—sideburns, cowboy hat, boots, and all.

I was so furious at being treated like a heifer, I couldn't even speak. Through clenched teeth, I finally managed, "Let. Me. Go."

"Pretty darn good aim, don't you think? Especially since I was standin' way over yonder by the laundry—"

"Let me go!"

I did not relish providing amusement for the passing Malaysians and tourists.

"Whoa, there. Simmer down," Hanks said as he loosened his lasso. I quickly pulled the rope over my head, whipped it out of his hand, and threw it into the brown river in one smooth move.

"Hey!"

Without speaking, I turned and strode down the road, searching desperately for an available trishaw. Where were they now that I needed one?

"Now that wasn't very nice," came his voice behind me.

"Lassoing someone isn't very nice."

"All righty. Next time I won't save your life."

I ignored him and just walked faster. But I could hear the *click-click* of his boots right behind me.

"That was my favorite lasso."

"I'm sooo sorry."

"Don't sound like it."

I waved my arms wildly at a passing trishaw. Occupied.

"What are those?" Hanks pointed at the Spring-Zs I was carrying. "Are they for real?"

"They're extremely comfortable walking shoes."

"I think they'd work better on your feet." He grabbed my arm. "Whoa. You better put them on or someone's gonna need a tetanus shot."

That got me. I leaned against a *kedai* wall to put them on.

"Next time you wanna visit Mr. Tee-Tee the Ear Nibbler, let me know," he said. "I'll escort you."

"What? You mean he's done that to other girls? That's disgusting. In America, he'd be arrested."

"He's just senile. And has a thing for a pretty gal's ears—especially if she's Thai or Dutch. He probably thought you were college age. You know, your height adds a few years."

"Uh-huh." I finished tying my Spring-Zs, then pressed

record on my PTP: "June 4th, 2:15 p.m. Note to self: Report one Mr. Tee-Tee of Mr. Tee-Tee's Villa to the local auth—"

"Cheer up. The old geezer thinks you're a looker—"

"Excuse me!?" I clicked the off button.

"I said *looker*—"

The Muslim call to prayer sounded. I turned to see we were standing right in front of a mosque. But Hanks didn't seem to notice.

"Aren't you going to . . ." I gestured toward the mosque.

"Uh, I'm Chinese. As in Buddhist. Not that I'm practicin'."

"Oh. Right. Chinese Malay."

"Yep. Then we got the Indian Malay who are Hindu—"

"And the Malay Malay. The real Malaysians."

"You could say that. Got many Asians in Seattle?" Was he trying to hide a smile?

"I live in Port Ann, across the Puget Sound from Seattle, and take the ferry to the Seattle Academy of Academic Excellence." Then: "Did I say something funny?"

"Nope. Any Asians in Port Ann?"

"Why wouldn't there be?"

I tried to hail a second trishaw. Occupied.

"Do you know any?"

"Yes."

"Who?"

"What?" I said, stalling for time. Who did I know?

"Who do you know?"

"Mrs. Kawasaki!" I said triumphantly. "Laurel's piano teacher."

"That's one."

"I'm sorry, there just aren't that many different ethnicities in Port Ann."

"Uh-huh . . ." Again, he tried to hide a smile but failed. What did he find so funny? Was he mocking me?

I rummaged around in my briefcase for a Handi Wipe and thoroughly cleaned my right ear.

"What are you doin'?" he asked, this time not hiding his laugh.

"I'm not taking any chances."

He shook his head and unwrapped a sucker. "Chupa?"

"No, thanks." Then: "Are you following me?"

He rubbed his pointed sideburns and squinted into the distance, his eyes becoming crescents. On his right hand he wore a silver horseshoe ring. The muscles of his upper body rippled under his blue cowboy shirt with white piping.

He ever so slightly gestured with his fingers, palm side down. Within seconds a trishaw a block away pulled up in front of us. After helping me onto the red vinyl seat and handing me my briefcase, he spoke to the driver. Then he turned to me, shifting the sucker to the side of his mouth, the white stick sticking out like a cigarette.

"He's takin' you to MCT, little lady."

"How did you know—" But the trishaw already pulled away.

CHAPTER SIX
The "Artist" at Work

MODERN COMPONENT TECHNOLOGIES WAS LOCATED on the edge of town in a white modern building flanked by two ornate colonial-era hotels. The trishaw deposited me at the front entrance. Now why did Grandma Gerd want me to meet her here, of all places?

Sanitizing my ear with a second Handi Wipe, I rushed through the glass doors into a giant lobby with black-and-beige modular furniture, potted palms, chrome wall sconces, and an oversize stone-slab coffee table. There across the room in front of a huge bare wall was Grandma Gerd standing with her hands on her hips, head tilted to the side, watching three men in white smocks brush a clear, gooey substance on the concrete.

A tall, forty-something Japanese man with grey-streaked hair and a 1960s-style suit watched Grandma Gerd as he smoked. There was evidence he'd worn a tie earlier in the day, but it had since disappeared. His face was worn and thin, with a dark smudge under each eye.

"Hey, kiddo," said Grandma Gerd. "Just in time to see us prep the wall—"

"We need to call the police!"

"Police? What are you talking about?"

"First I need to use the restroom. Urgently." I threw the Handi Wipe into a nearby pedestal ashtray.

"Breakfast disagreeing with you?"

"No, I need to wash my ear with soap and hot water. *Really* hot water."

She and the Japanese man exchanged looks, laughed, and said in unison, "The Ear Nibbler."

I stared at them. "How did you know?"

"Everyone in Melaka knows Mr. Tee-Tee," said Grandma Gerd. "He's an institution around here. Gives female tourists something to write home about."

"It's not funny. *Anything* could have happened—"

"In Melaka? The only place safer would be the Vatican."

Let her get accosted by a dental-challenged reprobate and see how it feels!

She smiled. "Believe me, you wouldn't be telling the police anything they don't already know."

"Why don't I show her where the restroom is," said the Japanese man. His voice was languid and mellow, like an overnight DJ's.

Grandma Gerd said to me: "This is Renjiro Sato, a Tokyo transplant. Co-owns Modern Component Technology with Zaki Biki, a local. He's the one commissioning this collage."

Renjiro meticulously extinguished his cigarette in a small silver box, slid it closed, slipped it into his front breast pocket, then shook my hand. His bony fingers were lightly yellowed with nicotine.

"Pleased to meet you . . . ?"

"Vassar."

"Vassar." Then: "So, Gertrude, is this your—"

"Granddaughter," Grandma Gerd said. "Sure is. She just flew in yesterday." She gestured toward the wall. "I wanted her to be able to visualize where the found art, photos, and stuff would be going. Fifty feet by twenty feet is a whole lotta space to fill, eh, kiddo?"

She was right about that. It would take quite a few strips of linoleum.

So this was her big art commission. And he was the sucker paying for it.

As Renjiro led me to the restroom, he pointed to a row of artwork on the wall at the opposite end of the lobby, each piece made out of hundreds of tiny silver and copper pieces.

"What do you think of those?"

"Close up, they seem haphazard. But from a distance, a picture appears. This one's a jungle scene, right?"

"Gertrude will be pleased."

"You mean . . . ?"

"These are the first pieces I commissioned from her."

I was surprised. Little of Grandma Gerd's art appealed to me. I couldn't get past the raw materials of the collages (bottle caps, twigs, shoe insoles) to see the creation.

"These are nothing like her normal work. I've never seen metal in her collages before," I said.

"Those are test chips that we would normally melt down for scrap. They're semiconductors, which are—"

"Oh, I know all about semiconductors," I said.

"How refreshing to find someone your age so informed. In any case, it was her idea to recycle them." He smiled at me, his eyes crinkling. "Your grandmother is an extremely talented woman. She has her own original take on things. Not to say I like everything she has done. The five throat lozenges glued to five slices of stale white bread entitled *Bread Coughs* was not to my taste."

I gazed at him. Maybe he wasn't a sucker after all.

"If Gertrude's collage turns out as good as we hope, I know two other businessmen interested in designs for their corporate headquarters."

So Grandma Gerd's art career wasn't just in her head.

I followed Renjiro through the side door, down a gleaming grey hallway.

"How did you meet my grandma?"

"In one of her ESL classes. It took months to unlearn what she taught me."

We passed a conference room—and there was Hanks, balancing on a stool, hanging a banner that read: MODERN COMPONENT TECHNOLOGIES WELCOMES YOU! He was sans cowboy hat and wearing a white smock with a blue MCT logo. But he still wore his boots. I could now see that his black hair was cut in a pompadour: short on the sides, full in the front.

What was he doing here? How did he get here so fast? Why was he everywhere I was?

Renjiro paused. "Hello, Hanks. I see your father has you busy preparing for the conference."

Hanks pivoted around on the stool. "Yes, sir." Then to me: "Hello, Spore. You made it. No more ear run-ins?"

"Mr. Sato, Miss Spore." The flat tones were unmistakable. Hanks visibly tensed as Henry Lee, Sr. walked in wearing a white smock and carrying a rolled-up plastic banner. He nodded at me, his wire-rimmed spectacles glinting. "Are you enjoying your visit?"

"Yes, thank—"

"Junior! The right side is higher than the left." The lines on either side of his nose deepened. "You must make an effort."

"Yes, sir," said Hanks in a flat tone that mirrored his dad's.

Mr. Lee watched him straighten the banner, his lips pursed. Then he unrolled his banner: THANK YOU, MR. FIELD REPS! OVER MILLION MACHINE SOLD! *"Hurry!"* He muttered under his breath and rapidly rolled it back up.

"Junior, return this. Tell them they have two hours to correct it before the opening night party or Mr. Sato will not pay for it."

"Yes, sir." Hanks climbed down off the stool, took the banner, but avoided eye contact with his dad. He nodded at us as he walked out the door.

"Poor Hanks," said Renjiro in an undertone as we

continued toward the restrooms. "If only his father weren't so set on him becoming an engineer."

"Isn't he too young?"

"This is just an internship for the summer. However, it is the last place Hanks would like to be. I attempted to convince his father that he is not the type to——" He broke off and sighed. "But it is futile to disagree with determined parents." He pointed. "The restrooms."

After scouring my ear with hot water, I sat in the MCT lobby typing up my day's experiences before they could fade in intensity. I had ample time while I waited for Grandma Gerd to finish her "prepping." Just wait till Denise, Amber, and Laurel read the chapter about the Ear Nibbler! But if Mom ever found out: Breakdown #2.

While I got ready for bed that night, I decided to be straightforward with Grandma Gerd. "I'm sixteen. I don't need a babysitter."

"What's the matter? You don't like Hanks?"

"It's not a matter of whether I like him or not. This is about the fact you think I need watching."

She was scribbling in her Everything Book while I washed my face—once again giving special attention to my right ear.

"Hey, I promised your parents I'd keep an eye on you at all times." Then she laughed and held up her Everything Book: a detailed sketch of me with a shocked look on my face and a perfect caricature of Mr. Tee-Tee daintily nibbling my ear—complete with glinting gold teeth.

"Very funny." I dried my face. "Anyway, I think Hanks is strange—not to mention annoying."

I drank the rest of my Pepsi before I brushed my teeth. Weird aftertaste. I'd heard that soda manufacturers often changed their recipes for different regions of the world. Well, I sure didn't like the Malaysian Pepsi version.

Grandma Gerd examined my face. "I think it's time for you to hit the hay. We're leaving for Cambodia first thing tomorrow."

"What? Tomorrow? I just got here. When am I supposed to explore Malaysia?"

"On the backend—after Cambodia and Laos. Take it from me, you'll appreciate the rest after Laos."

"What do you mean?"

"All in good time," she intoned mysteriously.

If Grandma Gerd's purpose was to pique my interest, it wasn't working. It succeeded only in irritating.

"Well, a little advance warning would have been nice! I have tons of packing to do! And which bags will I—"

"You'll have time in the morning."

"But—"

"Tomorrow." Her voice was firm.

Well, I *was* getting sleepy. Really sleepy. The day's adventures had obviously depleted me.

I brushed my teeth, flossed, and climbed into bed.

"Sweet dreams," she said.

CHAPTER SEVEN

Spring-Zs No More!

WHEN I WOKE UP THE NEXT MORNING AND TOOK OFF my eye mask—something didn't feel quite right. Odd. My PTP alarm hadn't gone off—I'd overslept by three hours. I'd never overslept by three hours in my entire life! My head felt fuzzy. Just where was my PTP? I could have sworn I'd left it on my bedside table. I plucked out my earplugs and reached for my glasses. Then blinked rapidly three times. The room was completely bare except for a large shabby black backpack, a smaller shabby black day-pack, and black buttpack.

And there was Grandma Gerd just about to tiptoe out.

"Whhttttssss—" I removed my retainer. "Where are Bags #1 through #10!?!"

She whirled around, caught. She gave me a big smile, accentuating the web of wrinkles around her emerald-green eyes and the whiteness of her teeth.

"Morning, kiddo! Everything's been sent home, where it'll be safe and sound and fungus-free."

"Everything? What do you mean *everything*!?" I jumped

out of bed and frantically rummaged through the backpack. "My jeans! My pumps! My one nice dress!"

"Just be happy I let you keep your guidebooks—which in my opinion are just crutches that prevent true exploration. And those Latin quotes you seem to get a kick out of. Anyway, one large backpack and one daypack are all you need. That's all I ever take when I travel. I wash out my blouse and underwear each night so I don't have all that fabric weighing me down. Add a few toiletries—no need to be odor-challenged—some vitamins, Chap Stick, and a hat. Now *that's* how to travel."

My cheeks flamed with the injustice of it all. "Well, lucky for me my Traveler's Friend Hygienic Seat was in my money belt under my pillow!"

Grandma snapped her fingers. "Balls. And I thought it was in the bag with your teeth-whitening kit and spare slips."

"And where are my Spring-Zs?" I looked under the bed. "Don't tell me you sent home my official walking shoes!"

It would be on her head if I got varicose veins.

She patted me briskly on the back. "We'll get you some sandals. They're much more practical. All those temples."

Temples?

"I've left you two pairs of pants, two button-down shirts, two T-shirts, two pairs of underwear, two bras, one pair of shorts, pj's, and all your toiletries. That's more than triple what I usually take. Once we get to Cambodia, I'll buy you some fisherman's pants like mine—I guarantee you'll never go back to regular pants. So baggy, so comfortable, and one size fits all."

I couldn't believe it. I collapsed onto the bed. The rampant injustice was making me light-headed. *Of all the diabolical—*

"Aaaaahhhh!"

I jumped up and gazed down at the empty space next to my nightstand.

My briefcase with my laptop was gone! And with it—my novel! The notes dictated on my PTP—gone! My cell phone—gone! ALL GONE! I hadn't realized that Grandma Gerd was really truly crazy. But there was no doubt about it—she *was*! And now we were supposed to go traipsing around Southeast Asia together. WITHOUT A PLAN! The idea was such a strong attack on my sense of order and preparation that I felt sick. SICK!

"How *could* you!? Mom and Dad are going to be furious! Just how am I supposed to finish my novel!?!"

"You have heard of pen and paper?"

"Longhand is the most inefficient mode of—" I choked on my own spittle.

"I think you'll like it once you give it a try. There's nothing more organic than creating with the most prosaic tools."

Still seething, I examined the backpacks. "These packs aren't even new! They're all worn—look, this one even has a tear!"

"They have character. A history. Nothing new is ever interesting—"

"Oh, no! It's not enough for an object to be useful, now it requires a *history*! And don't even think about buying anything with a bar code! Right? Am I right!?"

"Why don't you sit down? I think you're overheating."

"And my credit and ATM cards—where are they?"

"I told you, this vacation's on me. I'll pay for everything. If you need money, just ask."

Something dinged in my head. "Wait a minute! How could you have disposed of all my luggage without waking me up, unless—"

Grandma Gerd smiled and shrugged. "Caught me there. I slipped a couple Xanax into your Pepsi last night. Believe me, it was for your own good. All that baggage was just bogging you down."

My heartbeat accelerated, and I felt a flush cover my body: My very own grandma gave me knock-out drugs! I was furious, confused, disoriented, and slightly nauseated. Oh, for one of Dad's Tums . . .

"And since you overslept, we'll be taking the evening flight."

Overslept!

Although normally a super-positive person, I couldn't even look at Grandma Gerd without wanting to throw something at her. This was not the right attitude to have about my traveling companion for the next two and a half months. I pondered the idea of flying home right then and there. But the thought of Wendy already making headway in AP English, Advanced Latin Camp, and Sub-Molecular

Theory stopped me. I had no choice: I *had* to write my novel. In *longhand*. Then type it up chapter by chapter at Internet cafés. The rest of my life depended on it.

I was at the mercy of an unorthodox, unpredictable senior citizen who didn't seem to realize she was a senior citizen. I could never, ever trust her again.

And I would never, *ever* forgive her.

Vassar Spore's Goals for the Day

1. Do not hate Grandma Gerd.

2. FIGURE OUT WHAT SHE'S BLACKMAILING MOM & DAD ABOUT ALREADY!!!

3. Do not hate Grandma Gerd.

4. Email parents an update (with positive spin) and friends the latest chapter.

5. Do not hate Grandma Gerd.

6. Buy a notebook and pens.

7. Do not hate Grandma Gerd.

8. Never let my Traveler's Friend Hygienic Seat out of my sight for a second!

9. Do not hate Grandma Gerd.

10. −100. Do not hate Grandma Gerd.

Amber: *We're LOVE LOVE LOVING the novel!*

Laurel: *We can't wait to read each chapter!*

Denise: *Can't you write faster? Email more frequently?*

Amber: *Man, if only your real trip is half this interesting!*

Laurel: *How funny about the Ear Nibbler! Where'd you dream him up?*

Amber: *We LOVE the Malaysian Cowboy character. Can you package him up and send him home?*

Laurel: *Spoon update?*

Amber: *Oh, and Aunt Aurora ROCKS!*

CHAPTER EIGHT

Why Am I Surprised?

"*F*INAL BOARDING CALL FOR ANGKOR AIR FLIGHT 51 TO Siem Reap, Cambodia," crackled the loudspeaker over our heads. It was 8 p.m., and the flight left in five minutes. Grandma Gerd and I sprinted down the corridor toward the gate, wearing our backpacks and carrying our daypacks. She had on her standard uniform: Vietnamese hat, baggy orange fisherman's pants, a billowing chartreuse blouse with a fringe, and her most recent creation: a choker made out of silver semiconductor strips. And I wore what remained of my downsized travel wardrobe and my big white hat. We were late per usual, thanks to Grandma's failure to grasp the concept of time.

"Hurry!"

"Relax. The odds of a Cambodian airline taking off when scheduled are ninety to one. Make that a hundred to one," she panted as she caught up with me. "Kiddo, you're not supposed to wear socks with sandals."

She pointed at the white socks I'd bought at the *kedai* next to The Golden Lotus before we left for the airport.

"You do if you don't want to get blisters. Which will

most likely happen since I didn't have *time* to break them in, seeing as someone so kindly *just* bought them for me and disposed of my *already* broken in and *highly* comfortable Spring-Zs—"

"Oh, you'll thank me later."

She stopped suddenly, her attention captured by a passing Malaysian woman wearing a colorfully embroidered linen shirt.

"Isn't that the most fantastic shirt you've ever seen? What an unusual Cubist pattern. Obviously handmade. Check out the embroidery. Meticulous, but not too meticulous. Flawed just enough so that you know it's not machine made. Think of the history in that shirt. The years of memories soaked into that cloth!"

Here we go again.

"Grandma, come on!" I said, striding ahead.

But Grandma Gerd had already waylaid the woman. The woman stared at her incredulously and pointed to her shirt in disbelief. Grandma Gerd nodded with such enthusiasm, she almost sent her tortoiseshell glasses flying. The woman's female friends covered their mouths and laughed. But they stopped when she pulled out a wad of Malaysian *ringgit* and started bartering.

Grandma Gerd is literally buying the shirt off a woman's back. She's capable of anything.

"Final boarding call for Angkor Air Flight 51 to Siem Reap—"

"Grandma! We've got to board—*now!*"

"I'm running to the restroom to swap shirts, so you go on ahead—"

"What? But the—"

"Go on. I'll meet you on the plane. I'll be two minutes max—right behind you. Wait. Carry my daypack, will you? I need two hands for this." She handed it to me.

"Fine, fine, just hurry!" I felt like a pack mule with my backpack and the two daypacks weighing me down.

"Tell 'em to hold the plane!" she called after me.

Right.

"Hurry! Don't waste motions!" I commanded over my shoulder. Then, as I handed the flight attendant my boarding pass: "This extra carry-on is my grandma's—she's right behind me."

She just smiled and *salaamed*.

The rickety aircraft had only two rows of seats on either side of the aisle. I headed toward 12A, catching my breath and trying not to whack fellow passengers in the head with the packs.

I stuffed my backpack and daypack in the compartment above and shoved Grandma Gerd's daypack under the seat in front of me.

Garbled admonishments came over the sound system in at least three Southeast Asian languages, then finally in English: "Please secure safety belt and all item stow under seat. *Aw kohn*—thank you."

Where was she? I craned my neck to look down the aisle. Cutting it close—as usual.

How can she live like this?

To distract myself, I pulled out my *Genteel Traveler's Guide to Cambodia*. I skimmed through the introduction—then realized we were moving!

I peered out my oval window, scanning the terminal for any sight of—wait! There she was! Wearing the "fantastic shirt" and waving at me cheerfully.

I leaped to my feet and waved desperately for the stewardesses. But they were already buckled in and gestured for me to sit down. "Must sit, please, miss. Plane taking off."

I sat down and rebuckled.

Fuming.

The plane pulled away from the terminal, and the tall, lanky figure with the unruly silver-grey mop of hair grew smaller and smaller. I couldn't believe it. Oh, yes, I could. Figures Grandma Gerd would mess things up. She was always messing things up.

Just when I didn't think I could be angrier at her—she did something else.

Suddenly, fear took hold: I didn't know where I was going, where I was staying! Grandma Gerd had all that information in her head. What was I going to do?

Calm down. Look in your guidebooks. Thousands of tourists do just that, don't they?

With shaking hands I flipped to the town of Siem Reap. I knew where I was going. That was something, at least. There seemed to be a lot of very affordable hostels—

Uh-oh.

Grandma Gerd had the money.

I had maybe two dollars' worth of Malaysian *ringgit*. No credit card, no ATM card.

An overwhelming sense of dread filled me: *You've never been totally on your own before, Vassar.*

I pushed Grandma Gerd's pack to give myself more foot room. Hold on! Maybe she kept some money in there.

I lifted the pack onto my lap and unzipped it: a large bottle of echinacea. A glue stick. Double-sided tape. Her Polaroid camera with extra film. And—no wonder it was so heavy—her Everything Book, still barely held together with the help of that giant rubber band.

But no money.

I felt hot and prickly. I was going to hyperventilate if I didn't distract myself—NOW!

The Everything Book.

Most of the pages were covered with rough pencil sketches, flowers, leaves, and random bits of trash that I'd glimpsed every now and then when she'd cracked it open to shove something inside. Like that Polaroid of me with the *kopi* stain.

There were photos of Grandma and others in a sort of multilayered, multipage collage. My late grandpa wearing his plaid golf pants and squinting at the camera. Grandma eating sticky rice with a beaming Thai lady. Grandma in a pouffy A-line dress. Grandma balancing a giant cabbage on her head. Dad as a boy wearing his little blue suit and jabbing a calculator button with a pencil.

Then I flipped the page to find endless photos of ME! Photos from toddler to teen that my parents must have sent her over the years without me knowing. There I was, dressed as a giant bran muffin for my fifth-grade play on the food pyramid. And there again "Shufflin' Off to Buffalo" during a tap-dance recital. Then there was my fifteenth birthday photo, which was the first photo of myself that I ever really liked: My braces were off, my dark hair cut shoulder length, the cowlick in my bangs flattened with extra-strength hairspray, and my eyes eye shadowed and mascaraed—making me look "exotic" instead of "schoolgirl." Under that one, Grandma had scrawled: *Almost a Womb.* No, wait: *Almost a Woman.*

Grandma carried photos of me wherever she went? I had no idea. She'd also kept all my letters and notes. Even my latest one, a thank-you for last year's birthday gift:

Dear Grandma Gerd,

Thanks for the birthday collage. It's hanging above my bed. Does the deflated rubber ball signify anything in particular? I'm assuming the fifteen swizzle sticks were meant to symbolize my age.

In answer to your questions: No, I don't have a boyfriend as I haven't yet been on a date. Mom says I'll have more than enough time for that after *college. And no, I haven't yet read Graham Greene's* Travels with My Aunt. *What with my rigorous AP schedule, fencing classes, after-school Latin and Trig study groups, National Honor Society duties,*

membership in Toastmasters, and community service hours—
not to mention my regular school workload—I have little
time for recreational/light reading.

Once again, I appreciate your thoughtfulness in remem-
bering my birthday, albeit five months late.

Sincerely,
Vassar Spore

Yikes. Was I really as smug as I sounded on paper?

Feeling guilty for prying, I closed the Everything Book
and returned it to the backpack.

Dread once again overwhelmed Sarah: What am I going
to do in a Third World country with no guidance, no
reservations, no money—and no clue?!!

PART THREE

Cambodia

CHAPTER ONE

My Guardian

IT WAS PITCH-BLACK WHEN THE PLANE LANDED IN SIEM Reap, Cambodia. There were no lights other than the tiny ones on the runway to guide the plane. I pulled on my backpack, slung a daypack over each shoulder, and headed down the aisle. Then panic set in. I froze. Took a series of deep breaths.

"Move along, little doggie, you're cloggin' the aisle."

I whirled around.

Hanks, the Chinese Malay Cowboy!

Relief flooded me.

"You!"

"Howdy!"

"What are you doing here?"

Although Hanks was hatless, he still wore his standard Western shirt and jeans. And his sideburns were there in all their glory.

"Gerd thought I'd make a good guardian."

"Guardian? You're my age!" My relief turned to indignation.

Hanks said, "Actually, I'm two whole years older than you, Spore. Makes a world of difference."

So Hanks was babysitting me again.

"I've toured Angkor before. And I speak conversational Cambodian—my aunt's from Phnom Penh. So I'm darn qualified to be your *guardian*."

Then it hit me: "I bet she missed the plane on purpose! This was all *planned*! And she says she doesn't plan!"

"Now why would she do that?"

But there was something odd in his voice.

"What about your internship?"

"Renjiro thought I deserved some time off for good behavior."

Hanks pulled his cowboy hat out of an overhead compartment and plopped it on his head. Then he took my daypack and slung it over his shoulder and picked up a duffel bag—which was topped with a lasso. "Move along, move along." He smiled at the flight attendant. "And I thought I wasn't gonna get in any herdin' practice."

She just smiled blankly and *salaamed*.

Why had Grandma asked *him* along? We didn't even know each other. And now we were supposed to be travel buddies? Wait, make that: *guardian* and *ward*?! What was she up to?

"I hope you have money," I said.

We disembarked down a set of metal stairs. The heat and humidity assaulted us as we made our way across the tarmac into the airport, which resembled a set from a 1950s movie—and was probably built in that era. Stoic custom officials wearing tan uniforms dotted with metals stamped our passports and checked our visas.

Then Hanks led me outside, where a bevy of taxi drivers—each of them nursing a stub of a cigarette—jockeyed for our business. He smoothly negotiated, and in a matter of minutes, we zoomed off into more darkness, the headlights weakly illuminating just two feet in front of us.

Barely visible Cambodians on bikes and motorcycles shared the road with us, casually moving out of the way as we chugged by. Brightly colored sarongs and rubber flip-flops seemed to be the common garb for both women and men. The town of Siem Reap itself was no brighter. Like Melaka, it had a river cutting through town, though this one was much narrower and flanked with benches. Electric lightbulbs shone weakly above café tables and reflected in the water. Backpackers roamed the streets with flashlights, navigating their way down the dirt roads and into the guesthouses and restaurants.

"Bet you could use some grub." He handed me a package of peanuts.

"Okay. Just what's the deal with the cowboy act? Where did you learn your English?"

He shrugged. "In school, like everybody else."

"But you talk like—"

"Uncle How."

He flipped open a buckskin wallet and flashed a creased photo of a Malaysian guy wearing chaps over his jeans in mid-flight off a bucking bronco. It was hard to tell what he looked like other than airborne.

"He was an engineer like my dad. Until he invented a new kind of wire bonder machine. With the money he made, he bought a cattle ranch in Little Creek, Wyoming. I've spent every summer with him. Picked up Little Creek–style twang from him—along with how to ride, shoe a horse, lasso, and chew."

"Then why aren't you visiting him now? It's summer, or hadn't you noticed?"

"Man, someone's mighty testy. . . ." He shoved his wallet into his back pocket.

It was like he was half-putting on the cowpoke accent, but half-not. He really did have a slight drawl even when he wasn't "working it." He was like some sort of weird Far East–Wild West hybrid.

But I'd much rather be with a weird hybrid than all alone.

The taxi pulled up to our guesthouse, the sign proclaiming: PRETTY TREE GUESTHOUSE. "Accordin' to Gerd, it's the best deal in Siem Reap for anyone travelin' under twenty dollars a day," said Hanks.

"I bet she didn't make reservations."

Pretty Tree Guesthouse was a large central bungalow encircled by six smaller bungalows, painted light green and peach, and each one with an upstairs room and a downstairs room, making twelve rooms in all. Hanks entered the largest bungalow, which was a combined check-in, lobby, lounge, and dining room. A drowsy clerk who had been re-clining on a mat lethargically stood up, smoothing his rum-pled black hair.

A few minutes later, Hanks had a key in hand. "Grab your gear and follow me, *ward*."

He headed over to the picturesque Bungalow #4, sur-rounded by banyan trees and overlooking a small lily pond. The sounds of cicadas filled the night air. He led the way up the stairs to the top room, which sported the usual teak floors, white linen curtains, white linen sheets, and mos-quito netting over each twin bed. But this one had a panoramic black-and-white photo of the ruins of Angkor on the wall and a lotus blossom floating in a stone bowl.

Hanks tossed his duffel onto the nearest bed.

"Ah. So this room is yours," I said. "Thanks for letting me drag this stuff all the way upstairs." I picked up my day-pack and backpack and turned to go back down.

"Ours."

"Hanks, I'm tired. Just tell me which room you want."

"This is all they got. What we get for comin' at the height of the tourist season without reservations. Least it's a whole lot better than the last time I was here. So packed, I ended up sleepin' in a hammock by the river." He took out a plastic Ziploc bag that held toiletries. "So if I were you, I'd choose the room. The hammock gets really old after a while. Major rope keister. And all those mosquitoes. Take it from me, malaria's no fun. Neither is dengue fever."

Malaria!? Dengue fever!? Did I take my malaria pill today?

He headed into the bathroom, leaving me standing motionless in the doorway.

But even more scary: sleep in the same room as a boy? Alone? Me? Who'd never, ever even been on a date with a boy and now was expected to share the same bedroom with one? In beds a mere four feet apart and no partition?

What choice did I have? It was 10:30 p.m. already—in a Third World country, no less. This was all Grandma Gerd's fault!

I walked into the room, dropped all my packs on the floor with a thud, and flopped onto the other bed.

And what about the whole sharing-the-bathroom/getting-ready-for-bed thing?

What if he snored? What if *I* snored?

CHAPTER TWO

Bunkin' with a Cowboy

FROM THE BATHROOM CAME THE SOUNDS OF BRUSHING teeth, gargling, and showering—and humming. The tune sounded vaguely familiar. Oh. Right. "Home, Home on the Range."

Hanks walked out of the bathroom wearing cut-off jeans and a white T-shirt—and still wearing his boots. Water dripped from his black hair, down his nougat skin.

Didn't I read somewhere that cowboys slept with their boots on?

"It's all yours, Spore." He was now meticulously wiping off his black boots with a hand towel.

I took out my toiletries, then carefully relocked every lock on my backpack.

He laughed. "What? Don't ya trust me?"

"After what's happened to me, I trust *nobody*."

I entered the bathroom, then stopped short. "Where's the toilet?"

Hanks sauntered back in and pointed to a porcelain sink set into the floor. "Right where I left it."

"That's a toilet?"

"Squat toilet. You mean you've never used one?"

The smirk on his face was too much.

"Of course I have. Now may I have some privacy?"

"Be my guest."

I made sure to lock the door behind him.

This was a toilet? The white porcelain formed a shallow oblong, thicker on the sides with a sort of grid etched in it. Strange. How could it be even remotely comfortable? Next to it sat a large red bucket of water with a plastic green bowl floating in it.

I wished I hadn't skipped the section on hygiene in my guidebooks.

You must adapt, Vassar. I removed my Traveler's Friend Hygienic Seat from its sanitation case, inflated it, and laid it on the opening. Then I pulled down my pants and sat way down—and almost slid in!

"Aaah!"

"Need some help?" He didn't bother to hide the amusement in his voice.

I ignored him.

This was not conducive to peaceful urination. I tried again—how absurd I must look sitting on the ground with my knees up to my chin.

After I finished, I folded up my Hygienic Seat and stuck it back into the sanitation case. There was no flusher. My sea of yellow just pooled in the shallow toilet. How embarrassing. Oh, well.

"Did everything come out all right?" he called.

"It's the most uncomfortable toilet I've ever sat on."

What was that strange wheezing?

"You're supposed to *squat over* it, not *sit on* it. Didn't you notice the grid marks? The porcelain bit is for yer feet, not yer seat."

"There's absolutely no way that—"

"Next time, relax into a squat and let yer keister hang to your heels. . . . It all comes out easy as pie."

Was this just one big practical joke?

"And did ya pour a bowl of water in there to flush it down?"

"Of course I did."

Then, as quietly as I could, I poured a bowlful of water into the toilet.

I could still hear him chuckling.

Embarrassed, I changed into a T-shirt and shorts. There was no way I was wearing my pajamas in front of *him*.

My nighttime routine took a good hour, so by the time I finished, Hanks was already asleep. He was in bed, and the lights were off. His boots stood at attention at the foot of his bed.

Good. I could crawl into bed without his prying eyes.

The crisp white sheets felt cool to my skin, a nice contrast to the heat of the room. I pulled the mosquito netting down around me. Above my head, two geckos (*chincha* in Cambodia) ran across the ceiling, dodging the creaking fan. Soon I could hear their clicking sounds from the corner. *Chincha*—their name sounded like the noise they made.

Should I wear my eye mask and earplugs? Or would it behoove me to be extra alert?

"So, why did your parents name you Vassar?" Hanks's voice was even more gravelly when he was sleepy.

Great. Small talk before bed. But I removed my retainer. "I'm named after a quality women's college."

"Lemme guess, your brothers are Princeton, Harvard, and Yale?"

"Very funny. I don't have any brothers or sisters."

"Do you like being an only child?"

His question triggered a memory from ten years earlier. Dad had been coaching me how to set the table in two minutes flat. When I asked him why I didn't have any brothers and sisters, he said, "We prefer having just one little girl, Vassar. Because you know what the perfect geometric shape is?" He positioned the three knives.

"The triangle?"

"Exactly. You, Mom, and I—we three create the perfect family shape. After all, we don't want to be"—he added another knife—"*square,* now do we?" And we both had a hearty chuckle.

"Hey. I said: 'Do you like being an only child?'" Hanks sat up on one elbow. Without my glasses he was just a shadowy form through the gauze of the netting.

"I like it. What about you? Do you have any brothers or sisters?"

"Mom said that once she had a son, her work was done. You know, the whole Chinese thing."

Okay.

"Do you have a g . . ." *Stop! He'll think you're interested!*

"What?"

"Nothing."

"Come on, spit it out. What were you going to ask?"

"I forgot."

"If I had a girlfriend?"

Mortification!

"Isn't that right?" I could tell he was smirking.

"No! I was just wondering if you had a *g*-alloping horse. I was wondering if you had a *horse* you could ride for practice and . . . and all that." *Swift, Vassar. Real smooth.*

"Don't gotta horse. And don't gotta girl. My last one dumped me four months ago. Said my chops itched. What about you? Do you have a dude?"

"No, I don't have a *dude.* I have a boyfriend. His name's John Pepper." I wouldn't let him get the better of me.

"Really now."

Was that amusement in his voice? "John and I happen to be very serious."

"Meaning you two might just think about goin' out on a date one of these days?"

"Excuse me?"

"Gerd mentioned you'd never even been on a date. So in the States they put the cart before the horse, do they?"

"Good night."

He laughed.

I reached for my earplugs and eye mask.

"Just how many boyfriends have you had, Vassar?"

I didn't answer.

"Vassar?" His voice was softer, huskier.

I feigned a gentle snore. He laughed again, then turned over. Soon the sounds of deep breathing came from his bed.

And now I was wide awake. I needed a distraction.

I opened my new red notebook where I'd written down the words—longhand.

Bubble. Birth. Too young. Rubber ball. Dying. Egg.

"Watcha doin'?" asked Hanks.

Why couldn't this guy just sleep?

I was about to tell him to mind his own business—then paused. Maybe Hanks knew something. After all, even though he was annoying, he wasn't stupid. I gave him the full story of the blackmail as succinctly as I could.

"Hmm . . . Were your parents hippies?"

I laughed.

"Too bad. It coulda been something about drugs. Like they got caught with marijuana sewn into their bell-bottoms and did prison time."

The mental picture of Dad and Mom in bell-bottoms was so absurd, I laughed even harder.

"Or maybe they're wanted for tax evasion."

I bristled. "My parents are the most honest, upstanding people alive."

"Whoa, there. Just makin' suggestions."

"Actually, you can help by telling me everything you know about Grandma Gerd. Every single detail. For example, how and when did you meet her? At MCT? Did you ever take one of her ESL classes? Have you ever heard her say anything odd or mysterious? Would your dad be familiar with her story? What about Renjiro? Have you ever discussed—"

Gentle snores filled the room once again.

Thanks for nothing.

Well, I guess I could work on my chapter.

Sarah was shocked to find herself sharing a room with Wayne. Highly inappropriate. Even if she did find him strangely attractive—

I stopped and put the notebook on my bedside table. I'd wait until I had a good night's sleep, because right now I obviously wasn't thinking too clearly.

CHAPTER THREE

Chasin' Snakes

ROOSTERS.

Cock-a-doodling.

Right inside my brain.

Where was I?

I pried open my eyes in time to see a blurry flash of flesh walk by.

What the heck? I put on my glasses.

Hanks. Wearing only a towel.

"Do you mind?" My voice sounded thick and lumpy.

"Mornin', sunshine. It's daylight in the swamp. What happened to your face?"

My face? I jumped out of bed and dashed into the bathroom. There, reflecting in the mirror, was a girl with FIVE big red bites on her face! I looked like I had the pox. And last night I'd even applied bug repellent in addition to the mosquito netting.

After my shower, I tried to disguise them with extra foundation and cover-up. The effect wasn't perfect, but was better than before.

"Hurry on up. I need to shave." Hanks's voice wafted

through the wooden slats of the bathroom door.

"You? Shave?" I asked as I walked out.

"Sure," he said in a hurt tone, rubbing his hand over his baby smooth skin.

I bet he didn't even take the plastic protector off the razor.

"Wait a minute—something's different," I said, examining him. "Your sideburns! Where did they go?"

"They're chops," he said brusquely, and closed the door behind him.

When he reemerged, he smelled of Old Spice and his chops were back in place. So he obviously took them off at night and reapplied them in the morning after his "shave."

"Hey, do you know how long it would take an Asian to grow chops this good?"

"I didn't say anything." But I hid a smile.

He went to work on his boots, buffing first the right, then the left. His long bangs, usually pushed back in the pompadour, hung in waves over his forehead, Elvis-style. He put on one boot and held up the other—tilting it this way and that, making sure he got every last speck of dirt.

"You know you're obsessed with your footwear."

"And why not? These are mighty special," he said, slipping the other one back on.

"They're just boots."

"*Just* boots? *Just* boots!?"

He threw down the rag and strode into the bathroom. And emerged holding my bar of Dial soap.

"Come here."

I backed away.

"Someone's mouth needs a good washin' out." He shook the bar menacingly.

"Hey, wait a minute—stop—" I stumbled towards the bathroom.

"You can run, but you can't hide."

Blocked!

For the next five minutes Hanks chased me around and around the room, his boots clacking up a storm on the teakwood floors. Who knows how long he'd have gone on if the German tourists below hadn't banged on the door and shouted, "*Was ist los?* What goes on in there?"

"Chasin' snakes," said Hanks through the door. "They're mighty slippery."

"Die Schlangen?!" We could hear their rapidly departing footsteps.

Hanks turned up the ceiling fan as high as it would go and flopped on his bed. I flopped on mine. We were both dripping with sweat, and I was panting. Hanks's hair was damp, and his left chop was peeling off his face.

"You're melting," he said.

I felt my face. All my foundation had dripped right off. My red bug bites were probably glowing like beacons. Oh, well. It was just Hanks.

"Now where were we? Oh, right." He held up his foot. "These here are bench-made 1940s Godings with fancy red-and-white cut-outs, deep-scalloped kangaroo shafts, and square box toes. Got that?"

"I don't know; they look like *just* boots to me." I couldn't help it.

Commence Round Two.

"Berhenti!" I stopped short. Hanks ran into me, which sent me skidding across the slick teak floor facefirst into the wall.

The pain wasn't as disturbing as the giant purple bump that appeared on my forehead.

"Sorry about that," said Hanks. "I didn't mean to—"

"Now everybody will *see* what a brute you really are."

Once again, I reapplied my makeup and attempted to cover the bump with extra foundation.

"I'm going to check with the lobby if Grandma Gerd left any messages," I said as I picked up my daypack. "And try to call her. And see if they have another room available."

"Go right ahead," said Hanks. "Can't have you sharing a room with a guy you find 'strangely attractive.'"

I froze.

Mortification!

"That's private!"

"What would John Pepper say about his non-dating girl-friend?"

"How dare you read my—"

"Sorry, didn't mean to. But you left it lyin' there open on the table—"

"See why I need my own room?"

"Yep. So you won't act on this 'strange attraction'—"

"It's fiction! It's a novel! It's not even real! Sarah and Wayne are *characters*—"

"Then what's all the fuss about if I read how 'Sarah' has the hots for 'Wayne'—"

"Oh, shut up!" I grabbed my hat and glasses. He just stood there, smirking at me. "As if Sarah could really have the 'hots' for a wannabe cowboy with faux facial hair!"

I stormed out the door—straight into Grandma Gerd.

"Ahhh!"

"Hello, kiddo." She wore her backpack—and the "fantastic" blouse—and had exchanged her silver nose stud for a jade hoop. Under her arm was a roll of rusty wire fencing. Found art?

"What—where did you just—"

"Caught the early flight. Had to get up at six a.m. The things I'll do for my granddaughter."

I didn't trust myself to reply.

"What were you two doing in here? Sounded like a rumble."

I followed her back into the room. "You planned this, didn't you? You missed the plane on purpose." I tried to keep my voice steady.

"Why would I do that?"

"Probably because you thought it'd be highly amusing if I were forced to sleep—*room*—with a guy."

My words fell on deaf ears.

"Howdy, Gerd," said Hanks.

"Has your ward been behaving?"

"She's feisty, but fairly obligin'."

"Good. I'll leave my stuff in here until we can see about another room." She dropped her backpack to the floor and leaned the fencing against the wall.

"Got my daypack?" she asked me.

I handed it to her, eyes averted. Would she notice I'd read her Everything Book?

But she just set the daypack on top of her backpack and headed for the door. "Who's ready for some ruins?"

So she thought she could just pick up where we left off. After all she'd done.

"I'm checking my email," I said stiffly.

So while Grandma Gerd and Hanks arranged for a taxi and Angkor Wat day passes, I used the computer in the guesthouse lobby to email my latest chapter, reassure my parents, and check if I had any messages.

I wish I hadn't.

Amber: *BAD NEWS ALERT! Vassar, it sucks to have to tell you this, but it turns out that the girl from our Advanced Latin Study Group that John Pepper wanted to take sailing (to Crescent Island for camp-outs) was—Wendy Stupacker!*

Laurel: *This has completely squelched his appeal in our eyes.*

Denise: *Maybe his laser surgery was faulty after all and he thinks she's you.*

Laurel: *Or maybe he just has the worst taste in the world.*

Denise: *Or maybe his IQ is really 104 instead of 140. P.S. Keep those chapters coming—vent your anger and disappointment by writing.*

CHAPTER FOUR
The Churning of the Ocean of Milk

**We advocate frequent rests throughout the day, with
plenty of bottled water. Don't overexert or you'll
succumb to heat exhaustion. Take care of yourself.
Yes, Angkor is a treasure—but so are you!**
—*The Savvy Sojourner's Cambodian Guidebook*

I SLID INTO THE BACK OF THE TAXI NEXT TO HANKS.
Grandma Gerd sat up front loading sepia film into her
1930s Brownie camera.

Our taxi lurched into the crowd of bikes, motorbikes,
and pedestrians. We were on our way to Angkor Wat.

Hanks ran his hand through his pomp and replaced his
cowboy hat. One of Grandma Gerd's Polaroid cameras
hung around his neck. He shifted the Chupa to the other
side of his mouth. "So, how's John Pepper doing today?
Did he send you a love letter?"

I ignored him.

"Or was it one of those 'Dear John'—"

"Would you shut up?"

Grandma Gerd looked back at Hanks and they exchanged "My, someone's testy today" looks.

I pulled out a guava I'd bought at a stall near the guesthouse, washed it with antibacterial soap, then ate it as I stared out the dirty window at the scenery.

But I sure wasn't in the mood for sightseeing. When I tried to focus on Angkor, images of John and Wendy wearing white nubby sweaters with ocean spray glistening in their hair floated before my eyes.

Wendy Stupacker. Of all the girls at the Seattle Academy of Academic Excellence, he picks *her*.

Denise was right: There is no God.

I opened my *Savvy Sojourner's Cambodian Guidebook* and forced myself to read:

Mysterious Cambodia! Land of intrigue, blood-soaked earth, imperial kings, and revolutions. Angkor—magical, enchanting, most splendid Angkor—renders banal the pyramids and the Taj Mahal. A mere four miles outside the sleepy town of Siem Reap, Angkor is a wonderland of relics. There a stone tower peeking through the jade foliage! Here a spectacular temple! And there—is it merely a wall? No, it's a row of elephants! And this, is it a balustrade? No, no—it's a naga with scales and fins! Nothing is what it seems. Angkor with its endless ancient cities, temples, and palaces is simply one of the WONDERS OF THE WORLD!

I closed it, a touch heady from all the hyperbole. How could it possibly live up to all that?

Easily.

The majestic stone ruins of Angkor Wat rising out of the lush green jungle left me speechless. Immense pinecone-shaped towers silhouetted against the sky. Emerald rice paddies glistened beyond. I felt like a captive in *The Arabian Nights* and expected to see a prince with pointed slippers (like the ones Grandma Gerd had sent me) soaring overhead on a flying carpet. The ancient Cambodian temple was surrounded by a moat, which we crossed on a huge causeway made of sandstone blocks.

The spectacle distracted me from John Pepper. And it almost distracted me from the heat. Almost, but not quite. For if the heat in Malaysia was a warm, wet towel wrapped around you, here it was five sopping-wet sleeping bags suffocating you.

Oppressive.

"Non calor sed umor est qui nobis incommodat," I muttered in Latin.

"What did you say?" asked Grandma Gerd.

"It's not the heat, it's the humidity."

Hanks wiped his face and neck with a red bandanna, then tucked it into his back jeans pocket. "Conserve your energy, little lady. Take it slow."

He was right. We'd barely spent an hour exploring Angkor Wat before I wanted to curl up into a ball under the nearest tree. With the combined humidity and heat, my energy was so depleted, my lips could barely form words. My big white hat and sunglasses weren't shielding me enough from the sun. A line of Japanese tourists passed us: All the women carried umbrellas, and some even wore long white gloves. Now they were onto something!

And Angkor was not solely Angkor Wat, but seventy-seven square miles of ruined temples and palaces scattered throughout the countryside. If I was going to survive, I'd have to pace myself.

Monks dressed in saffron and novices dressed in orange strolled by. (*"Notice the novices, boys who live the monk lifestyle for a short period of time. . . ."*)

Suddenly, we were surrounded by rambunctious, dark-haired, dark-eyed Cambodian kids touting souvenirs.

"Hey, Mista, you buy hat? See, gold towers. Handsome, handsome. Four dolla'."

"No, no buy from her, buy from ME!" An older girl pushed a younger girl out of the way and shoved her hat toward Hanks.

"Bracelets cheap cheap! Two dolla'!"

No one seemed to sell in the Cambodian currency, *riel.*

"Do you have any spoons?" I asked, guiltily remembering my promise to Laurel.

"Spoon? Lady hungry? Tasty tasty food this way. . . ."

Spoons turned out to be a highly unpopular souvenir in Southeast Asia.

"Cowbell one dolla', cowbell one dolla', cowbell one

dolla'," intoned a tiny, bored boy shaking a crudely carved wooden cowbell. On his head was a peaked hat made entirely of green leaves.

Grandma bought the cowbell. And his peaked leaf hat.

"Souvenirs?" I asked.

She seemed surprised. "No, for the collage. I don't believe in souvenirs. That's what memories are for."

A boy missing his front teeth climbed up Hanks's leg like a bear cub on a Sequoia tree. He refused to let go until Hanks bought an Angkor Wat-*ch*—a black wristwatch with the towers of Angkor Wat painted in gold on the face.

"Buy Angkor Wat-*ch* for lady friend, she like very much," said the boy, grinning at me as he clung to Hanks's leg.

Hanks laughed and asked, "So, *lady friend,* would you like an Angkor Wat-*ch*?"

"Tell them I'm *not* your lady friend."

"We slept together, didn't we?"

The kids all giggled.

"You're so immature."

"Well, didn't we?"

"We just happen to share the same accommodations—"

"She your wife? Buy Angkor Wat-*ch* for wife?"

"Hurry up, you two," called Grandma Gerd. "There's something I want you to see."

After we finally extracted ourselves from the children, we followed her down a narrow passageway to a series of bas-reliefs—stories told through stone carvings.

Grandma Gerd stopped short and flung out an arm. "My absolute favorite bas-relief in all of Angkor: *The Churning of the Ocean of Milk!*"

I gazed at the meticulously carved stone drama before me. Male figures, some facing left and some facing right, gripped a large snake under their arms. They seemed to be in a standoff. Below them was an ocean of marine life: schools of fish, eels, alligators—even a fish cut in half. Numerous nymphs danced in the sky.

"Is it fantastic or what?" Grandma Gerd asked, snapping photograph after photograph with her Brownie while Hanks took Polaroids.

"What does it mean?" I asked as I fanned my moist face with my white hat.

"It's called *The Churning of the Ocean of Milk.* What more do you need to know?"

"Well, it's a good thing I happen to have my *Savvy Sojourner's Cambodian Guidebook* handy." I flipped to the correct page, then read aloud:

"'The Churning of the Ocean of Milk *depicts devils and gods playing tug of war using a serpent, and in so doing, churning up the sea in order to extract the elixir of immortality—*'"

The guidebook fell onto the stone floor. I clutched my stomach.

"Go on," said Hanks, peering closely at the serpent's head. "Oooh!"

I dropped to my knees, groaning. My stomach was churning! Churning like the Ocean of Milk!

Grandma Gerd turned to see me in a fetal position at her feet and said impatiently, "Must we? I've never liked charades."

Hanks peered at me: "Worm? Snake? Pastry?"

"Guava!" I groaned. Why did I risk eating fruit without peeling it?

Hanks cocked his head. "Guava? I don't see it . . ."

I scrambled to my feet. "I've got to go!"

Grandma Gerd frowned. "But we just got here. You haven't even taken the time to really absorb—"

"The bathrooms are way over there, by the temple," said Hanks, finally grasping the situation. He gestured off in the distance toward a Buddhist temple where monks were going about their daily business.

I leaped down the steps and sped across the grass, through the group of umbrella-wielding Japanese tourists.

Hold it, Vassar! Almost there, almost there! Hold it!

Wheezing, I careened around the corner of the wooden makeshift lavatories. Slamming the door shut, I made it over to the squat toilet—remembering to squat instead of sit—

Just. In. Time.

I felt relieved. Literally and metaphorically.

That is, until I realized there wasn't any toilet paper . . .

And I didn't have any Kleenex left.

That's it, Vassar, you are never, ever eating anything ever again.

My eye fell on the plastic bucket of water with its floating plastic bowl. The extremely detailed paragraph in my guidebook describing the way the locals used the bathroom appeared before my eyes.

You have no other choice.

I prepared to do the unthinkable (use water and my left hand) when—

Ding!

I hoped Hanks wouldn't notice.

"What happened to your socks?"

Why, oh why, couldn't I ever get a break?

Fssst!

He snapped a Polaroid of my bare ankles.

"I think I'll call this one *Sacrificial Socks.*"

I walked faster, ignoring him.

He caught up with me. "Maybe this will make you feel better. . . ." He put something around my wrist. The Angkor Wat-*ch*. ". . . *lady friend.*"

We finished the day atop Phnom Bakheng, a set of ruins facing Angkor Wat, to watch the sunset (after I made sure my Imodium kicked in). My guidebooks had blathered on and on about how intense and extra colorful sunsets were in Southeast Asia. I'd been skeptical. But they weren't exaggerating. This one was beyond merely colorful—the colors were so vibrant, so intense, so pure. Like Kool-Aid. I attempted to capture the vision for my novel.

Recipe for a Glorious Cambodian Sunset: Simply open one box of cranberry–flavored Jell–O and smear the granules across the dusky sky.

Pretty good, but slightly . . . smug.
I tried again.

Intense pastel reds, blues, yellows, and pinks dissolved into the horizon like Easter egg–dye tablets.

Nearby, Grandma Gerd was snapping photos with her Brownie. But where was Hanks? I scanned the crowd of sunset watchers and finally spotted his cowboy hat. He was taking Polaroids of the distant Angkor Wat towers backed by rice paddies and fringed by palm trees. The streaks of pink, blue, orange, and purple began to fade. A female backpacker with curly gold hair and a Celtic ankle tattoo approached Hanks. She said something, he said something, she laughed, he laughed, she touched his arm, he—
Why did he let her take his picture?
Who cares? It's just Hanks. Annoying, drawling, wannabe-cowboy Hanks.
But I couldn't pry my eyes off them, silhouetted against the molten sky as the golden sun submerged into the silver of the paddies.

CHAPTER FIVE

Frangipani

WE'D BEEN EXPLORING THE RUINS OF ANGKOR ABOUT A week when Grandma Gerd said:

"I want a Girls' Night Out. Just the two of us. Hanks can fend for himself, he's a big boy."

So Hanks grabbed a bowl of noodles and spent the evening packing up Grandma Gerd's found art to send back to MCT—the amount of trash she'd already accumulated for the collage was astronomical. (Of course to her it wasn't trash, it was Art with a capital A . . . a capitalized, italicized, boldface **A**!) And he was getting her sepia-film photos developed. That way, if some didn't turn out, she'd have a week to take more before we flew to Phnom Penh. I wondered how much Grandma Gerd was paying Hanks for his services. Or was Renjiro the one footing the bill?

I wasn't too excited about the proposed one-on-one time with my grandma. Although we now shared a room, we were typically so exhausted by the end of the day, we barely managed "good nights" before passing out. Which eliminated the need for small talk or pretending to enjoy each other's company.

However, perhaps tonight's familial bonding would shed some light on The Big Secret. . . .

Grandma Gerd and I navigated our way down the dirt road into town using my trusty Maglite flashlight. We ate dinner in one of the Siem Reap cafés that catered to the Angkor tourists. Or rather, Grandma Gerd devoured *lak* (meat) and rice while I tentatively sipped clear broth, the only thing that didn't seem to send my stomach into a tailspin. We sat outside under a large leafy tree with white flowers strung with twinkling lights.

"Nice watch," said Grandma Gerd. "Souvenir?"

Figures she just noticed it, Ms. Absorbed in Her Own World. "Hanks gave it to me." I added pointedly: "It'll come in handy now that I don't have my PTP anymore."

Grandma Gerd grinned and drank her Merlot.

I decided to use this time with Grandma Gerd to pick her brain about The Big Secret. I figured that if I kept bringing it up, bringing it up, bringing it up—she'd finally give in and tell me. My version of Chinese water torture.

Just as I was about to start the "dripping," a sturdy woman traveler with a long brown braid caught my attention. After the waiter presented her with a plate of rice and stir-fried meat, she promptly pulled out a bottle and sprayed it completely. Then, ignoring the dumbfounded waiter, she shoved a big helping of meat into her mouth and chewed away—mouth open.

"She reminds me of a sow I once came across in Chang Mai," said Grandma Gerd, swatting at a mosquito.

"I think she's onto something." I got up and walked over.

"Excuse me, but what did you just do to your food?"

She grinned, puffing her bulging cheeks out even more, allowing me the privilege of witnessing the rice and meat in mid-mastication. Then she bellowed, spraying bits of meat at me: "Foreign Food Sanitation Spray! I swear by the stuff. It works something wonderful. You just saturate your meal with it—and bingo! It's safe to eat!"

"Really?"

"No diarrhea, no gas, no stomach pains. Nothing! The spray kills anything alive—any critters that could pose any sorta problem! Zap! Gone!"

I gazed in wonderment at the metal spray bottle with bronze lettering next to her plate. The woman noticed and clasped her meaty fingers around it protectively. "Sorry, missy. Only got the one. But I can give you the Web site. They retail for thirty dollars a bottle, but it's well worth it. Everything's been coming out in firm little packages, if you know what I mean. . . ."

"She wouldn't part with her Foreign Food Sanitation Spray. Not even for fifty dollars," I said as I slumped in my chair.

"Hey, that's my money you're throwing around. Go easy. Besides, if it kills everything alive, what's it gonna do to your insides?" asked Grandma Gerd.

As I watched the woman joyfully shovel spoonful after spoonful into her mouth, my eyes narrowed and my thoughts darkened. What about mugging her for the spray? Jostling up against her in the dark, muddy street, causing her to drop her bag—"Oops, so sorry." Anything to have a normal eating life again.

Grandma Gerd paused, her wineglass halfway to her mouth. "Don't even think about it, kiddo."

How did she read my mind?

And, another thing:

"How come you always call me 'kiddo'? Why don't you ever call me by my real name? Do you not like it or something?"

She put down her glass and leaned back in her chair. "Okay. You caught me."

"Really?"

"I've never liked your first name. It's elitist, exclusionary, not to mention it sounds like '*vasectomy*.' So, now that you bring it up, mind if I call you by your middle name instead?"

Stung by her assault, I said, "Well, I happen to like my name. Like that it symbolizes excellence. Like that it connotes achievement. And maybe if you'd shown a little more interest in your only grandchild, you'd know that I don't have a middle name."

"Sure, you do. Picked it out myself."

I just stared at her, stunned by her capacity for fiction.

"Check your birth certificate if you don't believe me. I convinced Leonardo—okay, *bribed* him—to let me choose it."

"But my passport doesn't have a middle name, and don't they use the birth certificate to . . . ?" I pulled my passport out of my money belt and handed it to her.

As she read it, a spasm of pain flickered across her face. Then she snapped it shut and slapped it on the table. "Vassar Spore. So they legally erased your middle name. Balls." She took a big gulp of wine. "I would expect Althea capable of such deception—but not my Leonardo."

"What was—"

"Let me tell you—legal or not, you *really* did have a middle name. A name is incomplete without the three parts. It's like a story with a beginning and ending but no middle. No meat. No heart. Come on, which sounds better: Gertrude Spore—or Gertrude *Valhalla* Spore?"

I couldn't believe she was taking it so hard. So personally.

"I'd still like to call you by it, anyway," she said, straightening her mollusk hat.

I mentally cringed at what sort of name Grandma Gerd would have chosen.

"Don't worry," said Grandma Gerd, reading my face. "It's lyrical and musical and a fairy tale rolled all in one. You'll love it."

I very much doubted it.

She exhaled dramatically: "Frangipani."

It was worse than I expected.

"It's a flower—this flower, to be exact." She picked up something off the ground and handed it to me. A cream-colored, five-petal flower with a yellow edging and center—and a flamboyant tropical odor. "You'll find them growing on trees like this one all over Southeast Asia."

"Frangi . . . ?"

"Pani. Frangipani—got a nice ring, don't you think?"

"I prefer Vassar."

"You have been brainwashed, haven't you? Okay, how about Frangi? Shorter, but still with a lilt."

I shuddered and opened another bottle of water.

"How about this: If you let me call you Frangipani, then I'll let you know when you've guessed The Big Secret. Even though I promised your parents I wouldn't tell you. But, hey, they weren't exactly aboveboard with me, now were they? And now that I've met you in person, I think you can handle the truth. Personally, I think you're entitled to know since you've turned sixteen. But only if you figure it out. Deal?"

Why was I surprised at her unorthodox and unethical behavior?

"But how do I figure it out?"

"Use your intuition. Your deductive reasoning skills. Put that 5.3 GPA brain of yours to work."

"You'll honestly let me know if I've uncovered The Big Secret? You're not just trying to—"

"Promise. I'll even throw in some clues. A clue every day or so. To make it sporting. How does that sound? Fair?"

"I guess so," I said. What other choice did I have?

"Then it's a deal, *Frangipani!*" she said, and cheerfully pumped my hand. She tore off a piece of toilet paper from the roll in a plastic dispenser—all over Southeast Asia they used toilet paper for napkins. She wrote something on it with a green felt-tip pen.

She handed me the scrap. "There. Your first clue."

"What's this supposed to be?" I said as I examined it. "A hill?"

"No, it's a D."

"D? As in the letter D?"

"Is there any other kind?"

"Like a grade?"

"You have school on the brain, don't you?"

"Is it an initial? Or a monogram? Or—"

"That's what you're going to figure out, isn't it, *Frangi*?"

I winced. "Am I allowed to ask questions?"

"As long as they're just yes or no—shoot."

"Does it have to do with prison?"

She poured more wine. "Prison? Nope."

"Does it have to do with money?"

"Nope."

"Does it have to do with Grandpa?"

Picking a bug out of her glass: "Nope."

I narrowed my eyes. Her attitude was a touch too nonchalant. *She better be telling the truth.*

The next ones were long shots, but Hanks had planted the seed: "Are Mom and Dad wanted? Do they have disreputable pasts?"

"Althea disreputable?" Grandma Gerd laughed.

I took it as another "nope."

Was the "D" just a red herring?

CHAPTER SIX

The Apsara

Keeping in mind that Cambodia only recently finished a savage civil war, savvy sojourners steer clear of land mines by staying on designated paths and refraining from removing intriguing, half-buried metal objects from the dirt. . . .

—*The Savvy Sojourner's Cambodian Guidebook*

THAT NIGHT, GRANDMA GERD AND I SILENTLY GOT ready for bed, each of us absorbed in our own thoughts—which were punctuated by Hanks's footsteps above. His boots *did* make a lot of noise. (We'd moved into the room that the German tourists vacated—"Too much *Schlangen* chasing," they told the clerk.) But the sound was somehow reassuring and added to the music of the night: the clicking sounds of the chinchas on the ceiling, the croaks of the toads in the pond, and the buzzing of a flying beetle repeatedly hitting the screen.

I wanted to question Grandma Gerd further on the "D," but simply didn't have the energy.

The next morning I awoke to find I'd gotten six more bites on my face. That made a total of eleven red welts—not to mention the purple protuberance that still hadn't faded in intensity. I couldn't understand it. I had completely saturated myself with extra-strength bug repellent.

And my attempt at disguising them with makeup was useless. Within thirty seconds of stepping into the heat, anything on my face melted completely off.

Fsssht!

"Did you know that your bites form the Big Dipper? And that there big bump of yours is the sun," said Hanks as he analyzed the Polaroid photo he'd just taken. He pulled out a Sharpie and carefully labeled it *Vassar #5: Solar System.*

"Grandma Gerd won't be happy when she finds out you're wasting all her film."

"I don't know. This would look mighty fine on Renjiro's wall. . . ."

By now I'd grown resigned to the fact he'd continue taking my picture whether I liked it or not. My plan was that at the end of my trip, I'd somehow confiscate his entire stack of "Vassar Photos"—and burn them. But for now, I'd simply bide my time and ignore him. I refused to give him the satisfaction of annoying me. Otherwise every minute of every day would be one of perpetual irritation.

"Do you mind tryin' to cover up your affliction? After

all, I do have to be seen in public with you. . . ." He handed me my white face mask.

"Very funny."

We were walking down an overgrown path toward Ta Prohm, a Buddhist temple built in 1186 but since then overrun by the jungle. Grandma Gerd was already way ahead of us, snapping photos with her Brownie and picking up various leaves and rocks.

A red sign up ahead caught my attention: a white skull and crossbones.

"What does that mean?"

"Watch out for land mines."

"Land mines!?"

"Yeah. The Khmer Rouge left their callin' cards everywhere. Don't worry. Most of them have been dug up."

That put a wee damper on my mood. I scanned the well-trod dirt in front of me. What did a land mine look like, anyway? Solution: I'd just follow right behind Hanks—let him go first.

"Watch your footin'—*Frangipani*," said Hanks.

Uch. I would *never* get used to that name.

While Angkor Wat had been practically pristine, Ta Prohm was one big *mess*. A hodgepodge of foliage and stone that had remained untouched for centuries. No attempt had been made to restore it. Banyan and fig trees had spread their giant trunks and roots through the stone blocks, splitting apart walls and foundations, and toppling towers.

"This is my absolute favorite ruin, Frangipani," said Grandma Gerd.

To my surprise, Ta Prohm turned out to be my favorite, as well.

Grandma Gerd stepped over a dozing guard in uniform and paused in a doorway. She pointed to a row of dancing women carved above the door frame.

"Look: *apsaras*. Celestial nymph dancers, courtesans of the sky. They seduce men with their perfect beauty—"

"Something you won't have to worry about, Miss Mass of Bites," murmured Hanks in my ear. I jabbed him in the stomach with my elbow. "Ooof."

The *apsaras* mesmerized me with their mysterious yet whimsical expressions and their graceful in-flight positions. These were the most glorious creatures I'd seen in any of the bas-reliefs. There was something beckoning about them. When I blinked, I could have sworn I saw one kick up her heels. I wanted to sit and just drink them in.

"Watch out!" Hanks grabbed my arm before I sat down on a flat bit of rock.

"Land mine!" I shouted as I scrambled away, arms flailing.

"No. Somethin' a tad less explosive . . . ," said Hanks, pointing.

There, exactly where I would have sat, was a centipede—a *foot-long* centipede! I staggered back at the thought of that segmented, thick, reddish-amber-colored body with its multiple legs under my derriere.

"Supposedly its bite is worse than a scorpion's. Highly painful," said Grandma Gerd cheerfully.

"Thanks for the warning," I said. I eventually counted eleven of these despicable creatures on the ground, on walls, and in the crevices of Ta Prohm. My *Savvy Sojourner's Cambodian Guidebook* identified them as the Vietnamese giant centipede (*Scolopendra subspinipes*), common in Southeast Asian countries. Their bite was not only excruciatingly painful—it could even be lethal. (*"Savvy sojourners steer clear of these creatures and refrain from attempting to pick them up or take them home as pets."*)

We split up: I to jot down notes for my novel, Hanks to take Polaroids, and Grandma Gerd to get rubbings.

"When are you going to pull your weight around here?" Grandma Gerd asked me. "Found art doesn't find itself."

"I'll look," I promised. "After I write up my chapter."

I found the perfect writing spot: a square chunk of stone covered with light green-and-orange lichen—but centipede (and land mine) free. Before getting to work, I applied more sunblock and pulled my hat down over my nose. No need to court melanoma, as Mom would say.

I opened my notebook and gazed around me. Now to encapsulate Ta Prohm vividly:

Sarah sat contemplating the tentacles of trees raping the ruins of rock.

Not bad. I was about to continue when something half-buried in the dirt by the stone wall caught my eye: a partial remnant of a stone *apsara*'s face. About the size of my palm and about as thick. It must have come from the row of dancing *apsaras* above.

She smiled up at me. Even though most of her right eye and cheek were gone, she managed an enigmatic expression. The lips sweetly curved, the eyes twinkling.

On the lintel over the doorway, relatively new chisel marks pocked the stone around the now faceless *apsara's* body. *What were the guards paid to do around here?* Obviously someone had recently attempted to chip off the entire *apsara* when no one was looking. Maybe they'd been scared off and just left the damaged relic in the dirt.

Grandma Gerd wandered by, carrying a parchment paper with a rubbing of what looked like a sea serpent.

"How do you like this *naga*? Check out his nostrils—"

"Look," I said, pointing to the *apsara*. "Anyone could just pick that up and stick it in their backpack!"

Grandma Gerd looked at the *apsara* and slowly rolled up her parchment. "You're absolutely right, Frangi."

I glanced around us: a group of backpackers videotaping each other, a middle-aged Scandinavian couple holding hands, and an elderly Cambodian nun with a shaved head and a face like a shrunken apple. Bent over at the waist, she swept, swept, and swept the same space of ground over and over and over with her broom made of twigs.

Any of them could potentially pocket the treasure.

I turned back to the *apsara*. It was gone. "What!?!"

And there was Grandma Gerd cinching her oversize woven bag.

"Grandma Gerd!"

"Good work, Frangipani! Now that's what I call found art."

"But I wasn't . . . that's not what I meant. . . ."

I couldn't believe it. My very own grandma blatantly stealing a priceless relic from one of the Wonders of the World. I couldn't fathom stealing. I'd never stolen anything before in my life—not even a lip gloss from the drugstore back in junior high when Wendy Stupacker tried to peer-pressure me.

"Put it back!" I'd hissed. But she'd just walked away.

I snatched up my daypack. A guard in a wrinkled uniform strolled by—wrinkled because he'd probably just woken up. He paused. Gave me a piercing look.

Don't look at me, I wanted to say, *the culprit is the silver-haired delinquent in the mollusk hat!*

Before bed that night, Grandma Gerd and I washed our shirts and underwear in the bathroom sink. After she finished, she removed the *apsara* from her bag.

"There you go, you enchanting creature you," she said, positioning the stone fragment on her bedside table.

I clipped my bra to the portable clothesline we'd strung

across the bedroom, in hopes the ceiling fan would facilitate drying. "I still can't believe you stole it."

"She'd have just been taken by someone else, who'd sell her on the black market or turn her into an ashtray. Think about it: Those snoozing guards have allowed thousands of antiquities to be pilfered over the years."

"But that doesn't make it right."

Grandma Gerd snapped photos of the *apsara* first with a digital camera, then her Brownie. "At least with me she'll be prominently displayed in a Southeast Asian collage, as a tribute to Southeast Asia—*in* Southeast Asia."

She could rationalize anything.

I headed back into the bathroom to get ready for bed. When I returned, Grandma Gerd was already asleep—early for her—and there was an "A" on my pillow made out of matchsticks.

Nice try, Grandma Gerd. Trying to distract me from your crime with clues.

For hours I lay awake staring at the *apsara* through the filmy gauze of mosquito netting, hypnotized by the languorously swirling ceiling fan.

Thief . . . thief . . . thief . . . thief . . .

The *apsara's* one eye stared solemnly at me.

We both knew what I had to do.

CHAPTER SEVEN

Two Wrongs Don't Make a Right—
But What Do a Wrong
and a Right Make?

T HE NEXT MORNING THE THREE OF US ATE BREAKFAST AT the Angkor Wat Café and Bar. Mine: yogurt. Theirs: fried eggs, toast, and coffee. I cleared my throat and then said as casually as possible for a non-actor: "Oh, hey, I think I'm going to . . . uh, ahem, head back to Ta Prohm." Then quickly before they could ask why, I added: "I found it so tranquil yet, uh, mystical that I'd, uh . . . well . . . I'd like to sketch it."

Grandma Gerd stared at me a moment. I shifted in my chair and stared back—at her forehead. I couldn't quite look her in the eye.

"Well, well, well," she said to Hanks. "Some of my artistry has rubbed off on Frangipani."

"Like grandma like granddaughter," said Hanks.

"Whatever artistic talents I may have did not come from Grandma Gerd," I said. "We're not blood related. Dad was adopted."

"You don't say," said Hanks as he stirred cream into his third cup of coffee.

Grandma Gerd got up and hoisted her woven bag over her shoulder. "Do whatever you want. I'm going to the Bayon. I've got to take lots of photos there since it's Renjiro's favorite ruin."

"Well, since Ta Prohm's *my* favorite ruin," drawled Hanks, "I'll go with your granddaughter. Keep her outta trouble."

"I can go alone. I'm not a baby. I'll just hire a taxi—"

"Don't forget I'm your *guardian*. Gotta keep an eye on my *ward*." He winked at Grandma Gerd, who laughed.

"Then I'll take the Polaroid camera, Hanks," said Grandma Gerd, picking up the camera next to his plate. "Since you'll be guarding my non-blood-related relative."

She snapped a candid Polaroid of us sitting at the table. Then handed it to me.

"Memory."

Actually, it was a pretty good one of me—in that light, you could hardly see my bug bites. And Hanks didn't look bad. For him. I slipped it into my daypack.

Breaking away from Hanks in Ta Prohm was harder than I'd anticipated. While I sketched, he stuck to me like the adhesive on his faux chops. I simply couldn't shake him.

He leaned over my shoulder to examine my rendition of Ta Prohm. "Why all the noodles?"

"They're not noodles," I said stiffly. "They're roots."

"Well, they look like noodles."

Desperate because it was only ten minutes before clos-ing, I blurted out: "I need to be alone." Then cringed at how gauche I sounded.

He pushed back his cowboy hat and gave me a look. A discerning look? I quickly turned away. I wish he'd stop staring, staring, staring.

"Sure thing." Then he disappeared around the corner.

After confirming there were no stray tourists heading my way or lackluster "guards" snoozing nearby, I swiftly unzipped my backpack and pulled out the *apsara*. I'd taken it when we left the guesthouse that morning—I pretended to return to the room to get my sunglasses.

I scrambled over a mound of stone blocks and was just about to tuck the *apsara* into a hidden crevice when I heard:

The crunch of footsteps behind me. Why couldn't he just leave me alone?

I subtly slipped the stone fragment down the back of my pants, then whirled around. "Would you leave me—"

I froze.

For it was not Hanks the Malaysian Cowboy who stood behind me, but a guard. A non-sleeping guard. A guard in his fifties, with iron-grey hair and pockmarked cheeks, wearing a crisp uniform and a stern expression. "Remov-ing relics from Ta Prohm is against law."

My tongue didn't want to cooperate. "But . . . but . . ."

He pointed to the bulge in my butt. "Give to me, please."

"I was putting it back—not stealing it!"

He just stood there, hand extended.

Awkwardly, I pulled the *apsara* out of my pants and handed it to him. He examined it closely. Then looked up at the chipped lintel. I could see him putting two and two together.

"No, it wasn't me! I swear! I noticed someone had defaced the stone and the *apsara's* face had come off and—"

He took me firmly by the arm. "You come with me, please."

"Wait! I didn't steal it! I really didn't!" My voice squeaked.

By now a small group of backpackers and tourists had gathered. I turned toward them. "Can someone do something—please! He thinks I stole the *apsara*. But I didn't! It's circumstantial evidence!"

But they all just stood there solemnly shaking their heads at me, giving me the nonverbal version of the "tut-tut." One of them said, "Thinks she can get away with it because she's American."

Where the heck was Hanks!?

In a voice as calm and reasonable as I could muster, I said, "I'm underage. I have a guardian—he'll tell you I'm totally innocent. Can't we wait for him? Please?"

He said nothing, continuing to escort me through the ruins, his eyes focused straight ahead, his gait measured.

What should I do? What *could* I do? Everything pointed to me being a thief. I couldn't see any way around it. It was my word against his—and his word was a whole lot more convincing. He even had "Westerner witnesses." I'd arrest me, too—if I were in his shoes.

I scanned the groups of tourists as we walked. "Hanks? Hanks!"

The guard tightened his grip on my arm and said, "No comment, please."

Figures my "guardian" was nowhere to be found the one time I actually needed him.

The guard led me out of Ta Prohm and down the jungle path toward the waiting taxis, motos (motorbikes with drivers for hire), and milling tourists who were bartering with drivers, buying souvenirs, and drinking beverages in the shade of the banyan trees. Instead of heading to the parked police car, we veered toward a wooden guard-shack where one guard snored in a hammock and the other smoked and read a newspaper. My guard said something in Khmer to the "awake guard," who glanced at me with mild interest, then went back to his paper. He sat down next to him and put on bifocals from his breast pocket. Then he removed some papers from a black briefcase on the bench between them. He motioned for me to sit on another bench several feet away under a banyan tree while he painstakingly filled out the paperwork with a ballpoint pen.

Well, Sarah thought. This is it. You're being arrested and will probably face prison time. Prison time for a crime you didn't even commit. In a country you didn't even want to come to—

"Passport, please," the guard said a few minutes later without looking up.

I untucked my shirt, relieved to have something to do. Anything to stop that depressing train of thought. Just as I was about to unzip my money belt:

"Pssst!"

I swiveled around. There behind another banyan tree was Hanks! Sitting on the back of a running moto. The driver was a skinny teen with a cutoff T-shirt and arms covered with tattoos. He revved the engine and grinned at me. Hanks gestured for me to jump on the back.

Is he crazy!?! As if I'm not in enough trouble as it is!

Hanks gestured again, then mouthed: "It's your only chance."

My heart started to thump-thump-thump in a deafening bass.

I looked at the guards. One still slept, the other yawned as he turned the page, and my guard peered closely at his form. Apparently there were so many tourists milling and motors running that they didn't notice a thing.

What did I have to lose? I remembered the horror stories I'd heard about teens put in prison for life for drug trafficking in Southeast Asia. And teens stealing irreplaceable relics probably didn't fare much better. After all, I realized, the only way I could prove I wasn't stealing was for Grandma Gerd to admit she had. But I didn't want her to get arrested either. Catch-22.

Hanks waved his hand urgently. As in: DO IT NOW.

My body tensed, my adrenaline surged. I slowly pulled my daypack over my shoulders . . . then stood up like I was stretching . . . inched around the bench . . . behind the tree . . . *and ran for it!*

One second I was on the bench, the next I was zooming off on the moto, gripping Hanks's shoulders. The driver circled the perimeter so he wouldn't have to drive past the guard shack.

I glanced behind me: The guards hadn't even noticed I was gone!

"Don't look back! Here. Put this on." Hanks snatched my big white hat and replaced it with a blue baseball cap with CAMBODIA embroidered on it. "Shove your hair up in it." Then he handed me his red bandanna. "Tie this around your face."

I did as I was told.

The smells of gasoline, exhaust, and Old Spice mingled together in my nostrils.

Hanks craned his neck. "Here they come—hold on tight." Then he spoke to the driver in Khmer. I threw my arms around Hanks's waist just as the driver put it into the highest gear and sped onto the main road. With casual dexterity he navigated around taxis, motos, bikes, and pedestrians.

I darted a look behind me. The police car was only a couple blocks away—heading in our direction.

Our driver sharply turned down a side road, where we missed flattening two kids on bikes and a skin-and-bones cat by inches. Then we took an abrupt left into a maze of narrow alleyways that crisscrossed through a residential neighborhood. We finally emerged onto a busy street where we blended into the crowd of taxis, motos, and bikes. Many of the drivers and passengers wore face masks and bandannas to keep from inhaling too much exhaust. And I looked just like them. There was no way the police could track us down now.

I could feel Hanks's muscles relax.

"Thanks," I said, semi-muffled by the bandanna. "I don't know what I would have done—"

"I shoulda let you serve time. That'd teach you not to steal."

I yanked down the bandanna. "It was Grandma Gerd! I was putting back what she stole!"

He turned. His eyes searched mine. Then he pulled the bandanna back up over my nose. "You're durn lucky I was keepin' an eye on my ward."

"So you were watching me the whole time?"

"I'm your guardian, ain't I?" Then he laughed. "Contraband down your pants. Wish I coulda gotten a Polaroid."

It took a while for Sarah's heart to stop thumping. Could Wayne hear it? And a while to process what just happened: I—Sarah Lawrence—have narrowly escaped from the clutches of the Cambodian police!

When our moto driver dropped us off at the guesthouse, Hanks paid him $20 of Grandma Gerd's money for his role in the getaway. He gave us a grin and a thumbs-up, then roared off, dirt billowing in his wake. As Hanks and I walked toward our bungalow, I removed the baseball cap and bandanna and handed them to him. "Wow. I don't know what to say. . . . I really appreciate how you . . . you . . ."

"All in a day's work." He stuffed the bandanna into his back jeans pocket. "Although I think I'm due for a raise."

"Frangi, have you seen the *apsara*?" called Grandma Gerd from the doorway of our room. "I can't find her anywhere."

Hanks and I exchanged looks.

It took a while for Grandma Gerd to fully comprehend the situation. She paced our room in her bare feet, her baggy fisherman's pants making swooshing sounds, running her fingers through her disheveled hair and fingering her jade nose hoop. When she finally faced me, she said, "Well, I'm glad you're okay. You're lucky Hanks had his wits about him."

"I know, I told—"

She continued as if she didn't hear me: "But I'm having a hard time forgiving you about the *apsara*."

"It was for your own good. What if you got caught in customs? After all, I almost went to prison for putting her back where she belonged."

"I didn't ask you to. In fact, I wish you didn't."

"But—"

"I would have been fine. The *apsara* would have been fine." She put on her Vietnamese hat and slipped on her sandals. "Yes, I'm happy—*fantastically* happy—you're fine. But I'd rather you be fine *and* have my *apsara* back."

I opened my mouth. Then closed it. It was futile to explain that it wasn't *her apsara.*

Hanks cleared his throat and said to Grandma Gerd, "It's probably a good idea for us to head outta Siem Reap first thing in the a.m. In case one of the backpackers or tourists turns her in—or one of the security guards spots her around town."

Grandma Gerd picked up her woven bag. "So we're moving on to Phnom Penh a whole week early? There goes seven more days of found art and material gathering in Angkor down the drain."

And she slammed the door on her way out.

Hanks looked at me. "Where's she goin'?"

I sighed. "Probably to 'get a glass of red.'"

I went to check my email on the guesthouse lobby computer.

First, my parents:

Dad: *Thought I'd drop you a quick line before we start dinner. (Which isn't half so enjoyable without you by my side grating the Parmesan or zesting the lemon.) Your mom is feeling far better these days. Still concerned about you, though. So keep those optimistic emails coming! Principal Ledbetter called today at 3:45 p.m. She was curious to find out how your novel's coming along. I told her you had it well in hand. You do, don't you?*

Mom: *Now that you're in Cambodia, I want you to be extra diligent about your safety. Don't let Gertrude pressure you into doing anything even remotely risky. (Like staying at an unrated hotel.)*

By the way, Amber's making good progress. She's finally nar-rowed down her Life Goals—unfortunately they're all "arts" related. (Open a gallery, join an Elizabethan mime troupe, de-sign a line of knitwear, etc.) I've resisted the urge to sway her to-ward the more practical—after all, it's her life, her choice. Now if only she'd decide on a college major. . . .

And then my friends:

Amber: *I LOVE WAYNE!*

Laurel: *We can't decide who our favorite character is: Aunt Aurora or Wayne.*

Denise: *I must commend your regularity in emailing the chapters.*

Why wasn't I—ahem, *Sarah*—their favorite character?

I wrote about Aunt Aurora blatantly stealing a priceless relic and her conscientious niece Sarah attempting to make resti-tution by putting it back. Her sacrificial love for her aunt at the risk of her own freedom. Almost going to prison for righting a wrong.

It was my best chapter to date.

This time they couldn't help but see Sarah's winning qualities.

CHAPTER EIGHT
Full Moon in Full Squat

HANKS DIDN'T THINK WE SHOULD RISK FLYING TO Phnom Penh—too many security guards and police. "Who knows—they might have a wanted poster of Relic Thief Vassar Spore hangin' over the check-in desk. And those connect-the-dots bug bites of yours are darn hard to miss. . . ."

So our mode of transportation was the Tonlé Sap Lake and River via bullet boat, an ancient hot-dog-shaped vessel so jam-packed with passengers that some had to sit on the roof. A virtual death trap with no escape if it should submerge. Not for the claustrophobic.

I wore the blue baseball cap with my hair tucked up into it and Hanks's mirrored aviator sunglasses. I was taking no chances. Fortunately, none of the backpackers on board looked familiar—nor did any of them give me a second glance.

I sat on the vinyl bench seat next to Hanks, who was reading a worn paperback entitled *Dustup at the Double D*. I attempted to write my latest chapter. Grandma Gerd sat in front of us pasting found art into her Everything Book with a glue stick—ignoring me. I couldn't believe she was giving me the silent treatment for trying to put her *apsara* back. What, were we in third grade?

Out of the corner of my eye I watched Hanks subconsciously spin his horseshoe ring around and around his middle finger as he read. Around and around. I forced myself to look away.

Grandma Gerd abruptly turned and handed something to Hanks. "Would you give this to *her*? Not that she deserves it."

Hanks handed me a Fanta bottle cap with the letter "D" etched in it. "What's all this about?"

I shrugged. I rolled the cap around in my fingers. D. A. D. Dad? Did the Big Secret hinge around my father? I'd have to wait to ask her since she was obviously not too communicative right now.

I went back to my chapter.

"And how are Sarah and Wayne doin'?"

"Just fine," I said stiffly.

"You're really serious about this novel business."

"It's my only chance at valedictorian, which means Vassar, which means a lot to Mom and Dad."

"But not you?"

"Of course it does. But it means more to them. It's only natural. They've been looking forward to me attending Vassar for years. For *years*."

In front of me, Grandma Gerd made a sound like a "harumph."

"But it's your life, not theirs."

What was the use arguing with someone who didn't know a Latin suffix from a prefix?

He offered me a Chupa sucker. I shook my head. He popped it into his mouth.

"I know how you feel. My parents pushed me for years. No grade was good enough, no score high enough. They kept comparin' me to my cousin, a nuclear physicist. But I'm no physicist. The fact I was good at sports didn't count. Finally I got fed up and told them I wasn't going to college. Period."

"What happened?"

He shrugged, then laughed flatly. "Dad disowned me."

"Really?" It was obviously a wound that still smarted.

"Yep. Wouldn't talk to me for months. Acted like I wasn't there. Wrote me out of his will. Keep in mind, I was 'dishonoring' the entire family. To the Chinese, there's nothin' worse than that. Mom, my aunties, my grannies, even my cousin, all went to temple day after day to light joss sticks, hopin' our dead ancestors would change Dad's mind."

"And did they?" How sad!

"No, but Renjiro tried. Turned out, when he was a kid, he had pushy parents who pushed him into engineerin' when he wanted to major in art. He convinced Dad to at least talk to me. I agreed to go to college—as long as it was Little Creek Community College in Wyoming. That almost killed him. But I told him he'd lose face worse if I didn't go to any college. No sale. But I'm still workin' on him."

"What would you major in?"

"Major in? You mean study?" He shrugged. "Oh, I don't know . . . ranchin', agriculture, or maybe I'll take some veterinary prerequisites. I like horses."

"Then what are you doing at MCT?"

"Doin' an internship there was part of our compromise. Somethin's gotta make Dad realize I'm not engineer material. So, Missus Vassar Spore, I know darn well what it's like to have pushy parents. Chinese, Japanese, Australian, American—all parents are pushy parents."

"My parents aren't pushy. They're just super-supportive."

Grandma Gerd snorted.

Hanks smiled. "Uh-huh."

"No, really. Goals, plans, valedictorian, Vassar, Pulitzer—all my ideas."

Hanks just kept smiling.

Were Mom and Dad pushy? *Were* my goals actually *their* goals?

Hanks grabbed an empty water bottle from under his seat.

"Be right back," he said, slipping past me and disappearing into the luggage hold. A few minutes later he returned with the bottle half-filled with something yellow. He surreptitiously tucked it back under the seat.

I couldn't believe it.

He grinned. "Hey, I'm recyclin'."

"I don't think that's what they had in mind. . . ."

"I got an extra bottle. There's no one in there, so you'd have the 'facilities' to yourself, if you know what I mean."

"You have heard there's a bathroom onboard?"

"If you wanna call it that," he said in an ominous tone.

"You wouldn't catch me 'recycling'—even if I were a guy."

But I realized—once again—I did have to use the bathroom. *Why must every waking minute of every day in Southeast Asia concern relieving oneself?* Never would I take a toilet seat and bowl for granted again. Never.

I wobbled down the aisle toward the back of the bullet boat. A young Cambodian girl came out of the bathroom as I approached and smothered a giggle. I soon learned why.

"Bathroom?" Ha! A medieval torture device was more like it. The room was the size of a phone booth and housed a waist-high wooden box with a circular opening. *How on earth do I get on top of that?* I managed to use what meager upper body strength I possessed to hoist my lower body up onto the grimy, peeling linoleum that covered the top of the box. Trying to touch as little as possible, I maneuvered my way into the requisite squat over the opening—which required me to hunch over since the ceiling was so low. Even average-size Cambodians with their smaller builds would find this torturous. No wonder the girl laughed at the thought of all five feet ten of me pretzeled in here—my chin touching my knees and my butt extended.

You've squatted before, Sarah coached herself. Stop rocking back and forth. Relax—don't hit your head.

I'd just about relaxed when someone knocked on the door.

"Occupied!" I shouted, and tensed up again.

Contorted like a human crab, I willed myself to "un-tense." Finally, just as my legs were so cramped, I almost blacked out, I produced a stream that turned into a torrent. Blessed relief! I refused to be hurried by repeated knock-ings on the door. Once the job was completed, I attempted to unfold myself. I moved this, moved that, un-tensed this, un-tensed that, stretched, shifted—until I realized: I was stuck, *stuck in a squat toilet on a bullet boat in Cambodia.*

How many minutes had I been in here already? At least fifteen.

Don't panic, Sarah! You obviously got up here, so you can obviously get down. What goes up must come down.

One would think.

Part of my problem was the fact that in this position, I was unable to pull up my pants. My bare butt was vulnerable—in close proximity to the nastiest and possibly deadliest of germs. And I refused to sit naked on the linoleum—I'd rather die!

Bang bang bang!

They were getting impatient out there. I couldn't blame them. Urgent Khmer phrases came through the door. I tried to inch my pants up slowly, painstakingly, but only got them as high as mid-thigh.

I started to cry. *Don't be such a baby!*

Bang bang bang!

"I'm stuck! I'm stuck!" I whimpered.

Murmuring voices. Then silence. Then: *Bang, bang, bang!*

"I said I'M STUCK!!!!"

"Hey, toilet hog!" came Hanks's voice through the door. "This ain't your own personal boudoir, you know."

Rescue!

"Hanks, I'm stuck!"

"Stuck? How could you—"

"Don't ask stupid questions—just get me out of here!"

"But the door's locked—"

"I don't care if it's locked. I'm going to pass out if you don't get me off this thing!"

"Hold on, little lady—Cowboy Hanks to the rescue!"

Rattling of the door. Shoves. Murmurs. Then:

BAM! BAM! CRASH! A cowboy boot—make that a *Goding*—exploded through the flimsy wooden door. Then the door burst open, missing my face by a half inch! And there I was, squatting, face-to-face with Hanks—and a crowd of Cambodians and backpackers all staring at me incredulously.

Mortification!

I didn't know which was worse: Hanks seeing me sans pants or the entire boat population witnessing my ineptness.

"I bet the bottle sounds pretty darn good right about now," said Hanks, holding out his hand to help me down. He gallantly averted his eyes as I toppled on top of him in my half-naked paralysis. *Well,* I thought, *at least he's being a gentleman about this. Most guys would take advantage—*

"Mighty fine mole you got there on yer keister," he said in an extra-drawly drawl.

Fsssht!!

Before I could pull up my pants, the Polaroid camera spit out a photo.

"This one names itself: *Full Moon in Full Squat.*"

Cretin.

From the crowd, a female backpacker with a sunburned nose scrutinized my face. "Hey, aren't you that girl from Ta Prohm? Who was arrested for stealing—"

I subdued the panic welling up in me and forced myself to gaze at her with complete disdain. "I've never stolen a thing in my life. Besides, even if it *were* true, this would be way outside their jurisdiction: We're halfway to Phnom Penh." Close call!

"Nice save," Hanks murmured in my ear—but the girl still eyed me suspiciously.

And as if all that wasn't bad enough, Hanks had to carry me back to my seat because my legs were numb.

And Grandma Gerd wouldn't stop laughing.

The rest of the boat trip I feigned sleep to both ignore the giggles of the Cambodians, the whispers of the backpackers, the chuckles of Grandma Gerd—and to avoid smug Hanks, whom I loathed. Absolutely loathed.

Flip-flop.

CHAPTER NINE

D.E.A.D.

OUR PEELING RED 1973 PEUGEOT TAXI PULLED AWAY from the docked bullet boat, inching its way through the swarming traffic. The cacophony of horns, random shouts, and gravel continually dinging the windows was getting on my nerves. And we always seemed *thisclose* to running over something with legs.

But I could finally relax now that we'd left the backpackers behind.

Phnom Penh: Secretive, dysfunctional, titillating, bruised. A dead count in the millions thanks to the Khmer Rouge guerillas and their militant Communism. The bloody past is not forgotten, no, it will never be. But the people of Cambodia determinedly look to the future with smiles on their faces and hope in their hearts!

Guilt, guilt, and more guilt! Westerner guilt at having such an easy life when these people have suffered. I slammed my guidebook shut. "Okay, and what the heck am

I supposed to do with all this information, editors of *The Savvy Sojourner's Cambodian Guidebook?* I'm only sixteen!"

"What's that?" Hanks turned to me. He ran his hand through his pomp, then replaced his cowboy hat.

"Nothing."

"Sensational!" said Grandma Gerd from up front, photographing a mound of Pepto-Bismol-pink pigs on the back of a truck—dead.

The thought of visiting a place with such painful memories depressed me. Well, the least I could do was respect the Cambodians' history by exploring the city of Phnom Penh like I did the ruins of Angkor.

Phnom Penh did indeed have a different feeling from Siem Reap and Angkor. It was hard to place my finger on exactly what it was, per se. A slight gloom. But the locals here seemed to go about their day like the locals in Siem Reap: Cafés and bars flourished; the souvenir hawkers and potential tour guides roamed in packs; land-mine-victim amputees begged outside hostels and guesthouses; giggling children in their white shirts skipped to and from school; mothers balanced babies along with vegetables, kindling, fabric, and rice on their vintage bikes.

We booked rooms on the second floor of the Smile Smile Guesthouse—a spacious place with antiques and a view of the Mekong River.

Grandma Gerd and I were again sharing a room. Great.

With the silent treatment, I'd even be willing to room with Hanks.

Grandma Gerd paused outside our door and turned to Hanks.

"Tell *her* I'm going to call Renjiro to give him the update that the lovely *apsara* is no longer part of his collage."

"And tell *her* that I'm taking a nap," I said to him.

Hanks rolled his eyes and carried his duffel into the room next door.

Without a word, Grandma Gerd entered our room and dropped her backpack and daypack onto the nearest bed. Then turned around and headed right back out the door.

I flopped on the other bed.

There was a knock on the door, and Hanks poked his head in. "I hear there's a place where you can rope a steer— okay, a cow. But I need all the practice I can get. Wanna give it a try?"

I shrugged. I wasn't feeling up to much. "I don't know. Maybe later."

"Lemme know."

He started to close the door, then paused. "Oh, and if you get stuck while using the facilities, just bang on our adjoining wall—"

My whizzing sandal just missed his head.

As I lay there, I noticed a corner of the Everything Book poking out of Grandma Gerd's daypack.

Since she didn't believe in moral scruples, neither would I—temporarily.

Besides I was curious what she'd been writing about me lately.

I pulled it out and opened it.

The odd phrase here and there sprang out at me that made no sense: *canisters (flattened), seeds, textured paper, dill, pacifier? All round, then some not round, square maybe? glue stick texturizer sepia # 7 for edges*

Iridescent Ruffled Beetle—focal point.

Various Polaroids affixed to the pages. Mostly of Ta Prohm.

Then, toward the end pages: *Frangi. Don't understand. Nothing like I was at sixteen. This new generation seems so much more . . . <u>serious</u>. But <u>maybe</u> we have more in common than I think. Time will tell. . . .*

But it was the last written entry that riveted me: *Both our lives will be changed forever. It's the end of my life as it's been.*

Then some pressed flowers, leaves, and the parchment rubbing of the *naga*.

And an "E" made out of rubber bands taped to the last page—obviously the next clue Grandma Gerd was planning to give me.

My mind raced.

The clues: D. A. D. E.

Her journal: "*. . . end of my life . . .*"

The mystery word: "*Dying.*"

Together equaled: *D.E.A.D.*

My mind reeled. Grandma Gerd had obviously convinced my parents to allow her to spend quality time with her only grandchild before she passed away. Maybe she had an incurable disease. Could she have contracted dengue fever? Malaria? TB? Leprosy?

"She doesn't look like she's dyin'," Hanks said after I barged into his room and showed him my clues.

"So maybe it's not leprosy. But there are a lot of diseases that don't show."

"She doesn't act like she's dyin'."

I was forced to agree with him. But Grandma Gerd never did things the orthodox way if she could help it. I ground my teeth to stop the tears. I hadn't realized how fond I'd become of Grandma Gerd despite her many, many, *many* faults. I vowed to be a whole lot more patient with her from now on. I'd miss her in my life. Miss knowing she was out there somewhere in the world . . . picking up scraps of linoleum. Now I saw the stealing of the *apsara* for what it was: the last desperate act of a dying woman. A cry for help? I groped through my buttpack for a Kleenex.

"Hey, now. Take it easy." Hanks awkwardly patted my shoulder. "You don't know she's for sure dyin'. It's just a theory. A hypothesis. You should know that, Miss 5.3."

He was right. It was just a hypothesis. But a "darn convincin' one," to put it in his terms.

"Besides, DEAD is past tense. Am I right or am I right?"

"It's more dramatic. She'd choose dramatic over technically correct any day."

When should I ask her? The sooner, the better. I couldn't handle the not knowing.

We heard Grandma Gerd putting the key in the lock next door.

I turned to Hanks. "I'll ask her to go to lunch with me—alone. Make up some excuse why you can't come."

Grandma Gerd averted her eyes when I entered. I covertly examined her as I unpacked my big backpack. She didn't seem any sicker than normal. Didn't look wan or wasting.

After I showered and changed, I felt better able to face the emotional exchange to come. It's easier to be magnanimous when you're clean.

"Grandma Gerd . . . can we stop this? I don't want to spend the rest of our trip not talking. We only have so much time to get to know each other."

She looked up from labeling her stacks of photos.

I sniffed—*Vassar! Don't be emotional in front of her! It's probably all she can do to not fall apart!*

"I still think I was right to try to put the *apsara* back, but I wouldn't have done it if I'd known it would have upset you this much. It wasn't fair to do it behind your back."

After what seemed like eons, she said:

"Hungry?"

"Yes!" My stomach lurched at the thought of food.

"Pick a place out of that guidebook of yours. I'm taking a shower."

"Do you mind if we eat American for lunch?"

"You choose. Tell Hanks."

"Oh, Hanks is out . . . researching cows."

I consulted my *Genteel Traveler's Guide to Cambodia*. Then cross-checked it with my *Savvy Sojourner's Cambodian Guidebook*.

"How about pizza?" There was a place called Peppy Pete's Pizzeria a block away from our guesthouse.

"Fine. You go ahead and order and I'll meet up with you. Order me a bottle of Chianti."

"I'm underage. It's illegal."

She paused in the bathroom doorway. "Anything's legal in Cambodia . . . for the right price. If only you'd thought to slip that guard a twenty . . ." She closed the door. Seconds later, I heard the shower running.

CHAPTER TEN

Peppy Pete's Pizza

AS I WALKED TO THE RESTAURANT, I TRIED NOT TO DWELL on Grandma Gerd's hypothetical death. I didn't want to get myself worked up. At least Western food would give my poor stomach a break. However, one of my guidebooks did warn that *"Western food in Third World countries is as Eastern as it gets."* I'd just have to face the fact my bowels would be a constant source of pain and embarrassment.

Or would I?

There, in a group of souvenir hawkers, was a toothless man selling postcards, baseball caps embroidered with big Cs, and—Foreign Food Sanitation Spray! He had six bottles at $5 each. Even though I could have probably talked him down, I didn't bother. For $30 I could buy six bottles to that female tourist's one. I stashed the spray bottles in my daypack. Nothing could touch me now!

Peppy Pete's Pizzeria was like every other faux Italian restaurant I'd seen dotted throughout Southeast Asia: circular tables with the ubiquitous red-and-white-checked tablecloths, bottles of Chianti with raffia bottoms, jumbo bread sticks. But it was all a little disconcerting considering that across the street an ex-soldier land-mine amputee begged for money. Uncomfortable reminders of the war with the Khmer Rouge sat on every corner.

Before I sat down, I ran over and dropped a wad of *riel* into his grimy army hat. He saluted me. My guidebooks said that amputees could become part of the normal work-force (as in relic reproduction for the bourgeoning souvenir market) but only if tourists stopped giving them money, which sapped their incentive to earn it. But I just couldn't sit there and eat a pizza without doing *something*. Those guidebooks needed sections on what to do about Beggar Guilt. Especially *Ex-Soldier Land-mine Amputee Beggar Guilt When You're an American Girl Who Has Everything Including Your Whole Life Planned Out.*

I swatted away the kamikazing bugs as I read the menu. Now this was more like it: starch, starch, and more starch (and rice didn't count). The ideal placater for a churning stomach.

When the overweight, shiny-faced proprietor—Peppy Pete himself, if you went by his shirt—came to take my order, I couldn't resist:

"Da mihi sis crustum Etruscum cum omnibus in eo," I said. Then: "Sorry about that. It's just that my friends—"

"Ah, Latin. You want a crust with everything on it, yes?"

A Cambodian speaking Latin? Just wait until I emailed Denise, Amber, and Laurel!

"How do you know Latin?"

"Classics education. Parents very proud. But no jobs. Pizza pays much better."

Wow.

"So, one large pizza with everything—okey-dokey! Extra peppy?"

"Peppy? Oh, no. Nothing remotely spicy or peppy for me."

"Okey-dokey!"

"Oh, and a bottle of Chianti," I said, but added hurriedly: "For my grandma."

"Okey-dokey smokey!" And he waddled off.

I discreetly sprayed both glasses with Foreign Food Sanitation Spray before I poured my Coke—sans ice. Then I opened my notebook and worked on the next chapter while I waited.

"Pizza actually does sound good," said Grandma Gerd as she slipped into the chair opposite me fifteen minutes later. "Haven't had it for years."

I quickly closed my notebook before she could read any of it.

Peppy Pete waddled back with a bottle of Chianti, which he poured into Grandma Gerd's glass with a flourish. She drank deeply and leaned back in her chair.

Now. Ask her now.

"Grandma, there's something I want to ask—"

"Have some." She slid her glass across the table.

I promptly slid it back. "Grandma Gerd, you keep forgetting I'm only sixteen. Besides, I don't see how you can drink alcohol in this weather. As if you weren't dehydrated enough from the humidity and sun. And you know it's not good for your *health*."

I paused to let that sink in.

"Okey-dokey smokey! Pizza with everything!" With a flash of teeth and a sprinkling of sweat from his forehead, Peppy Pete plopped the pizza onto the table. He picked up the Chianti bottle and topped off Grandma Gerd's glass: *"Bonum vinum laetificat cor hominis!"* Then whirled away to welcome a bunch of granola-type backpackers.

"What did he say?" asked Grandma Gerd.

" 'Good wine gladdens a person's heart.' It's Latin."

"I guess you are learning something at that posh school of yours." She put her glass down. "Not that this is 'good' by any stretch."

The pizza smelled amazing as only dough and cheese and tomato sauce can. A welcome change after rice, rice, and more rice.

Right as Grandma reached for a slice, I sprayed every inch of the pizza thoroughly with my Foreign Food Sanitation Spray. She jerked her hand away as if she'd been burned.

"What are you doing?"

"I'm not taking any more chances with my stomach. Remember, this eliminates every germ and bacteria. Don't worry, it's tasteless and odorless."

Grandma Gerd did not look convinced.

"Delicious," I said with my mouth full. "Just like home."

She shook her head. "When are you going to just LIM, Frangi?"

"If you'd had as many bathroom emergencies as I've had, you'd be spraying, too."

Grandma Gerd took a tiny bite of pizza. Then a bigger bite. "Not bad. Luckily you can't taste all the chemicals you just added."

"Be right back," I said, grabbing a slice and pushing back my chair.

I ran across the street to the amputee and bestowed him with the additional gift of starch. He was even more pleased than before and gave me a double salute.

"That was nice of you, Frangi," said Grandma Gerd as I slid back into my chair.

Before I could reply, I froze: There on my plate was the rubber band "E." A chill ran down my spine. Talk about perfect timing. *Too* perfect.

"Making any headway with the clues?" She asked in a casual voice. *Too* casual.

To mask my surging emotions, I devoured an entire slice of pizza in three bites.

Now. Tell her NOW.

"Grandma, I want you to know, that . . . that I *know*." I squeezed my eyes shut, holding back the tears that were trying to push their way out of my lids.

"Know what?" she asked with her mouth full. "What's wrong with your eyes? Do you have a headache?"

She was going to actually make me say it?

"I've figured out the clues."

"You have?" She sounded skeptical. "Already?"

"I know that you're . . . you're . . ."

"Spit it out."

"Dying."

Silence.

"D-E-A-D. Dying. End of life." I blew my nose with some of the toilet paper roll on the table, then continued on, ignoring the fact that my voice was squeaking. "You wanted to spend your last remaining days bonding with your—"

I was interrupted by a snort. A big snort.

I opened my eyes, releasing the tears, which sped down my cheeks. Grandma Gerd was laughing.

"You mean you're not . . . *dying*?"

"Of course I am! Aren't we all? Once we're born, life is just one long journey toward death. Or haven't you gotten to 'Death & Dying' yet in your AP/AAP classes?"

Was she just being cavalier to protect my feelings?

"Are you dying *sooner* rather than later is what I'm asking."

"No sooner than your average sixty-year-old."

"You're not lying?"

"I'm not lying and I'm not dying. I'm in better health than most senior citizens. There's no lower blood pressure to be found in any bingo parlor anywhere."

Then *what* was The Big Secret? If she wasn't using her impending death to coerce Mom and Dad, what else could it be? Was Hanks right after all? Had Mom and Dad actually done something so unethical, they'd allow Grandma Gerd to blackmail them rather than have me find out? But no, she'd already said they hadn't done anything disreputable.

"Then what—"

"Come on, Frangi. You're a smart cookie." She blotted my wet cheek with the checkered tablecloth. "If at first you don't succeed, try, try again. Isn't that right?"

"But you wrote in your Everything Book that . . ." Ooops.

"That what?" She didn't seem angry.

" 'Both our lives will be changed forever. It's the end of my life as it's been,' " I quoted verbatim.

"Ah," she said. "Our lives *will* be changed. But not in the way you think. And for me, it *is* the *end* of an era. . . ."

My head felt strange. My entire body felt strange. A tingly sensation rippled across my skin. A faint ringing in my ears. Lights seemed brighter and blurred around the edges. My stomach suddenly cramped.

I dropped my glass of Coke right onto the pizza, speckling my shirt and Grandma Gerd's tortoiseshell glasses with red sauce.

"I feel . . . funny. . . ." Could what I had feared actually come true? I pushed back my chair and swayed on rubbery legs. "Malaria! I've contracted malaria! Or . . . or is it dengue fever?"

Grandma Gerd shook her head and blinked rapidly. She, too, looked strange. "Whatever it is, it's not dengue fever. . . ." She abruptly clutched her stomach. "Oooh."

"Done with lunch, gals? The steers need a-ropin' and the taxi's a-waitin'."

There was Hanks walking toward us, his footsteps gunshots on the ceramic-tile floor.

"What's wrong with you two?" Hanks quickly looked at me. "Was your hypothesis doubly correct?"

Grandma Gerd weakly gestured toward my Foreign Food Sanitation Spray. "I think we're having a chemical reaction."

Hanks picked up the metal bottle of spray. The bronze print rubbed off on his hands. He sprayed a little on his forearm, smelled it, then tasted it with his tongue. "How much have you had?"

"Enough," she said.

"Oh, no!" I said. "The amp-amputee!" I unsteadily turned to see my friend the amputee teetering back and forth on his crutches, his one leg as wobbly as my two.

The rest of the afternoon was a blur. I followed Grandma Gerd and Hanks out of Peppy Pete's Pizzeria into a taxi. Despite my incoherence, Hanks figured out I'd also inflicted my spray upon the amputee, so he stuffed him into the taxi, too. I remember little of the hospital other than it was crowded, less than clean, and a place I wouldn't wish on my worst enemy (Wendy)—or toughest SAT competitor (Wendy).

Apparently my cheap Foreign Food Sanitation Spray knockoffs contained a cocktail of chemical substances that aren't supposed to be inhaled, much less ingested. We were given charcoal to bind the chemicals—then had our stomachs pumped for good measure. An experience that would not be on my List of Trip Highs.

"That's what you get for buyin' black market goods," said Hanks as he paced back and forth at the foot of my bed. He clenched and unclenched his jaw and wouldn't look me in the eye. "You're lucky you're not bein' nailed into your coffin right this minute." This was the first time I'd seen him upset.

We were sharing a hospital room with twenty-five other patients. At least Grandma Gerd and I had beds next to each other. The amputee was six beds down. And he most certainly wasn't happy with me—even after I had Hanks tell him I'd pay for his stomach pumping.

Grandma Gerd was even worse off, thanks to the mix of chemicals and alcohol in her system. With her eyes still closed, she said, "Next time I'll just play along and say, 'I'm dying, I'm dying,' and save you the trouble of knocking me off."

"That's not funny!" I could barely croak it out.

"Come on, we all know you have death on the brain." She coughed. "Or is this your way of punishing me?"

"I better keep a closer eye on your granddaughter," said Hanks. "She's dangerous to your health." And then after a glare at me: "And her own."

CHAPTER ELEVEN

SHOOT 'EM UP SHOOT 'EM UP BANG BANG!

*I*T TOOK ABOUT THREE DAYS OF R & R AT THE SMILE SMILE
Guesthouse before I felt back to my normal Vassar self—
other than a raw throat from my bout with the plastic tube
and a bruised ego from acting like a complete idiot. But
Grandma Gerd appeared frayed around the edges. Even
when awake, she lay in bed with her eyes closed and winced
at the slightest sound.

I was sitting in bed writing up the Peppy Pete's Pizza adventures as my latest chapter—a difficult task since much of
it was hazy—when Hanks knocked, then entered our sick-
room without waiting for a reply.

"How 'bout ropin' some steers?"

Grandma Gerd groaned and pulled the sheet up to her
chin, eyes still firmly shut. "I'm not leaving this bed for
twenty years. But you two go ahead."

Her voice was raspy.

"No, I'll stay and keep you company."

My voice was raspy.

Grandma Gerd opened her bleary eyes. "Frangi, I really
need some alone-time today."

I was hurt, but I tried not to show it.

"If you're sure—"

"Sure I'm sure. You two go on and rustle cattle. Don't forget to keep a lookout for found art. Oh, and one more thing . . ." Grandma Gerd dropped a gum wrapper into my hand.

It contained no gum . . . only a faint "P" written in pencil.

Before we left, I typed up and emailed the latest chapter in the lobby of the guesthouse and checked what was going on stateside.

Amber: *Guess what? Garrett FINALLY asked Laurel out! Sure, it was a free outdoor concert at Seattle University, followed by a Mini-Mart hot dog and Cinnabon dinner, but . . .*

Laurel: *A date's a date!*

Amber: *BTW, hope you're not still hung up on John Pepper. Anyone who prefers a Stupacker to a Spore is a BORE.*

Laurel: *Has Denise mentioned that her parents made her sign up for ballroom dancing lessons?*

Denise: *They seem to think that being "cotillion-ready" will some-how make me more marketable to the opposite sex. Do I leap off the ledge before or after the humiliation?*

Laurel: *Did Amber mention she won another chess tourney?*

Amber: *Your mom's bugging me to invite my parents to the next one. Says that once they see me in action, they couldn't help but be proud. RIGHT. The last time they were REMOTELY inter-*

ested in anything I did was when I was named Tetherball Queen of sixth grade. . . .

Denise: *Keep those chapters coming!*

I felt a pang—their lives were continuing without me.

However, the final email from Amber confused me:

Amber: *That wild Aunt Aurora! LOVE her! What will she do next? We all think Sarah's acting like a goody-goody, though. Total PRIG. Have her loosen up, why don't you?*

What did that mean? Exactly how was Sarah a prig?

There was an email from Mom:

Mom: *It sounds like you're having such a good time—so restful and peaceful. I'm glad to hear Gertrude is actually behaving herself for once. It certainly sets my mind at ease. I'm sleeping without medication now. Amber is making quite good headway. (Although her parents continue to impose their sports agenda on her. Such a travesty!) I bought some fuchsias yesterday. Remember how much fun we had potting the hanging baskets for the patio last summer? I miss you.*

Another pang. I realized I missed her, too. And Dad. Their predictable ways were so comforting. There was definitely something to be said for routine.

An hour later, I sat behind Hanks on a rented motorbike that was more rust than paint. We bumped down a dirt road on the outskirts of Phnom Penh, narrowly avoiding potholes the size of Fiats. Every part of my body vibrated: my toes, my teeth, my clavicle. We weren't wearing helmets.

And we were going very fast.

This would be so illegal in the States. Thank goodness my parents couldn't see me now—Dad's stomach would probably implode.

I soon forgot about the speed as the dust billowed around us. I squeezed my eyes closed so the grit wouldn't get under my contact lenses. Thank goodness I'd taken off my big white hat or it would be long gone by now.

"Hold on," said Hanks. "Tight."

He dodged yet another barking mutt that magically appeared out of nowhere. I threw my arms around Hanks's waist instead of gripping the seat handle behind me. The familiar scent of Old Spice filled my nostrils. I was hyper-aware of his muscles beneath his brown cowboy shirt.

"Tighter," said Hanks.

I squeezed Hanks as tightly as I could.

"Tighter."

Flip-flop-flip-flop.

What was the deal with my stomach?

And what the heck was spelled with the letters "DADEP"?

Hanks passed a field where a herd of cows grazed and pulled up next to a bamboo hut with a roof made out of corrugated tin. An elderly man wearing a sarong and a red-and-white-checked *krama*—the traditional Cambodian cloth—around his head squatted out front, smoking a cigarette.

"He's gotta be the owner. Wait here."

Hanks walked over and squatted next to him. They conversed in Khmer for a few minutes. The owner gestured toward a teapot on a blue plastic table. Hanks looked over at me quizzically. I shook my head. How could they drink hot liquids in 100 percent humidity? I was already damp. The owner pointed at Hanks's boots. Hanks shook his head. The owner grinned and shrugged.

After Hanks paid five dollars to practice roping for the entire afternoon, he untied his lasso from the back of the motorbike.

"He wanted to buy my Godings. The geezer's got taste."

I had to laugh at the thought of that old man wearing Hanks's boots.

After practicing on a fence post until his arm and shoulder were loosened up, Hanks climbed over the fence into the field. I waited in the shade of a papaya tree.

"You gotta creep up on cows so as not to spook them," he whispered over his shoulder.

"The sight of you would spook anybody."

"Shh. Quiet now. Cows have darn good hearin'. They don't like loud or jarrin' sounds—like that voice of yours."

He slowly walked toward the nearest cow, which didn't pay him the slightest bit of attention. He started to throw his lasso—then stopped. Started to throw his lasso—then stopped again. Was it stage fright? I laughed. Hanks's back stiffened. Then he threw the lasso and ringed the cow right around the neck.

"Bravo!" I called, and applauded.

"It would be a bigger challenge on a horse, but he doesn't got any," Hanks said after lassoing a few more cows.

"What a strange way to make money: renting out your cows to be lassoed."

"He raises them for that place over there." He pointed to a large wooden shack a few hundred yards away painted with giant yellow letters: SHOOT 'EM UP SHOOT 'EM UP BANG BANG!

"For what?"

"What do you think?"

"You're kidding." He couldn't be serious. No way.

"Hey, where are you goin'?"

I strode briskly past a mound of garbage, past a chicken coop, past a line of rented motorbikes, and into the shack. The place was jammed with twenty-something backpackers, mostly Caucasian males, sitting at wooden tables reading menus. Attached to the back of the shack was a bunker where the sporadic sounds of gunfire could be heard. A lanky Cambodian boy with a straggly mullet cut, camouflage pants, and a Def Leppard T-shirt handed me a laminated piece of paper. It looked like a menu, but it sure wasn't selling food. *AK-47, thirty rounds: $20; M16, thirty rounds: $25; Grenade/RPG: $50; and there it was: Grenade with Live Cow as Target: $100!*

So it was true! I glared at a table of backpackers, who were animatedly trying to decide what "appetizer" to start with.

"What to choose, what to choose . . ."

"The M16 sounds finger-lickin' good."

"RPG!"

"Hmmm . . . I think I'll go for thirty rounds with the AK-47 with an RPG chaser."

I cornered the mullet-haired Cambodian. "You don't really use live cows, do you?"

He shrugged and walked away. Bored with the question? Couldn't understand English?

A chunky guy my age with a shaved head and combat boots stood in the bunker wearing protective ear coverings and goggles. He aimed his M16 at a target: *BOOM! BOOM!*

The echoes ricocheted in my ears.

"What a rush!" he said, stopping to take a break. He grinned at me. "Wanna try?"

Before I could respond, the cool, hard metal of the M16 was in my hands and I was propelled toward the bunker. "Wait—I'm just—I'm not—"

"What? Scared?"

"No—"

"Then try it—it's on me."

Shoot a gun? Me? My intellectual curiosity momentarily distracted me from my quest. This would show Amber that Sarah's no prig!

"It's easy. Put these goggles on. Now just put your finger here, look through there, and aim there! That's all there is to it!"

It was as if I were watching a whole different Vassar from above.

"A testosterone cocktail, that's what it is!" His giddy voice spiked the air. "Whatta rush!"

Sarah's sweaty finger gripped the trigger. She squinted through the "sight" at the black silhouette on the paper target—so distant and so tiny. She strained to hold the chunk of metal steady. It was surprisingly heavy. BOOM! The gun kicked back against her shoulder and shook her entire body—adrenaline gushed through her veins, and her hands started to shake. What a rush was right!

BOOM! BOOM!

"Look at that! You've hit the target twice! Atta girl! Go for the brain!"

BOOM!

Then—kachink! It locked up. I tried squeezing the trigger again. Nothing.

Impatiently, the mullet-haired Cambodian grabbed the M16 and shook it, banged the butt on the ground. He then took a long metal rod and jammed it down the barrel—and peered down it! *Am I seeing what I'm seeing?*

My intestines constricted. I slowly backed away from them, trying to catch my breath.

"You okay?" asked the chunky teen.

After my breathing finally regulated, I snatched a menu off the nearest table. "This is a joke, right?" I asked, pointing to the part about the cow.

"No. It's for real. He's done it." He pointed to a runty guy with braces drinking a bottle of Orange Crush. Before I could stop myself, I strode over and slapped him over the head with the menu.

"Murderer!"

Then I slapped Chunky Guy on his shaved head for good measure.

"What's her problem?"

"Hey! You come back here—"

But I was already out the door.

My adrenaline raced. My heart pumped. My mind whirled: *There's absolutely no way I'm gonna let those beautiful cows be grenaded by slacker backpackers using this struggling country as their own personal playground. It's sick and wrong and just not gonna happen.*

Hanks didn't notice my return. He was too busy teaching the cow owner how to lasso a stump.

The cows had drifted toward the far end of the field. I grabbed a rusty piece of corrugated metal off the garbage heap. Then I walked along the fence examining the dirt until I found what I was looking for: a large rock.

After checking that no one was looking my way, I unlatched the gate and left it wide open. To propel the cows through the opening, I'd have to situate myself behind them. Ideally they'd stampede *away* from me, not *over* me! Remembering what Hanks had said, I crept around the herd until I was on the opposite side. I held up the piece of metal—out of the corner of my eye I saw the owner waving his arms at me and Hanks staring at me, his mouth open—then, WHACK! I smacked the rock against the metal sheet over and over and over again. To say the cows were spooked was an understatement—instead of heading through the open gate, they crashed right through the fence!

Ooops—not exactly what I had planned.

All twenty hightailed it across the neighboring field, past SHOOT 'EM UP SHOOT 'EM UP BANG BANG!, past the neighboring bamboo farmhouses, and off into the distance until all that remained were clouds of dirt suspended in the air.

At least now they were safe. Vassar Spore to the rescue!

The owner was stunned by my actions—and at my philosophy. He just squatted in front of his hut, shaking his head incredulously. "Cow is meat," he said. "When blow up, no waste. Meat go straight to market. For to eat."

Still, it wasn't right.

"What isn't right is deprivin' this guy of his income," said Hanks. "What's the difference if they're killed by a grenade or by the butcher's cleaver?"

"Hanks, you know there's a big difference." But I began to doubt. Was he right?

A couple cows meandered back. Hanks said: "Odds are

most of 'em will find their way back eventually. Cows are used to their routines—like someone else I know."

I ignored his smirk.

The owner turned to Hanks:

"Your woman cause much trouble. Break fence. Lose cow. I call police."

Uh-oh.

We helplessly watched him walk toward his hut. His call would trigger my second run-in with the Cambodian police in less than a week.

"I didn't mean to damage your fence!" I called after him. "Honestly!"

But he kept going.

"How about fifty-three dollars?" I held up the cash Grandma Gerd gave me to last until Laos.

The owner paused and turned around. Then shook his head.

"A silver medallion necklace inscribed in Latin?" I pulled it over my head and waved it enticingly. "*Nulla dies sine linea.*"

Once again he shook his head.

"What *do* you want?" asked Hanks in a wary tone.

The owner pointed. At Hanks's Godings.

"Boot. I no call police."

"No way."

"I call police." He continued toward the hut.

Hanks and I tried everything, but the owner was adamant, his weathered face unyielding. "No boot, no deal."

Hanks lifted up his hat and ran a hand through his pomp. He looked down at his boots. Then at me. "Okay."

One by one, Hanks took off his bench-made 1940s Godings with their fancy red-and-white cutouts. He gazed at them, rubbing his hand tenderly over the leather. Then he handed them to the owner—who immediately pulled them on and strutted around like a rooster, chest out. Hanks grimly stripped off his socks and walked barefoot down the road toward the motorbike.

He looked naked.

I'm the reason Hanks is walking Goding-less down a Cambodian road! Why hadn't I mentally prepared a Pros and Cons List before causing the stampede? At home, I'd never have acted so impetuously without careful consideration. What had gotten into me? Wait, I knew what had gotten into me: Cambodia. It had oozed under my skin and seduced me into behaving in ways as opposite Vassar Spore as I could get.

Hanks's eyes were opaque. Blank. This was worse than anger. I wished he'd chew me out.

"I'll buy you another pair of boots when I get back to the U.S. I promise."

He gave me a wan smile. As in: *Good luck finding 1940s vintage Godings in my size.*

His listless resignation brought a sick feeling to my stomach.

Say you're sorry. Just say you're sorry!

But every time I opened my mouth, the words got

lodged somewhere down in my esophagus. How could two little words be so hard to say?

Way to go, Vassar. First, you get arrested and almost imprisoned. Second, you narrowly escape from the Cambodian authorities. Third, you almost kill your grandma (and an amputee) with black market sanitation spray. Fourth, you chalk up two counts of assault—albeit with plastic menus. Fifth, you cause a stampede. Sixth, you separate Hanks from his most treasured possession, thanks to your impulsiveness. What's seventh, Vassar? Extortion, kidnapping, murder?

If I didn't get out of this country soon, there was no telling what damage I'd do—to myself or others. Cambodia was dangerous to my mental health and moral fiber.

As I rode back to the guesthouse, my arms around Hanks's waist, it hit me:

I'm in love with Hanks.

And now he hates my guts.

PART FOUR

Laos

CHAPTER ONE

Volo praecessi domus.

(I want to go home.)

*H*ANKS WAS ACTING JUST LIKE HE ALWAYS DID, BUT I COULD sense an invisible barrier between us. And someone unhappy with me because of my actions was something I'd never experienced before. It felt horrible. I'd never let my parents down, never let my teachers down, never let my friends down. (In Grandma Gerd's case, she was in the wrong—so that didn't count.) During our last two weeks in Cambodia, every time I saw Hanks walking in the cheap rubber flip-flops he bought from a street vendor, I felt a sharp jab in my chest. I couldn't appreciate sightseeing or concentrate on writing my novel.

I was miserable.

Really, I realized, it was all Grandma Gerd's fault. Her idea for me to travel through Southeast Asia, her idea for me to visit Cambodia—the country of my downfall. Now that she wasn't dying after all, what secret could possibly be important enough to destroy her granddaughter's life and future? D-A-D-E-P? What did it mean?

Who cared?

So it was a relief when we finally flew to Luang Prabang, Laos—a lush, incredibly beautiful country. Like Melaka, it had French Colonial architecture juxtaposed against a tropical backdrop. Thirty-two peaked *wats* (temples) dotted the town—each one more ornate than the last with their intricately carved bas-reliefs covered with gold leaf. Luang Prabang was an oasis of calm in the sea of Southeast Asia. But ironically, Laos was Communist. Highly intolerant about many things, though on the surface it seemed like paradise.

"Isn't visiting a Communist country promoting Communism?" I'd asked Grandma Gerd as we unpacked in our guesthouse. The Ever Charming Guesthouse—which was indeed charming. It was a two-story house with wraparound balconies and a view of a *wat* (complete with saffron monks and orange novices) directly across the street.

"I don't view it that way," she'd said. "I think the more visitors see what's going on, the better chance for change. The key is to take the road less traveled, getting off the usual tour routes and seeing the *real* Laos. Someday this country will have free elections like Cambodia—not that Cambodia's got its act together yet, but at least it's got the freedom to try."

But her real reason for coming to Laos:

The Iridescent Ruffled Beetle.

"It's the focal point of the entire collage," said Grandma Gerd. "The Holy Grail of found art. So elusive that very few ever find it. But I've got a lead. . . ."

I should have known we weren't here so I could experience Luang Prabang: the friendly smiles of the locals, the blue crystalline sky, the refreshing breeze, the architecture, or the flowing Mekong. Nope. It was all about her and her art. And that's how it always would be.

Suddenly, I was tired. Really, really tired.

I wanted to go home.

And I didn't even care if I ever learned The Big Secret. I ignored the voice in the back of my head that whispered, *You've never, ever given up on a problem, equation, or project. What are you? A quitter?*

No. I was sensible. Cutting my losses. Getting out while the getting's good—or as good as it was gonna get.

Amber: *Keep up the AWESOME work—you've got one HECKA imagination! How do you come up with this stuff? Must be all that tons of time doing nothing. You CAN'T come home until you finish this puppy!*

Denise: *You can't seriously be contemplating giving up. Because Vassar Spore is NOT A QUITTER! Sorry for the Amber-caps, but I'm irate. Not only have you not completed your novel, you haven't even figured out The Big Secret! How can your intellectual curiosity be appeased when ours isn't? How can you possibly forfeit your academic career at this juncture? Must I say those motivating words . . . WENDY STUPACKER!!! (Sorry, but someone needed to do it.)*

Laurel: *You can't come home yet—Sarah hasn't bought any spoons!*

⚜ ⚜ ⚜ ⚜ ⚜ ⚜ ⚜

A week later while washing my shirt in our guesthouse bathroom, I mustered up the courage to tell Grandma Gerd I wanted to go home. She'd just walked through the door after snapping photos of a *wat,* and I broke it to her before she even had the chance to put down her bag and camera.

It was surprisingly easy. Although she was a touch hurt, she knew as well as I did that the situation was impossible. Why didn't she attempt to stop me? Why didn't she convince me to stay? I expected at the very minimum: "Frangi, don't be a wuss. Travel is broadening. Experience! Opportunity of a lifetime! You only go around once! Adventure!"

But she didn't. She even helped me repack my backpack and flag down a three-wheel motorized *tuk-tuk* to drive me back to the airport.

"Well, you can tell me The Big Secret now, can't you?" I asked as the *tuk-tuk* pulled up.

She clicked her tongue. "Sorry. You knew the rules."

Figures. I threw my backpack and daypack into the back of the *tuk-tuk.*

She grabbed my arm. "Remember, Frangi: I love you—*no matter what.*"

I froze. Wasn't that exactly what Mom had told me in the airport?

"I love you, too," I mumbled. *I love you, but I don't always like you.*

"Hey." Hanks walked out of the guesthouse, a sucker tucked in the corner of his mouth. He wouldn't quite look me in the eye as he solemnly held out his hand—the one with the silver horseshoe ring—and said without a trace of expression:

"See ya."

What? No "Mosey on, little lady"? No "Happy trails"?

I found myself saying in an artificially high voice as if I'd just inhaled helium:

"I'll send you some new Godings, I promise." Then I climbed into the *tuk-tuk*. I faced straight ahead as we drove off, refusing to look back at the two of them. Not even to wave.

Once I was out of eyesight, I cried.

"I'm coming home," I told Mom and Dad on the airport pay phone.

"You are?" Mom couldn't disguise the elation in her voice. "Leon! Vassar's coming home!" Then: "We absolutely understand, Vassar. There's a limit to how long a sane person can handle Gertrude Spore."

"And don't worry: I have more than enough material to finish my novel when I return—"

"We're not worried about that! Academics, you can handle. But an unpredictable, unconventional grandmother isn't so easy." Then her tone turned apprehensive. "Unless . . . is there, well, any *special* reason you're returning early?"

I reassured her there wasn't.

Grandma Gerd had given me just enough money to pay for the ticket to Singapore and the fee to change my return ticket to Seattle from August to July. Finally, I was doing what I wanted to do, when I wanted to do it. I was in control of my own destiny—for once.

I set my daypack and backpack down in front of the Laos Air ticket counter. The sparsely mustached clerk smiled and said: *"Sabadii."*

"Sabadii, sir. Are there seats available on the two p.m. flight to Singapore?"

He checked the computer.

"Yes. It will be one hundred fifty U.S. dollar."

"I'll take it."

"Passport, please."

Zip-zip. My driver's license, receipts, and return airline ticket.

But no passport.

I checked again. I'd never misplaced anything in my life. It had to be in there.

It wasn't.

I ripped the flesh-colored money belt completely off my waist and emptied the contents onto the counter. The clerk helpfully organized the items into tidy piles. He seemed apologetic for inconveniencing me.

No passport.

I couldn't believe it. My money belt was *never* out of my sight. Ever. I even slept with it around my waist. Had an especially adept pickpocket brushed up against me on the street? Had a sneaky guesthouse clerk slipped into the bedroom while I was showering?

Neither of those seemed feasible.

What was I to do? I obviously wasn't going anywhere. I'd have to apply for a new passport at the American Embassy. And who knew how long that would take? Hanks had said most embassies in Southeast Asia suspected young Americans with "lost" passports of selling them to locals for thousands of dollars.

As the clerk's thin fingers deftly straightened the stacks of Cambodian currency and receipts, I noticed a folded piece of paper with smeared pencil handwriting. With a sense of foreboding, I opened it:

I know. You're upset. But you'll thank me later. GG

The clerk and I were equally surprised at the profanity that spewed out of my mouth. I didn't even know what some of the words meant.

When I returned to the Ever Charming Guesthouse, Grandma Gerd was conveniently out, but there was a manila envelope on my bed. It contained another note:

Tomorrow we're going on a six-day trek through the jungle in search of the Iridescent Ruffled Beetle. Pack light and get a good night's sleep. If you follow directions, you'll get your passport back. But the more stubborn you are, the more

uncomfortable this whole experience will be. So why not . . .
LIM? GG

Hanks was right. When I called the American Embassy in the capital city of Vientiane, they didn't look favorably upon my situation.

The impatient male voice on the other end snorted, then said: "You don't really expect us to believe your own grand-mother stole your passport? Come on, you can do better than that."

Even though there were two backpackers waiting to use the guesthouse lobby phone, I made another call.

"What do you mean you're not coming?" Mom's voice escalated.

Patiently—more patiently than I was feeling—I explained it all again, to the annoyance of the backpackers. Before I'd even finished, Mom interrupted:

"We can't let her get away with this! We'll call the embassy—the U.S. ambassador—the White House—"

"Althea, there's nothing we can do."

"There's always something you can do!"

Dad's voice came across the wire, surprisingly firm: "No, Althea. This time there's nothing . . . you . . . can . . . do."

Mom hiccupped, then was silent.

"Here," said Dad. "Have one of these." There came the unmistakable sound of a bottle of pills being opened. "Vassar will go on the trek and have a good time. Won't you, Vassar?"

"Yes, Dad." I said. Then I added for Mom's benefit: "Now that I think about it, a trek actually sounds fun. *Really* fun."

Dad was right. I had no choice. I was a prisoner in Laos, and Grandma Gerd was the warden.

And there *was* a solution: Follow Grandma Gerd's instructions. The irony. She who abhorred plans was inflicting them on her granddaughter.

CHAPTER TWO

Bounmy

DO NOT HATE GRANDMA GERD. DO NOT HATE GRANDMA
Gerd.

Grandma Gerd handed me a chocolate bar. "Here. You
need some pep." The label read CRUNKY! "It's from Japan.
They're big into wacky brand names."

I took it without speaking or changing my expression
whatsoever. Wouldn't give her the satisfaction. This time *I*
was administering the silent treatment.

The three of us were walking along the Mekong to meet
our trek guide. We all wore daypacks (traveling light; the
rest of our luggage remained at the guesthouse) and new
green-and-black jungle boots Grandma Gerd had bought
us—along with hiking socks that wicked away moisture.

"You can't make this trek in flip-flops or sandals—even
if the locals do." The rugged jungle boots made a humorous juxtaposition against Grandma Gerd's fisherman's pants,
Cubist-patterned blouse, and Vietnamese mollusk hat—as
well as Hanks's cowboy hat and chops.

As for me, well. If Mom and Dad could see their only
daughter now: Gone were my stylish travel linens and trusty

Spring-Zs—replaced with baggy green fisherman's pants, a Laos Ale T-shirt, jungle boots, and a tan, which I'd managed to acquire despite repeat applications of 45 SPF. But I still had my big white hat.

Grandma Gerd's daypack bulged with extra boxes and cotton for all the Iridescent Ruffled Beetles she was planning on capturing. "This particular part of Laos is the only place they're found in all of Southeast Asia," she explained to Hanks.

Grandma Gerd abruptly dropped to a squat and groped through the dirt. After a moment she jumped to her feet clutching a smashed cigarette pack. She wiped it off on her shirt, leaving skids of brown across her chest. "Brilliant! Just look at the design: It's a lotus. A red lotus on a golden yellow background. Isn't that just sensational?"

"So we're taking the road less traveled," I said. Giving her the silent treatment was getting old. I shifted my daypack. My shoulders weren't used to carrying something so heavy.

"Frangi," Grandma chortled. "We're taking *no* road!"

I wasn't liking this.

"No Road Travel—we're taking their Trek Where No Trekker Has Gone Before!'"

"But my guidebook says that the Laos government doesn't allow overnight stays in the tribal villages—"

"*Unless* you're with a licensed outfit. And as it so happens, No Road Travel is the only licensed outfit in Luang Prabang. We're going to see the *real* Laos—not a tour simulation. Our guide, Sone, is *the* expert on Laos hill tribal areas. *The* authority on the Iridescent Ruffled Beetle." She dug around in the side pocket of her daypack.

"Now that you're talking to me again . . ." Grandma handed me a cluster of tiny pebbles glued together to form a "T."

"What makes you think I'm still interested?"

"That intellectual curiosity of yours."

D-A-D-E-P-T.

Bicycles, motorbikes, and *tuk-tuks* cruised past us. Outside a handicrafts shop, wooden boxes containing flattened paper pulp peppered with tiny orange flowers were drying in the sun. Grandma Gerd *oohed* and snapped a photo with her Brownie camera. Then bought eleven rolls of dried paper to be picked up on her return.

Hanks walked ahead of me, his cowboy hat pushed back on his head.

Why did he come along? I wondered. *I'd have thought the less time spent with me, the better.*

As if reading my mind, he glanced behind him. But I couldn't interpret his expression. His mirrored glasses just reflected me back at myself—and I didn't like what I saw. But at least my bug bites and purple bump had faded.

Come on, I tried to convince myself, *who cares if he doesn't like you—he doesn't even fit your prototype. He's not six feet five or blond or a surgeon-to-be. Doesn't own a boat or a white nubby sweater. And lives a zillion miles away. Not remotely boyfriend material.*

It didn't work.

✎   ✎   ✎   ✎   ✎   ✎   ✎

Below us the Mekong glistened in the morning sunlight. Blue and red and yellow long-tailed boats cut through the muddy water. We sat on a stone bench and ate croissants while we waited for Sone. The light and buttery croissants were a welcome byproduct of French colonialization (according to my *Genteel Traveler's Guide*). I was conscious of Hanks's thigh barely touching mine. But we both looked straight ahead as we chewed our breakfast.

A white *sawngthaew* (a pickup truck with two bench seats running down the sides of the flatbed) pulled up beside us.

A boy jumped out of the passenger seat and walked toward us, hand outstretched.

"*Sabaai dii*, madams and sir! I am your guide!"

He couldn't possibly be more than twelve. Even game-for-anything Grandma Gerd seemed taken aback. The three of us swiveled in unison, scanning for someone more suitable.

"You're Sone? The renowned hill tribes expert? The international authority on the Iridescent Ruffled Beetle?" asked Grandma.

"I am Bounmy, madam! I shall endeavor to please!"

He was five feet tall, wiry, with the usual cappuccino skin and jet-black hair. But unlike the usual Laotian attire of cool silk or cotton or linen, he wore jeans, a black T-shirt, and a thick jacket with NEW YORK YANKEES emblazoned on the back.

"Bounmy? I thought our guide's name was Sone?" I said.

"Change of plan, madams and sir!" he said cheerfully, lifting our packs into the *sawngthaew*.

"But do you know what the Iridescent Ruffled Beetle is?" Grandma Gerd's voice sounded strained. "And where it can be found?"

"Sone tell me," said Bounmy with a wave of his hand.

"Brilliant! Unpredictability! I love it already!" she replied with relief and popped the last of her croissant into her mouth.

"How old are you?" I asked.

"Old enough to like the ladies," he said, leering.

Who was this fellow? And where had he picked up his banter?

"So are you married? Got any kids?" asked Hanks with mock seriousness.

"Alas, I have not found my special lady," said Bounmy sadly.

After driving for fifteen minutes our *sawngthaew* driver turned down a bumpy dirt road that led to a clearing in the middle of the jungle. In the center of the clearing sat a battered helicopter. Grandma Gerd, Hanks, and I exchanged looks.

"What are we doing here? I thought we were going to the mountains?" I asked.

"Must take helicopter to start of trail," Bounmy replied, holding the door as we all squeezed out of the *sawngthaew*.

The helicopter, Bounmy explained, was an Air America

relic left over from the drug war. It looked soldered together—just barely.

"That doesn't look safe to me," I said to Grandma.

"But it is only way to reach trail, miss," insisted Bounmy. "Do not fear, Bounmy most capable guide!"

Bounmy opened the side door with a flourish.

"Hey, if it can survive a war zone . . ." Hanks trailed off as the door came off in Bounmy's hand.

After the pilot fixed the door with a bungee cord, I reluctantly followed Grandma Gerd, Hanks, and Bounmy into the helicopter. The pilot was a heavyset man who spoke no English. The blades whirled, and dust went flying. We jerked into the air. My knuckles turned white from gripping my armrest and Grandma Gerd's forearm. She didn't even flinch, just continued snapping Polaroids through the grimy—cracked!—window.

Now we were hovering over Luang Prabang. I never thought there could be so many shades of green. Rice paddies green, jungle green, mountain green. And dotted with gleaming gold peaks.

"Look at all the *wats*," said Grandma Gerd.

Fsssht!

Below us, the Mekong cut a path through the green-and-brown patches. I distracted myself by counting the *wats*. *One, two, three, four—no, that was a hotel—four, five—I'm getting nauseated!—count, count, oh, look—sick, sick, gonna be sick . . .*

The helicopter finally landed on the cleared section of a field at the base of a mountain. Nearby, workers macheting bamboo paused to watch us disembark. I rushed over to vomit onto a pile of discarded stalks.

As I wiped my mouth with a Kleenex, the helicopter rose into the air, its blades hurling pieces of bamboo into our faces. I shrieked. Anyone who wears gas-permeable contact lenses understands the excruciating pain even the tiniest of fibers can cause when it becomes embedded under the lens. Quickly, I popped my right contact lens out of my eye and put it into my mouth, hoping my saliva would rinse the offending particle off.

Then I felt a big thump on my back and Grandma Gerd said: "There. Feel better? Got it all out?"

Gulp!

I choked and coughed, working up phlegm to enable the contact to ride out on it like a wave. I jammed a finger down my throat to induce more vomiting. But I just gagged over and over . . . my mental self knowing that my physical self had nothing more to regurgitate. It wasn't to be fooled. For a full five minutes, I alternately swore and jammed my finger down my throat. Grandma Gerd, Hanks, Bounmy, and the bamboo harvesters watched as if I were performing some sort of tribal dance.

I whirled around to face Grandma Gerd.

"You made me swallow my contact lens!?!"

They had no idea how unbalanced and off-kilter the world looked through one lens. And, wouldn't you know, I suddenly realized, I'd left my spare pair of glasses behind in my big backpack at the guesthouse.

"When are you going to get soft lenses like the rest of the world?" asked Grandma.

"Gas-permeable contact lenses happen to prevent my eyes from getting worse," I said, clenching my jaw so tightly, I got an instant headache.

Bounmy stared at me expectantly—probably wondering what nasty bodily function I'd perform for an encore.

"Bounmy, I need you to call back the helicopter. I can't go on the trek with just one contact."

He smiled encouragingly. "Sorry, miss! No phone here. No phone for entire trek. Very natural and rustic as requested."

I attempted to control my mounting impatience. "No, with your cell phone."

"Cell phone?"

"What? You don't carry a cell phone—or even a walkie-talkie?"

He laughed delightedly. "No, miss. The helicopter shall return in six days as planned. No need for phone when have good plan."

Right.

"Did you hear that?" I asked Grandma Gerd. "What if something happens?"

"You shall experience the bounties of the coquettish Mother Nature. Relax, please, and enjoy. Ready, miss?" Bounmy held out my daypack. "Must hurry to see the most lovely beetles."

Then he hoisted an enormous backpack full of food onto his shoulders, topped it off with four rolled-up rubber mats, and picked up two plastic bags bulging with water bottles and said, "Shall we go?"

"You're not really carrying all that?" Grandma asked.

"Let me help," said Hanks.

Bounmy looked like a snail in an oversize shell. "I shall be fine."

"Do me a favor and let me take some of it," insisted Hanks.

Bounmy finally gave in: "If it will enhance your enjoyment." And he handed Hanks one of the bags of water.

"Madams and sir, if you endeavor to maintain a good pace, I shall regale you with a most spellbinding sunset."

We followed him up a narrow, dirt-packed path. The harvesters returned to their hacking. Show over.

"So, Bounmy," said Grandma Gerd. "How many times have you led this trek?"

"First time."

"What?!"

I stopped dead in my tracks. Grandma Gerd quickened her pace, not eager to catch my frigid gaze. She said, "Interesting. So how do you know where you're going?"

"I follow Sone once. Look! Butterfly! Nature's little dancer!"

"Exactly where is Sone and why couldn't he take us himself?" I asked.

"Sone have accident. Ah, so many butterflies! Be warned: They follow beauty."

Like fingers that won't stop fiddling with a sore tooth, I kept probing:

"What sort of an accident?"

"Oh, he fall off cliff and break both legs. Mud very slippery. Such bad tragedy."

We all exchanged looks.

"When Sone get hurt they no want to lose business. So they ask me to go since I follow Sone on trek one time. So Bounmy take vacation from school to guide you most excellently!"

CHAPTER THREE

Trekking

*E*VEN GRANDMA GERD WAS STRUCK DUMB BY BOUNMY'S revelation. We were heading into the lush jungle that umbrella-ed us from the harsh sun but also insulated us from any refreshing breezes. My clothes were saturated with sweat. Bamboo, ferns, palms, and other greenery enclosed us with a stifling thickness. The smell of my namesake, frangipani, filled the air. Butterflies danced above our heads. And the path led us grindingly up a mountain, switchback style. Up, up, and up on a path so narrow, only one of us could fit on it at a time.

Okay, keep calm, keep calm. At least he seems to know where he's go—

"Stop please, madams and sir!" Bounmy said as he gracefully squeezed past us back down the way we came. We followed dumbly. When we reached the bottom of the trail that ran alongside the base of the mountain, he abruptly turned onto a trail offshoot. "Yes. Now we are correct!" His Levi-clad legs led us back up, up, up.

I grimly refused to comment, and Grandma Gerd knew enough not to say a word.

How could Bounmy carry all that when my small day-pack already felt like bricks?

Grandma Gerd stepped spryly for the first eight or so switchbacks, then downshifted into slow but sure strides. Ten minutes later she downshifted yet again into leaden Frankenstein steps.

"Bounmy, is there any wildlife we should be aware of— like anacondas?" I asked.

"Pardon?"

"Snakes."

"Ah, snakes. No bad snakes. Only friendly snakes. But we have many leech, spider, and scorpion."

"Does that relieve your mind?" said Grandma Gerd.

I tucked my pants into my socks and sprayed on extra bug repellent.

We trudged onward and upward.

"Hold on!" Behind me, Grandma Gerd stooped to pick something up off the ground: an iridescent rock. She dropped it and straightened up. "False alarm."

Hanks dropped back to wait with me as I paused for a rest. He took off his mirrored aviator glasses and put them in his breast pocket.

"Walkin' fast, then stoppin'—that's not good for the body."

"And?" I could barely speak I was panting so hard.

"Keep a slow, steady pace instead of rushin', then stoppin' to catch your breath. Think of your body as a car engine. Each time you start and stop it over and over again, it takes more and more energy and fuel. But by maintainin' a slower, constant speed you conserve energy. Got it?"

"I think so."

He rustled in the underbrush, then returned with two bamboo sticks. "Use these for support and balance. One, two, one, two."

I stopped. "Hanks."

A step ahead of me, Hanks paused. "Yeah?"

I looked up at him. His cowboy hat cast a shadow over his eyes. All I could see were his nose and mouth. Which made it easier to say what I had to say: "I'm really, *really* sorry about your Godings." My voice peaked at an unnaturally high pitch. I cleared my throat. "I really am . . . sorry."

A moment passed. Then he slowly smiled. He pushed the hat back on his head so I could see his dark brown eyes. "No problem. They were . . . *just* boots."

Flip-flop.

The heaviness I'd felt for days finally lifted and a surge of energy filled me. Now I could walk forever!

"Whoa!" If Hanks hadn't grabbed me, I would have stepped right over the edge. "That's the fourth time I've saved your keister. Don't let there be a fifth."

"Madams and sir, we shall stop here for refreshment!" called Bounmy from way up the trail.

"About time," croaked Grandma Gerd from behind me.

She was a sodden mass of laundry—her fisherman's pants, shirt, and socks were dripping. I was no different. After four hours of trekking, we were all sweat bags—make that starving sweat bags. Bounmy passed out a late lunch of squashed ham-and-cheese baguettes (another colonialization perk), but Grandma Gerd and I were so exhausted, we could barely chew. For once I sat down, my renewed energy left my body. The combined forces of altitude, humidity, and the exerting of muscles heretofore unexerted sapped me. Thus, no conversation. Just the soft sound of mashing of bread against the tongue.

Aunt Aurora's putting us all through this for some stupid iridescent beetle with ruffles, Sarah thought as she huffed her way up the mountain.

Hanks blotted his face with his bandanna. I watched with fascination as a drop of sweat ran along his jaw. His chops were peeling and his shirt clung to his chest. Highlighting every muscle.

Flip-flop.

Before we resumed climbing, Hanks cut us pieces of moleskin with his pocket knife. We applied them to our blisters—which all three of us had thanks to our new jungle boots.

Bounmy's energy was bountiful. "Enjoying trek, madams and sir? Such good flora and fauna we see today. And more to come. Butterfly!"

Our lack of enthusiasm did not deter him from pointing out each and every butterfly that crossed our path.

"Bounmy, I'd prefer you keep your eyes peeled for beetles," said Grandma Gerd, fanning herself with a napkin.

"Beetles, very nice. So pretty, so colorful."

"How much farther?" The effort of simply forming words made me want to curl up in a fetal position.

"Five tiny hours, madams! Five more hours of blessed views!"

I wished I hadn't asked.

What made people climb mountains? Those lunatics who climbed Machu Picchu, Kilimanjaro, Everest—what drove them to waste all that time and energy to simply get to the top of a land mass?

Dainty balls of perspiration rolled down Bounmy's temples. And his short black hair was damp, but he refused to remove his leather New York Yankees jacket. He pulled a pack of Lotus-brand cigarettes from his back pocket and lit up as smoothly as a forty-year addict. He inhaled deeply and expertly exhaled through his nose. Then he politely offered us the pack.

"Should you be smoking at your age?" I asked.

"Smoking is a gift everyone should enjoy! No matter how old," he added, nodding respectfully at Grandma Gerd.

The smoke mingled with the butterflies fluttering overhead.

CHAPTER FOUR

Mr. Vang's Hospitality

A homestay is a delightful way to immerse yourself
in the native culture. A home away from home
filled with people oh-so-different than *you*!
—*The Genteel Traveler's Guide to Laos*

BY THE TIME MY THIGH AND CALF MUSCLES WERE PULSATING
with pain, we reached the top of the first mountain
peak. Dusk approached. Yet another phenomenal tropical
sunset streaked the sky.

"We shall now enter genuine Hmong village," Bounmy
said.

The small village consisted of ten huts made out of
bamboo and wood, raised off the ground by stilts. A system
of hollow bamboo tubes procured water from a nearby
stream. Pot-bellied piglets and mutts roamed. Round,
graceful cages made of thin strands of bamboo housed
roosters and hens. Brown pieces of what looked like leather
hung on a line.

"What are those?" I asked Bounmy.

"Dried meats," he said.

"Beef jerky," said Hanks.

In the valley below us, terraced rice paddies gleamed golden in the glow of the setting sun. Mountains and hills surrounded us as far as the eye could see. As we followed Bounmy along the central dirt path of the village, the smell of smoke from hut fires filled our noses and the damp of night cooled our skin.

Both the adults and children of the village cheerfully welcomed us by *sompiahing* (like the Malaysian *salaaming,* hands pressed together chest high) as we went by.

"Hello!"

"Americano!"

The women wore blouses and brightly colored sarongs; the men wore shirts and short pants; both wore rubber flip-flops or went barefoot. They resembled the Laotians in Luang Prabang with their dark eyes and blue-black hair, but their skin was slightly darker from farming.

It was obvious Westerners had trekked this way before, but not enough to deflate their curiosity or goodwill. An elderly woman chopping sugarcane insisted on giving each of us a stick. Bounmy showed us how to chew it, suck out all the sugar, then spit out the fibers.

We passed by a pen with two brown cows.

"Don't get any ideas," said Hanks.

He was lucky my mouth was full of sugarcane.

Our first homestay was in the hut of Mr. Vang, a widower. His big grin offered us a gleam of white with gaps where eyeteeth should have been. His hair was neatly trimmed, and he smelled of aftershave.

"Hello! Thank you! God bless you!" he said in a jovial tone, shaking our hands one by one.

"Thank you for your hospitality," said Grandma Gerd. "We are—"

"Hello! Thank you! God bless you!"

"That is all the English he know. He speak Hmong and some Laotian," said Bounmy, who then conversed with Vang in Laotian.

"Mr. Vang say that you are very welcome and someday he will visit Disneyland."

"Hello! Thank you! God bless you!"

We removed our muddy shoes and entered the Vang abode.

Vang's bamboo hut was large and spacious and so clean, I could eat off the bamboo-slatted floor. He had somehow managed to bring an ornately carved bureau up the mountain, and it was topped with water bottles, pop bottles, wine bottles, and—a bottle of Polo aftershave. White plastic-molded chairs surrounded a large wooden table in the center of the hut. Enclosed bedrooms ran along the left wall, and a large area for cooking ran along the right. Wooden stairs led to a second floor that functioned as a sleeping loft. A lone lightbulb hung from the peaked ceiling—Vang was very proud of his little generator. It had taken many years of rice farming to save up for it. Apparently Vang was prosperous for a Hmong tribesperson.

Vang lived with his two married daughters (whose names loosely translated were Grace and Peace), their husbands, and five grandchildren. Unfortunately, the sisters' husbands were off buying a cow and wouldn't be back for a couple days. They'd be disappointed they'd missed us. The Vang family enjoyed hosting trekkers and welcomed them an average of twice a month. Various travel agencies repaid their hospitality with food and a stipend. But they really did it to make friends from all over the world. A large piece of cardboard hung on the bamboo wall covered with signatures of all the overnight guests they'd hosted from Maryland to Iceland. We took turns signing it with my red felt-tip pen. Instead of his signature, Hanks drew an HL tucked inside an upside-down horseshoe U.

"My brand," he said.

Over the bureau hung a Paint by Numbers of Jesus as the Good Shepherd. The colors were pea greens, dung browns, sausage taupes, and alarmingly white whites for the sheep and clouds. And it wasn't even finished—one of the sheep was completely devoid of paint.

Grandma Gerd's eyes lit up. "Fantastic!"

"Grandma . . . ," I whispered warningly. I could just see her trying to buy his only bit of décor. Or, let's be frank: stealing it.

"What?" she asked innocently.

"Would anyone like to wash?" asked Bounmy.

I could have kissed him.

After we'd all washed in Vang's makeshift outdoor shower of bamboo, banana leaves, and bucket of water, we changed into clean clothes. I was relieved to shed the perspiration-soaked T-shirt and pants. (Why was my sweat in Southeast Asia so much more pungent than my sweat in Seattle? A question for Denise, who'd won the science fair with her entry: "Identifying the Bacterial Enzyme That Releases Sulfur-Containing Scent Molecules in Sweat.")

For the first time since I'd arrived in Southeast Asia, I felt a touch chilly. My guidebooks said that it cooled down in the mountains and that at night, the higher altitudes could be downright cold. What a refreshing change!

In the kitchen, Bounmy cooked a makeshift meal, squatting beside the central fire. From his backpack came an endless supply of ingredients, Tupperware bowls, and utensils. Apparently the trek guide provided all the meals during the homestays.

Vang's older daughter, Grace, enthusiastically helped Bounmy, her quick, deft hands slicing mushrooms and chopping up a recently slaughtered chicken. She had a gold front tooth, and laugh lines around her eyes. Peace sat in the corner, nursing her baby, and seemed to be making good-natured fun of Bounmy's gourmet prowess.

"Peace say I make good wife," translated Bounmy, grinning. Although Peace was only a year older than me, she already had two children: a three-month-old and a two-year-old. She had a dimple in her chin like mine, and a mole under her left eye that looked like a brown tear. Both she and her sister wore T-shirts with their sarongs and held their hair back with scrunchies.

I tried to imagine Denise, Amber, Laurel, and me all married with children—at our age.

And failed.

Peace gestured toward Hanks, who was sitting in the main room of the hut next to Grandma Gerd. Vang was regaling them both with his mega collection of postcards sent by former trekkers. She said something to Bounmy in a soft, lyrical voice and pointed to her cheek.

"She want to know if his hair . . . how do you say . . . tickle," said Bounmy. He and Peace giggled. Grace reprimanded Peace, but she too giggled.

"Tell her I wouldn't know," I said. Would never know.

Then Peace asked Bounmy to ask me: "Is he your special friend?"

I glanced into the other room. Hanks was reading a "Salutations from Sausalito!" postcard.

Then I whispered to Bounmy: "Tell her I wish he was."

He did. Peace giggled again and nuzzled her face in her baby's hair.

Bounmy tasted his noodle-spinach concoction and made a face. "Need coriander," he said, and went outside.

The adults squeezed around the table while the children ate sitting on woven mats on the floor. Peace led me to the seat next to Hanks, smothering her mouth to cover a titter.

Hanks raised an eyebrow. I looked away before he could see my face turning pink.

I noticed that we were each given a metal Asian spoon, but there were no individual spoons for each of the five different entrées. Everyone just dug in with their own personal spoons. A germ holocaust waiting to happen! And as I was about to pull out my antibacterial soap to at least wash my spoon, I remembered I'd left it in my big backpack at the guesthouse.

While Vang prayed in Hmong for our food, I prayed I wouldn't catch anything. What the heck, it was worth a try. As soon as he finished, I was the first to load up my bowl with large helpings so I wouldn't be forced to get seconds from the "tainted" bowls after the family all started digging in for the second round. Hanks gave me a bemused look.

"Mmm . . . the spinach noodles are fantastic," said Grandma Gerd, literally gobbling down her food.

"It is the coriander, the gracious coriander," said Bounmy.

Then he passed around a woven basket.

"Purple sticky rice. Laos specialty."

We each took a handful.

Sticky was right. It was so gummy, it took a full minute to chew. But it was more flavorful than regular rice. And I liked the brownish-purple color.

"Dip sticky rice in food—no need fork!" Bounmy rolled a bit of rice into a ball and dipped it into a bowl of minced chicken and mint leaves. Then popped it into his mouth.

"Not bad," said Hanks, going back for seconds and thirds.

"Sticky rice rubbery like Lao time," said Bounmy, a cud of rice in his cheek. "To American, nine o'clock mean nine o'clock. To Laotian, nine o'clock mean ten o'clock. Rubber time!"

"Sounds like my kind of place, huh, Frangi?" said Grandma Gerd. Her silver-grey mop was more tousled than ever, and the greenish lenses of her glasses were smudged.

I smiled stiffly, then turned away. I still hadn't completely forgiven her.

The Vang family all expressed their enthusiasm for Bounmy's cooking.

"Feast, Miss Vassar! Enjoy banquet!" said Bounmy, noticing my bowl was now empty.

"Thank you, Bounmy, it's delicious—it really is. But I'm full."

He seemed stung, but I wasn't going to allow manners to interfere with my health.

With a flourish, Vang set a bottle and votive-size glasses down on the table.

Bounmy smiled and lit up a cigarette. "*Lao-lao.* Vang's very extra-special recipe." He passed the pack around. Vang took a cigarette—positioning it through one of his gaps where it stuck out like a walrus tusk.

"What's *lao-lao*?" I asked.

"A type of distilled rice liquor," said Grandma Gerd.

"Don't worry, it's not strong." From the look she gave me, I knew I'd be required to partake, so as not to offend our host.

Vang poured a glass for each of us, then held his glass aloft and toasted us in a melodic, singsong voice. Bounmy interpreted: " 'Thank you for honoring my home with your presence. You are always welcome here. God bless you, your families, and your future families.' "

We drank. I didn't know what to think. The only alcoholic beverage I'd ever had before was NyQuil. This was more delicate, much sweeter, and had less of an aftertaste.

Vang refilled our glasses.

"To Vang's hospitality!" said Grandma Gerd.

We drank. The glasses were refilled.

"To Bounmy's guidance!" said Hanks.

Toast. Drink. Refill. Repeat.

Then Vang looked at me and toasted. Bounmy snickered.

"He say: May you and Hanks have long life together with many little Hanks!"

I gasped.

"I'll drink to that," said Hanks with a grin and quickly downed his *lao-lao*.

CHAPTER FIVE
Freshly Brewed

AFTER GETTING READY FOR BED AND USING THE BAMBOO outhouse, we climbed the hut stairs to the sleeping loft. The mats were rolled out, each topped with a thick, fuzzy blanket, compliments of Mr. Vang. We laid in a row: Bounmy, Hanks, Grandma Gerd, me. The Vang family slept in the two enclosed rooms down below. Grandma Gerd's whistling snores and Bounmy's rhythmic breathing soon filled the air. Which didn't thrill Hanks.

"Got any more earplugs?"

"No. But here. You can have one and I'll have one and we'll sleep with our unplugged ears to the pillows."

He reached out a hand, then hesitated.

"What's the matter?"

"Ear wax."

"Your loss," I said, and put them both in my ears.

"I'm kiddin'! Wait! I kid! I kid!"

But his loud whispers were soon muffled by the expansion of the orange pieces of foam in my ears and I drifted off to sleep.

Two hours later, my bladder awoke me. I wasn't used to

drinking so much liquid before bed. I removed my earplugs to hear:

Rain.

Great. I'd have to go outside in *that*.

I groped around in my daypack for my toiletry bag and carefully put in my lone contact lens. Then grabbed my Maglite and Kleenex.

I gently made my way past the sleepers and down the squeaky bamboo ladder. No one stirred. How inconvenient to have only one entrance to a home.

I pushed the door. It didn't budge. I pushed over and over until I noticed that a length of wood held it firmly in place. I jiggled the wood, but I couldn't dislodge it.

What the heck? Why the barricade? After all, it was a hut, not the U.S. Treasury!

The pressure in my bladder was so great by this time, I was crossing my legs and squeezing.

I rocked back and forth and wondered if I should wake up Vang or his daughters. I didn't relish knocking on either of the closed bamboo bedroom doors and disrupting their sleep. I tried rattling the door in an attempt to somehow dislodge the wood barrier. There was no budging it. Reluctantly, I approached one of the bedroom doors. But just as I was about to knock, I had an epiphany.

I scampered back up the ladder, made my way back to my mat, and removed an empty water bottle from my backpack. If Hanks could do it, so could I!

First I double-checked that Grandma Gerd, Hanks, and

Bounmy were all still asleep. Then I turned off my flashlight and pressed myself into the corner farthest from my sleeping companions. It was dark enough that if one of them should stir, they wouldn't quite be able to tell what I was doing. I could pretend I had a leg cramp and was doing stretches. Or something.

I tied a sarong I'd bought in Cambodia around my waist for added protection from any accidental gaze.

Then positioned the bottle.

And willed myself to pee.

Nothing.

Peeing on command is hard enough, but peeing on command *in a bottle* when you aren't sure if you have *correct aim* is the hardest thing I've ever attempted—and that includes memorizing the entire Periodic Table.

Oh, to be a guy! How much easier their lives were!

I repositioned and tried again.

Behind me, someone coughed.

I froze.

Oh, please don't let it be Hanks, not Hanks, not Hanks!

"Gonna try recyclin' after all, eh?"

A thought crossed my brain. He wouldn't, would he?

"If you dare take my picture—" I said through clenched teeth.

The bamboo flooring creaked, and then he was right behind me.

"Here, I'll hold up the sarong around you. See?"

"Don't look!"

"I'm not. Just relax."

"But what if it overflows? I don't know if I can stop it once it starts."

"Take it easy. It'll be fine. Trust me."

"I can't do this—you're making me nervous."

"Come on. Pretend you're sittin' on your toilet at home, doin' your Latin homework. . . ."

Latin! If only it were as easy as Latin!

I closed my eyes and willed myself to relax: *Relax, relax, relax. Think soothing. Soothing. Sitting with Mom and Dad by the fireplace, drinking herbal tea, reading—conjugate "to read": egō, legere, lēgī, lēctum . . .*

Somehow I managed to fill the bottle and—*Euge!*—didn't need another.

I pulled up my pajama bottoms and breathed an enormous sigh of relief.

Hanks dropped his arms, and the sarong wall collapsed. A euphoric stupor enveloped me. I was completely relaxed—and drained.

"Screw the lid on tightly. We sure don't need any spillage," he said.

Gripping the warm bottle of liquid, I turned around—and found myself nose-to-nose with Hanks. Or, to be precise, *almost* nose-to-nose, since he was a couple inches shorter. His black hair hung in his eyes, and his chops were still on his cheeks.

"I'll get rid of that for you." His hand covered my hand as he reached for the bottle.

"That's okay—"

As I tried to pull away, his hand tightened over mine.

Which sent tingles racing across my entire body.

I suddenly felt like I had to pee again.

His normally mischievous eyes were intense. Like magnets. They seemed to suck my eyes into his.

In all my fantasies, I'd never foreseen the possibility of my first kiss taking place with a chop-wearing Chinese Malay cowboy named Hanks in a bamboo hut in a hill tribe in Communist Laos—all the while clutching a bottle of my own freshly brewed urine!

Hanks leaned forward.

I remained absolutely motionless.

Softer than I'd anticipated, with a slight flavor of *lao-lao*.

Flip-flop flip-flop flip-flop flip-flop flip-flop flip-flop flip-flop flip-flop flip-flop!

I'm kissing! I was melting from the inside out, there was a ringing in my ears, my stomach whirled, my eyes glazed, my skin secreted a pint of sweat. But Hanks didn't seem to notice. I was so hyperaware of his warm skin, the blood pulsating through his veins, the pressure of his fingers, that I unconsciously held my breath. *Could he tell this was my first kiss?* After a couple minutes, I let out a strangled half-choke, half-belch as I gasped for air.

Hanks laughed.

How romantic.

He touched the dimple in my chin.

"Let's try that again," he said in a husky voice.

My body seemed to have a mind of its own—suddenly I was clinging to him.

Tight. Tighter. Tighter.

"Frangi, what are you doing? It's two in the morning."

As Grandma Gerd rummaged around to find her glasses, Hanks and I jolted apart—dropping the bottle onto the bamboo floor.

"Careful," said Hanks, his voice even huskier than before.

Disappointment flooded me. That little taste wasn't enough—I wanted more!

"I was just . . . uh, giving Hanks one of my earplugs," I said. And then followed the words with the action.

He took it. "So that's all it took."

We crawled onto our mats. I removed my contact lens and put in my earplug—and the retainer I'd forgotten to put in earlier.

I never felt more awake, more *alive,* in my life.

On the other side of Grandma Gerd was a cowboy with my name on him.

"See?" whispered Hanks. "*Sarah* does have the hots for *Wayne.*"

Sleep would not visit me tonight.

CHAPTER SIX
Ta Prohm Revisited

ANOTHER ONE OF SOUTHEAST ASIA'S ALARM CLOCKS cock-a-doodle-dooed in my ear. Or at least it was so loud, it sounded like it. Morning. Pouring rain. My blurry eyes barely made out the figure of Grandma Gerd—about to drink from a water bottle.

"Shhhtop! Nhhooo!" I slurred, thanks to my retainer.

"What's the matter?"

Then I realized *my* bottle was still sitting safe and sound next to my mat.

Hanks found that extremely funny.

"Oh, don't mind her. She didn't get much sleep last night."

Grandma winked at me. "I know."

It was strange to awaken and realize I'd kissed Hanks.

Flip-flop!

I could barely make out Hanks's face, but I could tell that he was smiling. A big smile. And what would tonight's homestay bring? I couldn't wait to find out!

Then I moved. "Owwww . . ."

"Not used to hikin' nine hours straight, eh?" said Hanks.

"Here. Extra-Strength Tylenol," said Grandma Gerd, popping two gel caps and handing me two.

I found myself watching every move Hanks made. When he lifted his daypack, I noticed a fascinating muscle on his upper arm. Many times I'd labeled that muscle as the triceps brachii on muscular-system diagrams, but I'd never realized how appealing it was on a real-life specimen before.

I opened my Latin quote for the day: *Malum consilium quod mutari non potest.* (Pubilius Syrus) "It is a bad plan that cannot be changed."

As Grandma Gerd and I headed down the ladder for breakfast, I saw Mr. Vang remove a wooden peg from the hut door and effortlessly lift up the piece of wood that had barricaded me in.

"So that's it!"

"What?" asked Grandma as we sat down at the table.

"Oh, nothing . . ." No need to advertise my stupidity.

A whiff of Old Spice wafted through the doorway as Hanks walked into the hut fresh from his morning shower. His wet pomp glistened. His toned muscles rippled. His lips—

Hanks grinned at me. "Take a Polaroid, it'll last longer."

I turned away mid-gawk. No need to give him a big head. Make that a bigger head.

Over our breakfast of bananas and sticky rice, Bounmy giggled at a dramatic story Vang was telling complete with big flourishes and waves of the hand.

"What's he saying?" I asked, peeling a fourth banana. I

loved the variety of bananas in Southeast Asia, especially the pigmy ones, which were extra yellow and extra sweet.

"He talk about . . . how do you say . . . 'miracle,'" said Bounmy.

"What miracle?" I asked with my mouth full.

"Long ago when he was young man, missionary come to village and heal wife."

"Of what?"

Bounmy giggled again. "How do you say—stink breath? She have stink breath, stink like skunk. Man heal her—breath like flowers. Very nice."

They both laughed. Then Vang added something.

Bounmy grinned. "Then they make many children. Good miracle."

Vang beamed.

"It's a cute story," I said.

Fssshtttt!

"Don't you believe in miracles, Frangi?" Grandma Gerd asked, shaking a Polaroid of the Paint by Numbers Jesus. At least she wasn't going to try to buy or steal it. Her unscrupulousness did have limits, after all.

"Sure. I believe in the miracle of science and the miracle of modern technology and, of course, Miracle Whip." I laughed at my wit.

"You must keep 'em in stitches in Port Ann," said Hanks. "Bet that John Pepper thinks you're a laugh riot."

"Shut up!" I threw a peel at him. He caught it deftly in midair.

Grandma Gerd adjusted her glasses and gave me an inscrutable look. "There's more to life than the tangible."

"Must go," said Bounmy, getting up from the table. "Take two more day and night to reach beetle."

The three of us began to strap on our daypacks and replace our rubber flip-flops with boots.

"Tell Vang it's been a fantastic experience," said Grandma Gerd to Bounmy. "That his hospitality—"

"Eeeoww!" Hanks threw his jungle boot onto the bamboo floor and clutched his right foot. Bounmy hurried over and just as he was about to pick up the boot:

"No!" shouted Hanks.

Out crawled a *foot-long centipede.*

"Ta Prohm!" I said.

"No, centipede," said Bounmy. "Bite much worse than scorpion." Before he could smash it with the other boot, it escaped through the bamboo slats.

Hanks's foot swelled three times its normal size. His face turned red, and he sweated profusely. He seemed to have difficulty breathing.

Apparently this was the "normal" reaction to a centipede bite.

"It's a good thing he isn't allergic to the venom. With no medical facilities, he'd be dead before sunset," said Grandma.

"I told you this trip was a bad idea!" I found myself shouting. "That we'd be putting ourselves at risk! No cell phone, no help in emergencies, and Bounmy doesn't even have a first-aid kit!"

"We have Spider Flower weed," said Bounmy, pointing to Peace entering with a small wooden bowl of salve. "The root, it cool. The flower it dis-disin—"

"Disinfects?" said Grandma. "Good, good. Oftentimes the homeopathic cures are better than the commercial. And this is the next best thing to ice. Which we're sure not going to find up here."

Peace carefully applied the salve to Hanks's red bulbous foot. He winced. Grace blotted his forehead with a towel and gave him a drink of water.

"Why isn't anyone sucking the venom out of his toe?" I asked, exasperated. "It'll spread—"

"Calm down, Frangi. That's only for snakebites. And actually, I think that's been proven ineffective—"

"How do you feel?" I asked Hanks.

Hanks turned his head and vomited. All over my foot.

It was evident that Hanks wasn't going anywhere anytime soon. He had to stay off his foot, rest, drink liquids, and pop Grandma Gerd's Extra-Strength Tylenol every four hours. The fact he wasn't allergic lessened the urgency of the situation (although I refused to forgive Grandma Gerd or Bounmy or No Road Travel for putting him in it). Eventually, the swelling would go down and the pain would diminish. It didn't look like he'd be making the journey back down the mountain for at least three days.

So much for Homestay Night of Romance #2.

Hanks insisted Grandma Gerd, Bounmy, and I finish the last three days of the trek.

"Go on," said Hanks, in a hoarse voice. "Bond with your grandma. Don't know about you, but I wanna know The Big Secret."

"Are you sure you don't want me to stay—"

"What are you still doin' here? Get yer keister movin'!" That took his last ounce of energy. He flopped back onto the mat.

Grandma agreed. "We're not much use here, Frangi. Might as well finish what we started."

"Peace-nurse-*Your*Hanks," said Peace shyly in stilted English.

Your Hanks. I liked that.

As I turned away, Hanks reached out and grabbed my arm: "Wait."

Was he going to kiss me good-bye? Here, in front of everyone? How romantic!

"You forgot somethin'."

He handed me an empty water bottle.

CHAPTER SEVEN

Don't These Places Only Exist
in Nineteenth-Century Novels?

"I CAN'T BELIEVE YOU'RE DRAGGING US UP A MOUNTAIN IN search of a stupid beetle," I said as we paused for a break in the shade after a particularly grueling incline.

"Just . . . wait . . . till you . . . see it. It's not . . . just a . . . beetle . . . it's . . . it's a . . . work . . . of . . . art." Normally, this would have been said with vigor. But now Grandma Gerd could barely get the words out, she was panting so hard.

Without Hanks, the trek took on a subdued tone. Although she breathed and sweated heavily, Grandma Gerd managed to keep up with Bounmy and me. For his part, Bounmy smoked more and chatted less. When we paused at a crossroads of two similar trails, he seemed confused. His sassy self-confidence gradually dissolved into a slight pensiveness. Grandma Gerd didn't seem to notice, but I did. Especially when we passed the same waterfall twice.

"Bounmy, you're lost."

"Not lost: scenic route. Enjoyable beauty." But he wasn't convincing.

Rain began pitter-pattering on the banana leaves, a hollow sound. Bounmy gave us thin, transparent plastic ponchos. There's nothing worse than slogging through ankle-deep mud in pouring rain with 100 percent humidity—drenching you from the inside out. Even my underwear was dripping. What was the point of ponchos, anyway? The plastic just prevented the skin from breathing. I was sweating more than I was drinking since we had to conserve water.

Spots appeared before my eyes. I stumbled.

"Here. It's an electrolyte packet," said Grandma Gerd, grabbing me before I fell. "Put it in your water and drink it *now.*"

I followed orders.

"We have to be extra careful not to get dehydrated out here," she said, pouring a packet in her own bottle.

"Caution! Leeches!" sang Bounmy as he slogged through a deep puddle.

Was that something crawling up my leg? A foot-long centipede, maybe?

I forced myself to look down—just a floating piece of fern.

We made it to the next Hmong village by sunset. Bounmy practically melted with relief. "Here we are, madams!"

We were instantly surrounded by a group of children. Clustering around us, not for money or handouts, but just to watch us. No Road Travel was right: Very few Western-ers trekked this way, if at all. The children were mesmerized by our Western looks. And they actually jumped back when Grandma's camera spit out a Polaroid.

"Delight in the most spectacular of sunsets. I shall return," Bounmy said with a flourish of his cigarette, his confidence restored. We sat on large white rocks facing the descending burgundy lozenge in the pink-and-blue-striped sky. The children pressed in around us. Their hair smelled like smoke.

Grandma Gerd drew caricatures of the kids in her Everything Book. She pointed to a little girl with watery brown eyes and a big smile and said, "You!" and rapidly sketched her in a few broad, cartoony strokes. The kids giggled and squeezed around us tighter and tighter till they were breathing down our necks. Although they were adorable, they had runny noses and dirt covering every inch of skin. All I could think of was: *germs.*

"You!" Grandma pointed at a cheeky boy missing a front tooth. She drew him riding a giant pig. He laughed uncontrollably, literally doubling over.

I couldn't believe how genuinely entertained they were by mere pencil sketches.

However, two children contrasted with the rest: a three-year-old boy with watery eyes and a scratched-up face as if he'd fallen onto gravel. And a six-year-old girl with a tangled mass of hair and the dirtiest face of all, who carried around a bundle of pointed sticks that were some sort of game to her: She'd drop them on the ground and then pick them up one by one. Then drop them again and pick them up one by one. And *again*. When another girl tried to play with her, she screeched, snatched up all her little sticks, and ran away. The rest of the kids all exchanged knowing looks. As the kids turned their attention back to Grandma Gerd's next drawing, the girl carefully examined each stick to make sure it indeed belonged to her collection.

"Madams, prepare to meet your accommodation for the night," said Bounmy, coming toward us. We realized the coral-striped sunset had faded and darkness was falling. The children and their parents hurried inside their huts. Within minutes, Bounmy, Grandma Gerd, and I were the only humans outside.

A dog yowled.

I shivered.

"Animist tribe. Very superstitious. Scared of spirits—jungle spirits that come out at night," said Bounmy.

No wonder the aura here was different than the one at Vang's village.

A chill descended. The black palms silhouetted against the grey sky like a collage cut out of construction paper.

I shivered again. This time from the cold.

The first thing we noticed about our homestay was that the hut was positioned away from the rest of the village. Secondly, both Stick Girl and Scraped-Face Boy were among the children of the house. Thirdly, the parents and six other adult relatives who seemed to live there weren't exactly friendly. They weren't hostile, just standoffish and apathetic. And every single one had vacant eyes. They sat on odd wooden stools (which resembled a shoeshine boy's stool that had to be balanced carefully or you'd topple over) and stared at the two Western women who'd invaded their space. Space that wasn't even enough for all thirteen members of their clan, let alone the three-member trekking team. And fourthly, the hut couldn't have been more paltry (not to mention grungy): dirt floors, a central fire, and a rectangular, raised platform made of bamboo in the back corner. Our bed for the night.

"Voilà!" Bounmy said, waving his arm around the hut. "The home of Mr. Ly and family."

Mr. Ly was a sullen forty-year-old with matted hair, yellow teeth, and a prematurely aged face. He wore a soiled white T-shirt and black ripped shorts. Mrs. Ly was basically the female version of her husband with longer hair and a faded red sarong.

"Time for Bounmy to cook!" said our guide, trying to keep our spirits up.

During dinner, the family silently shoveled Bounmy's tasty noodles into their mouths. Stick Girl kept one eye on Grandma Gerd and me as she attempted to pick up rice with her sticks.

How I missed the Vangs.

As we finished our supper, a bony man dressed only in a tattered, black sarong drifted in and headed over to the bamboo platform. He stretched across it and rested his head on my backpack! Mrs. Ly got up from her stool and opened up a little wooden box. She removed a sticky brown substance, which she heated in a metal spoon over a candle.

"What is she doing?" I hissed at Grandma Gerd.

"Opium."

Opium!

Sure enough, Mrs. Ly set up the standard opium pipe you might read about in the more melodramatic novels, and the scrawny neighbor puffed away. A sickly, sweetish odor filled the hut.

I turned to Bounmy. "Look! They're doing opium— right there! On our bed!"

Bounmy looked up from his bowl of rice. "Ah, yes. He will finish before sleep time."

No wonder the only two "strange" kids came from this particular hut—it was the village *opium den*!

At that moment, Mr. Ly began smoking something from a bamboo tube, which he passed around to the adults in his family. And that certainly wasn't tobacco I smelled.

Bounmy said consolingly, "They are tribal people. They smoke opium and hashish. That is what they do."

"The Vangs didn't!"

But he wasn't listening.

"I thought opium dens went out in the 1800s," I said to Grandma.

"Oh, no. Still going strong. You get your good eggs in

Southeast Asia as well as your bad eggs. Doesn't help when it's sanctioned by the government."

I coughed.

"I think we'd better step outside for some fresh air or else you'll be experiencing something you'd rather not," said Grandma Gerd, getting to her feet. Unobtrusively, she slipped something into her fisherman's pants pocket—one of Stick Girl's sticks.

Really, she will stop at nothing!

We took advantage of the situation by getting ready for bed outside, using my Maglight. Neither Bounmy nor No Road Travel had prepared us for the lack of running water—no running water whatsoever. All we had were the bottles of water Bounmy carried, and we had to conserve those for drinking. We were sweaty, caked with dirt, and absolutely reeked—and forced to sleep that way.

I used a portion of our water supply to carefully wash my sole contact lens. Grandma Gerd directed the beam of light on my hands so I could see what I was doing.

The beam drifted away toward the bushes, leaving me in darkness.

"Hey!"

"Ooops, sorry." She redirected the beam back toward my hands. "Just thought I heard something."

After my contact lens had been safely put away in its plastic case, I said in exasperation, "What's the point of all this?"

"Hmm?" Grandma was still distracted by the rustling in the bushes.

"Why steal my passport? Why the trek? Why a ruffled beetle? Why spend all your savings to bring me out to Southeast Asia in the first place?"

She finally focused on me. I'd never seen her look so solemn. Her tanned face looked beige and strained. "You know, I'm wondering if it was such a good idea after all."

My stomach plummeted. Great. Perfect time to have second thoughts. When we're smack-dab in the middle of nowhere.

"Here's our culprit," said Grandma as a pot-bellied piglet emerged from the bushes and trotted on by.

As I crouched behind those same bushes while Grandma stood guard (the Ly family didn't even have an outhouse!), it suddenly occurred to me I was *squatting.* Effortlessly. After weeks of resisting, unable to do the "relaxing butt-to-heel position," I'd finally achieved it! And Hanks was right: It *was* easy. My legs weren't shaking or hurting. Now I could squat-squat-squat for hours. Had I become more limber?

When the last opium addict finally rolled off our bed, Bounmy rolled out our rubber mats. Matting had been spread across the floor and the Ly adults were already sleeping in a row, with their heads touching the thin bamboo-slatted wall and their feet pointing toward the center of the room. The children all slept in the one part of the hut that was an enclosed room, shut off from the rest.

The fire still crackled but barely took the edge off the chill.

The mountain air was now almost frigid.

I checked under the platform for any curled-up centipedes.

Bounmy deposited a blanket on each mat. "Dish towel" was more like it: four feet long and two feet wide—with all the heft of a Kleenex. It barely skimmed the tops of my ankles and ended at my chin. Vang's blankets had been gargantuan in comparison.

Grandma Gerd and I were exhausted and filthy—and now this. Our morale took a nosedive. But Bounmy explained that the blankets were all that No Road Travel had packed for us. Evidently, they still had some kinks to iron out in their "Trek Where No Trekker Has Gone Before" package. We rummaged through our backpacks and put on every piece of clothing we'd brought: pants, pj's, both shirts, both pairs of socks. Layered. But that didn't stop the cold from seeping into our bones. I'd never been so cold before when trying to sleep.

After shivering on our mats for twenty minutes, Grandma Gerd hissed: "Here. Take a Xanax. It's the only way you'll get any sleep. I have two left."

"No thanks." How hypocritical of her to offer me drugs—albeit prescription ones—after what we'd just witnessed!

"Sure? You've taken them before with no side effects—"

"Not of my own volition, in case you've forgotten."

She shrugged and popped them both. Then handed me a spearmint Life Saver.

"I already brushed my teeth."

"It's a clue."

"What's it supposed to be?"

"An 'O,' what else?"

"Admit it: You're just giving me random letters until I go home. At this rate, I'll have the entire alphabet in my carry-on."

"Nope. This is the last one. You now have all the letters to spell out The Big Secret."

For some reason, I couldn't get too worked up about it.

I turned the Life Saver over and over in my numb fingers. Anything to distract me from my freezing extremities.

D-A-D-E-P-T-O. Taped? Do? Addet? Pot? Deto? Top a ded? Peat odd? Todd Ape?

"Is it a name?"

But Grandma Gerd just exhaled in response. How could she be asleep already? I'd have to save it for another day. By now, my intellectual curiosity was waning. What could be that important, anyway? Knowing her, it was probably something anticlimactic. *Much Ado About Nothing.*

Although Bounmy had set up our bedding with our heads touching the bamboo wall, in line with the rest of the adults, I quickly repositioned myself so my head was nearer to the fire.

A few minutes later, Bounmy tiptoed over and said, "Please sleep this way, if you please." He moved me back around like the rest of them. "Use backpack for nice pillow. See? Most comfortable." He placed my backpack against the wall.

I was too tired to protest.

My backpack was lumpy. I couldn't get comfortable. My head itched. What if the opium addicts had lice? After a good scalp scratching, I jabbed in my earplugs, pulled on my eye mask, put on my face mask (no need to inhale any lingering hashish fumes), and willed myself to feel drowsy. But the icy night air slipped in through the bamboo slats and froze my head. Why had nobody informed me that it could drop to arctic temperatures at night? I'd have words with a certain No Road Travel representative when I returned.

Forget this. I sat up and turned back around so my head was nearer the fire. Much better.

A few minutes later I dimly heard soft foot patter, and Bounmy's small frame leaned over me. "Please, madam, you must please turn around."

I removed my eye mask, face mask, earplugs, and retainer. "But I'm freezing! I need my head close to the fire—"

"It is disrespectful. You must turn around. Please comply."

Muttering under my breath, I did so. Then put all my nighttime accoutrements back in place.

Bounmy padded back to his mat and I soon heard his childish rhythmic breathing mingling with the snores of Mr. and Mrs. Ly. Not one of them had a clear nasal passage.

I shivered and pulled my meager covering up around my chin, trying to eliminate air pockets. Finally, I forfeited one of my shirts to wrap around my damp head, keeping what little body heat I had from escaping. I must have finally dozed off when a couple of creatures skittered across my legs! Rats? Lizards? *Centipedes!?!* I didn't want to know.

My head shirt was soaked from the outside moisture. I slid off my eye mask and glared at Grandma Gerd's slumbering form with the anger that only a nonsleeper can have for the sleeper. Why hadn't I taken the Xanax? At least I'd be getting REM cycles instead of the flu. How could the fact that I merely wanted warmth constitute "disrespect"? It made no sense. I wiggled back headfirst toward the fire, crawling as close as I could without singeing. Ah, warmth!

My body being taken care of, my mind could now roam. And roam, it did—to Hanks. (*Flip-flop!* That kiss! Wait until Denise, Laurel, and Amber heard about it. Would they be jealous—in a good way. My first boyfriend ever! Now, if I could only somehow bring him home with me. . . .)

Then it roamed back to the letters. DTAEDOP. PODEATD. EATDDPO.

The letters formed, fragmented, then reformed. Each letter was branded into my brain. A kaleidoscope of—

I gasped.

It couldn't be. I tried it again. That had to be it.

I FIGURED OUT THE CLUE!

But it made no sense. What did it mean? How could it possibly be referring to me?

Bubble . . . birth . . . too young . . . rubber ball . . . dying . . . egg . . .

How did the clue apply to those words I'd overheard?

I reached over to tap Grandma's shoulder. But she was in such a deep sleep with a peaceful half smile on her lips, I didn't have the heart to wake her.

I'd just have to wait until morning to reveal my intellectual prowess.

CHAPTER EIGHT
Sleeping Wrong

THE NEXT THING I KNEW, SOMEONE WAS TUGGING ON MY ankle. I heard a distant, muffled voice in my dream saying, "Miss! Please, miss! Wake up, please, miss!"

Groggily, I pulled down my blue eye mask to see Bounmy, Mr. Ly, Mrs. Ly, and the rest of the stoners clustered around me, along with Stick Girl, who was still clutching—yep—her bundle of sticks.

A full minute passed before I comprehended this was indeed happening and not a dream. I tried to focus my non-contacted eyes on Bounmy, who was babbling wildly and waving his hands. Ly stood with folded arms, stone-like, with no expression whatsoever. My first thought was: *I hope they didn't mistake it for lemonade!* Then I realized I was now in the *other* village—in the village opium den.

Bounmy babbled on and on in pure gibberish until I plucked out my earplugs and heard:

"You turn around again! I warn you! I warn you three times! Three times I must tell you to turn around! Three times I tell you please must sleep head here and feet here! And now you anger the spirits! You disturb the spirits!" His former verbal dexterity was gone. He no longer looked like a confident boy but a scared child.

I slowly sat up. My joints were stiff from sleeping all tensed up. I removed my face mask and retainer. "What are you talking about?"

Bounmy pointed dramatically to the grim Mr. Ly. "Family much angry! Much, *much* angry! He see you sleep wrong! He see you disturb spirits by sleep disrespectfully! Disturb the *dab nyeg*—the spirits. He wake up and see you like this! Now . . ." Bounmy looked physically sick. "Now he say you . . . *you must pay!*"

I was an actor onstage who didn't know my lines.

I squinted at my Angkor Wat-*ch*: 5:03 a.m. I realized the shirt-turban was still wrapped around my head and I yanked it off.

"Hold on, hold on. Let me wake up Grandma."

Grandma Gerd looked like a bag lady stuffed with miscellaneous bits of clothing. She, too, had a shirt wrapped around her head. She lay motionless in the deep slumber of the self-medicated.

I nudged her. "Grandma Gerd! Wake up, Grandma!"

No response.

"Grandma Gerd?"

No response.

"Grandma!"

This time I shook her. Hard. With both hands.

"Grandma-Grandma-Grandma-Grandma!"

Grandma Gerd's head lolled around like a doll's head. Her arm flopped onto the dirt floor.

My heart drummed. Panic welled up in my throat like bile. *Dead!*

Thick. I felt thick. Thick and slow and protracted. Numb. Fuzzy.

I couldn't think. No thoughts were forthcoming.

Eventually, my mind slowly warmed up, the wheels greased themselves and began to turn.

I am in a hut. In a remote tribal village. On a mountain. In Laos. In Communist Laos. And my grandma is dead. And my grandma is dead. AND MY GRANDMA IS DEAD!

What-to-do? What-to-do? *What-to-do!?!*

And that serene smile was still on her face.

How dare she do this to me! And just when I'd figured out The Big Secret!

Then shock gummed up my mental machinery. I couldn't feel anything but that . . . *thickness.*

I wish I'd been more supportive about her rice bag skirt.

Thinking about her rice bag skirt thawed my frozen emotions, and I burst out crying.

The surly group standing at the foot of the platform took a collective step back.

Bounmy exchanged knowing looks with Ly, then said solemnly, "See? You make spirits very angry."

"Grandma! Grandma!" I grabbed Grandma Gerd's body and tried to lift her up with the superhuman strength born of tragedy, but she slipped out of my hands and her head whapped against the thick bamboo leg of the platform.

"Whaaaaaaaaat!?" A garbled moan came from Grandma Gerd's body.

I dropped her onto the dirt floor.

"She's alive!"

Her right eye slowly opened. Then the left.

"What's . . . what's going on? Who hit me? Why am I on the floor?"

She untangled her long limbs and stood up, pulling the shirt off her head. Her hair stood on end, like she'd been electrocuted.

Thanks to the Xanax (and NyQuil gel tabs, it turned out she'd also taken), it was a good ten minutes before Grandma Gerd had completely grasped the situation and her place in it.

"Grandma Gerd! I thought you were dead! *Dead!!!*"

"Well, I'm obviously not, Frangi. But I was dead to the world, finally getting some solid sleep, when someone whacked me in the head and threw me to the ground."

Same ol' Grandma Gerd. Well, I'd *never* take her for granted again, that's for sure. A rush of appreciation flooded me—appreciation for my grandma with all her colorful shadings.

Realizing she was lucid, Bounmy frantically gestured at her.

"Your granddaughter not listen to me! I tell her three time! Three time I tell her to turn! I tell her, she not listen! She anger the spirits!"

He then turned to me. "I tell you this, I tell you this. Why do you not listen to me? Family very upset, very upset! *You have brought a curse upon hut and village!"*

Grandma Gerd just stared at him as if he were an organ grinder's monkey.

I turned to Bounmy incredulously. "Curse? For sleeping the wrong way?"

"It big disrespect! Which you do three time! Three time! Bad number. And now you must pay!"

I was fed up. After having to endure uncomfortable and inhumane circumstances, I was now being harangued for simply wanting to be near the fire. I jumped off the bamboo platform, my growing sense of injustice spurring me to action.

"Are you crazy? It was survival! I was freezing! You gave us no suitable blankets and expected us to be able to sleep! My head, when it was turned toward the wall, was soaking wet! I'm sorry, but self-preservation is more important than sleeping protocol!"

Grandma Gerd turned to me. "Really, Frangi. I thought you knew the importance of respecting local tribal customs."

Oh, now *she* was going to lecture *me*? Miss Medicated Stupor Sleeper?

Bounmy was wringing his hands. "But now you must pay, miss. You must pay owner for sacrifice so the family can purify hut and village. Very important they purify to appease angry spirits since wife . . . how do you say . . . pregnant. They not want baby cursed."

Oh, please.

"Maybe it's not the angry spirits messing up their kids but maybe, just maybe could it be . . . their *drug use*!?!?!"

Grandma Gerd murmured to me, "Calm down. You must save face. Now, for Bounmy's sake, I think we should pay them. It would be worth five or ten dollars to smooth some ruffled feathers."

I took a deep breath and exhaled. Then I turned to Bounmy, who had developed a nervous tick in the corner of his mouth. "How much?"

Bounmy consulted Mr. Ly, then translated: "Three hundred and fifty dollar."

Our mouths fell open in unison, like two puppets. That was a large sum—for the U.S.! For a tribe in the jungles of Laos with no running water or electricity, where a family survived on barely a hundred U.S. dollars a year—it was astronomical.

"Seriously, Bounmy," Grandma Gerd said. "How much would do the trick?"

Bounmy inhaled deeply on his fourth cigarette of the morning, his hand shaking. But the chain-smoking was doing nothing to alleviate his tension, or his twitch. He was obviously intimidated by the Hmong hut owner. After all, this was a lot of stress for a twelve-year-old.

"The owner say three hundred and fifty dollar," rasped Bounmy as he segued into a coughing fit. Grandma Gerd patted his back.

I asked as calmly as I could, "How in the world could the monetary equivalent of 'sleeping wrong' equal three hundred and fifty dollars? Why that specific amount?"

"Family must purchase bull for sacrifice for two hundred and fifty dollar. And a rooster to chop off head—fifty dollar. Bull and rooster blood must be thrown in air outside hut and around village. Also must pay for chief of village to oversee ceremony, twenty-five dollar. And a *txiv neeb*—a medicine man, shaman—to chant, sing, dance cost twenty-five dollar. More if he must make *txib neeb*, metal rattle."

Grandma and I were both dumbfounded. But she finally asked: "How can a cow be worth two hundred and fifty dollars?"

"A cow support whole family in mountain tribe. Take much savings."

"Balls! There's no way we'd pay that—even if we had the money." Grandma Gerd rummaged around in her backpack and pulled out her echinacea with golden seal. She chewed a handful. The sharp odor made my eyes water.

Bounmy interpreted this for Mr. Ly, who literally snarled at us.

At this point, Bounmy became completely unraveled: "But . . . but you must please pay! If you do not please pay, they hold you hostage until they get money! Oh, Bounmy in much trouble! Much, much, much trouble!"

Hostage? Now it was just getting wacky. Where was the accordion music, the balloons, the bearded lady?

"Bounmy, is this all a big joke?"

"No joke! He lock door and not let you out." As if on cue, Mr. Ly slid a piece of wood across the only door (once again: one hut, one door!).

Bounmy whimpered. "They say you have disrespected the spirits and you must pay for purification." Then, in a whimper: "Please pay, miss! Bounmy be punished, very punished. Oh, such a very bad tragedy."

"But I have no money! We were going on a trek—why would I bring large amounts of cash with me? All I have in here"—I pointed to my money belt—"is my passport. And even if I did have the money, I wouldn't give it to them. It's wrong. It's extortion! We weren't warned about the spirits or religious customs in this tribe. It is No Road Travel's fault. *They* are the ones who should pay—if anyone!"

"Take it easy, Frangi," Grandma Gerd murmured.

"They hold you prisoner!" Bounmy was almost hyperventilating. His hand trembled so hard, he could hardly hold his cigarette to his lips.

"They couldn't really hold us here—"

"Yes, yes! They are tribal people with machetes and no modern knowledge as I have!" Then he moaned to himself. "I tell her . . . I tell her three times. . . ."

"I don't for one minute believe they'd try to hold us hostage," said Grandma Gerd and walked towards the barricaded door. Two of Ly's male relatives stepped forward, casually wielding machetes.

"I stand corrected," she said, backing away.

I whirled around to face Bounmy. "This isn't the village we were supposed to homestay at, is it? *Is it!?!*"

For a moment he seemed about to protest, then he crumpled. "Bad Bounmy, bad, bad, bad. He make lovely ladies lost. Such travesty!"

"And the only place who'd take us in was the local opium den, is that right?"

"So very misfortunate!"

"And," said Grandma Gerd, suddenly realizing, "you have no idea where the Iridescent Ruffled Beetle is, do you!?!"

Bounmy hung his head. "No, no, no!"

Mr. Ly spoke gruffly to Bounmy, who turned reluctantly toward us.

"Ly say: Old lady go back for money, girl stay."

I stared at him blankly. Grandma Gerd said, "Why not let us *all* go back and let Bounmy return with the money—"

"No good. He not trust you. Americans shifty, he say."

"Shifty!?! Where does *he* get off calling *us* shifty!? He's the one robbing us!"

Grandma Gerd nudged me. "Face, Frangi, face. The indignation routine that works in the States won't work here."

Bounmy stubbornly repeated, "He insist: Old lady go, girl stay."

Seething, I watched Grandma Gerd stuff her daypack. She handed me a plastic bag of Crunky bars and her extra clothes. "Those and my blanket should keep you warm tonight. . . ."

Tonight! Tonight I'd be sleeping *alone* in this creepy opium den!

I will not cry I will not cry I will not cry! My mantra kept my face frozen. I couldn't speak or I'd dissolve.

"Buck up, Frangipani." said Grandma Gerd. "I'll be back before you know it. Shouldn't take more than a couple days down the mountain. And once we're back in Luang Prabang, I'm sure we can hire that helicopter to drop us back on the mountain so we won't have to make the climb a second time. Isn't that right, Bounmy?"

He stared at her balefully. "Very dangerous to fly—"

Grandma Gerd hurriedly cut him off. "See this as an opportunity to gather more material for your novel. Why don't you start with the smells of opium and hashish."

"It's not funny."

"I'm not trying to be." Her voice cracked.

It dawned on me she was masking fear. She was putting on this jovial buck-up act so that I'd forget to be scared. But the normally invincible Grandma Gerd herself was *scared stiff*.

I threw my arms around her. She bear-hugged me back. Then reluctantly released me and hoisted her daypack over her shoulders. I grabbed her arm.

"You can't go before telling me The Big Secret!"

"Why don't we wait until—"

"You've made me wait long enough and you know it," I said. "And it would make my *imprisonment* a whole lot easier."

But we both knew these were just words. The subtext

was: *You'd better tell me now because you may never see me again.*

She put down her daypack. And I removed the letters from the front pocket of mine.

Bounmy moaned impatiently at the hut door. Grandma Gerd ignored him.

"Frangi, sit down. Or at least squat . . ." She gently pushed me onto one of the carved wooden squat stools.

"A-D-O-P-T-E-D," I said as I placed each letter in the dirt.

"Good work," she said.

I cleared my throat. "I know Dad was adopted, but how does that apply to The Big Secret? The blackmail?"

She placed both hands on my shoulders, squeezing them so tightly, her silver rings dug into my flesh.

"Vassar Frangipani Spore: *You're* adopted."

CHAPTER NINE
Who Am I???

GRANDMA GERD GENTLY SHOOK MY SHOULDERS.
"Frangi? Did you hear what I said?"

I blinked rapidly.

"It shouldn't come as that much of a shock," she continued. "You look nothing like either Leonardo or Althea. And you were a head taller than both of them at fourteen."

"But . . . not all children resemble their parents."

"True. But hasn't it hit you whom you resemble most?"

Wait.

It couldn't be.

"Not . . ."

"Excuse me, madam, we must go." Bounmy's strained voice seemed miles away.

"You?"

Grandma Gerd got up.

"But, wait! You can't go yet! How, when, why—"

Grandma Gerd is my birth mother!? How could I not have seen it? Both five feet ten, lanky limbed, with bad vision. Did Grandma have dark hair before she went prematurely grey? And that photo in her Everything Book of her wearing a pouffy A-line dress—it wasn't pouffy: She was pregnant with me!

My brain somersaulted around in my skull. My dad was no longer my dad—he was my *half brother*! But then again, he was also adopted, so what did that make us? My whole world had turned out to be a fabrication, a sham, an illusion!

"Dad's whole silverware triangle analogy was completely bogus!"

The hut and its occupants receded into the background. Grandma Gerd and I were the only two people in the entire world at that precise moment.

The right side of my brain said: *How exciting! Now you can conduct studies on nature versus nurture!* The left side of my brain said: *Uh-oh. What if I turn into Grandma Gerd!?*

I had to block both sides. I simply couldn't bear to think about it anymore. Blackness oozed around me. I quickly put my head between my knees.

"Madam! Please! Must go NOW!"

"In a minute, Bounmy," Grandma replied.

He groaned and wilted against the door frame.

"Then, who . . . who's my real father?" I asked in a muffled voice.

"You were conceived during my first visit to Malaysia. At a beach resort on Tioman Island. With a man I'd just met."

A sinking sensation in my stomach. A ringing in my ears. "Who was he?"

A sheepish look crossed Grandma Gerd's face.

"I don't know."

"What do you mean you don't know!?!"

"I was lonely, it was dark, and the gin and tonics were doing the thinking for me."

I was physically incapable of responding.

"Bounmy in much, much trouble!" moaned Bounmy, crushing his now empty Lotus cigarette pack.

"Hey, I'm not proud of my actions, but I am proud of the result." Again, she squeezed my shoulders. "Did you know Tioman Island is where they filmed *South Pacific*? But instead of washing the man right out of my hair . . ."

I remained motionless.

"It was all very escapist. His wife had just left him for a bass player, and I was still the grieving widow—after all those years. I woke up seven hours later, alone on the sand. Very ashamed and very sunburned. I never saw him again. Three months after that I was in Malta where—surprise! The rabbit died."

"Rabbit died?"

"You know"—she gestured toward her stomach—"pregnant."

The complete and utter mess of it all!

"Believe me: After that, I gave up recreational drinking—other than the occasional glass of wine. Which lately I don't seem to have a taste for, thanks to your Foreign Food Sanitation Spray."

"So you can't tell me anything about . . . my real father?"

She tilted my face toward her. "I can tell you he had eyes the color of a Hershey bar. And a couple of those." She pointed to my cowlick. "And that." She pointed to my chin dimple. "He loved discordant jazz. Oh, and he was Thai."

"What?!"

"He was Thai—as in Thailand."

"Are you positive? But . . . but . . . I don't look . . . Asian."

Was that me speaking? So calm and collected?

"That's not uncommon for a Eurasian."

Eurasian!?

Back went my head between my knees.

"Please, madam, I beg you!" Bounmy fidgeted in the doorway, almost in tears, his mouth twitching away.

"All right, Bounmy. I'm coming." She walked toward the door.

I unsteadily stood up. My legs seemed to be made of Silly Putty.

The right side of my brain said: *This proves life has infinite possibilities. It's not cut and dried and inevitable. There's a part of you that's an unknown variable. A mystery.* The left side of my brain said: *Danger! Alert! Chaos! Out of control! Messy! Unplanned!*

Bounmy handed me some line-dried beef jerky and sticky rice wrapped in a banana leaf. Then he gently pulled Grandma Gerd into the doorway.

"I can't believe this . . . I'm still so . . . shocked . . . so . . ."

"We'll talk more about it later, Frangi, don't you worry." She smoothed my hair—then pulled something out of it. "Saving this for later?"

It was a piece of sticky rice.

"Can't let your grooming go to pot just because you're a hostage. What would Althea say?" She tried to play it light, but her voice wavered. "Now don't forget to—"

"LIM," I finished weakly. My mind was still attempting to process it all. Then Grandma—*my mother!?*—hugged me tightly until Bounmy pried her off me and propelled her out the door.

As they disappeared around the corner of the hut, Bounmy's strained voice wafted through the air: "You exonerate Bounmy? You shall explain to my boss? And exonerate Bounmy?"

Ly firmly closed the bamboo door, slid the wood barricade in place, and gave me a look that said, "Don't even think about it."

And then, for the very first time in my life, I was . . . *alone.*

CHAPTER TEN

???

I'M ADOPTED!?!
   I'm Eurasian!?!
   I'm a hostage!?!

CHAPTER ELEVEN

I Wait

PART OF ME APPRECIATED THE TIME ALONE TO PROCESS. And being held hostage afforded a whole lot of quality-processing time. My life pre–Southeast Asia had been neat and organized. Everything in its proper place. Straightforward. All planned out.

And now. And now . . . it was as if someone had removed my glasses and I couldn't see one step in front of me. Speaking of seeing:

Very carefully and using as little water as possible, I put in my lone contact lens.

Stick Girl squatted near me, carefully counting and recounting her sticks—a puzzled look on her face. After a few times through, she turned and glared at me suspiciously.

"I didn't take it, but I know who did," I said, giving her a big smile.

But she just glowered even more at the sound of my voice.

The lackluster women of the hut all went about their chores, ignoring me. I could have been one of their wooden stools for all the attention they paid me. The morning opium customers filed in. They were mildly curious to see a soiled American girl sitting on a mat in the corner, but soon forgot me in their hazy reveries.

I opened my notebook. Perhaps writing it all up as a chapter would help me process. But my right hand remained motionless. So Mom and Dad had kept The Big Secret from me for *sixteen* years—and had kept Grandma Gerd away as well. What did I think about this? How did I feel? Overwhelmed—yes. Confused—yes. Numb—yes. Betrayed? That seemed too harsh. They all had probably kept the secret for "my own good."

And what would Denise, Amber, and Laurel make of it all? And here I'd thought getting my first kiss was big news!

I closed the notebook, too fatigued to ponder any longer, and gestured that I needed to use the bathroom. Ly opened the hut door but assigned Stick Girl and Scraped-Face Boy to tail me. They squatted on their haunches inches away from me as I urinated, their unblinking owl-like eyes watching my every move.

After I finished, I surveyed the village. The same gregarious children Grandma Gerd had sketched the night before now stared at me reproachfully. Why? For spoiling their fun? Obviously the news of my "disrespect" had spread. Even the friendly mothers kept their distance and didn't return my smiles.

Now I knew how Hester felt. All I needed was a scarlet "D" on my shirt.

From the Big P to the Big D—all in less than two months.

There had been joy in Vang's village. But in this one: oppression. Addiction. *Fear.*

I strolled a little way up the hill to stretch my legs, but Stick Girl followed me, poking me in the leg with one of her sticks until I turned back around.

Around six o'clock, Mrs. Ly and her fellow zombies prepared rice, vegetables, and mystery meat. But they didn't even offer me any. How inhumane! Especially since I'd eaten all my jerky and sticky rice for lunch.

As I sat on my mat in the corner, I scarfed down two oatmeal cookies, a handful of raw cashews, and a Crunky bar. Mr. and Mrs. Ly had commandeered their bamboo platform. Everyone continued to ignore me except Stick Girl, who kept trying to unzip my daypack. I finally had to lock it. She growled—then immediately started stabbing the lock with one of her sticks. No one even noticed.

That night I once again stuffed all my clothes in and around my freezing body and was grateful for Grandma Gerd's additional blanket. Just as I was lying down—yes, with my feet facing the *right* direction—surly Mr. Ly gestured for me to pick up my mat, daypack, and blankets. I slowly got to my feet and followed him. What exactly did he have in mind? My senses intensified. *If he tries anything, go for the eyes and the groin.* Mom had once instructed me exactly how to position my thumbs and apply pressure in order to pop the eyeballs out. I subtly removed the Maglite from my backpack and gripped it in my right hand. It wasn't much, but at least it was metal.

He led me into the enclosed room where the children had slept. But they were all now sleeping in the main room—except for Stick Girl. He motioned for me to sleep on the dirt floor. Then he backed out and closed the door—and secured it from the outside with a bamboo pole. Stick Girl and I were penned in for the night.

The moon shone through the cracks in the bamboo strips and highlighted her suspicious face. She lay on her bamboo mat, still clutching the bundle of sticks, completely motionless except for her eyeballs following me around the room.

Soon I could hear the deep breathing and snoring of the family in the main room—the walls of the room obviously more for show than privacy.

I switched on my Maglite, and the narrow beam of light fell on the bamboo-slated wall closest to me. I squelched my scream just in time. Thick white webs covered the wall, dotted with the wrapped bodies of dead insects—guarded by furry black spiders the size of bagels! Not only that, three cockroaches the length and size of chalkboard erasers clung to the parts of the bamboo not covered with web.

ICK! Ickity ickity ick ick! Don't think about it, don't think about it.

I moved as far away from the wall as possible without invading Stick Girl's space. The creatures didn't seem to faze her—maybe they stayed where they were. I gingerly removed my lone contact lens. Then I rummaged in my daypack for a piece of sugarless gum since I was too tired to brush my teeth and needed to conserve water. Instead, my hand closed on the Polaroid that Grandma Gerd had taken of Hanks and me at the Siem Reap café.

Hanks.

Flip-flop.

Just wait till Hanks finds out I'm Eurasian.

What irony, my first real boyfriend being Asian. Talk about foreshadowing!

Are you somehow supposed to feel different, once you discover your genetic makeup is not what you thought it was? Does it really make any difference if you weren't raised in that culture? And while we're at it, just what about nature versus nurture?

I, Vassar Spore, am a science experiment.

CHAPTER TWELVE

And I Wait

SOMETHING WET DRIPPED ON MY FACE. I OPENED MY EYES to see . . . blood spurting from the dangling severed head of a rooster!

"Disrespect! Disrespect!"

Ly cackled riotously as he shook it harder. I tried to sit up, but his dirt-caked children climbed on me, each sitting on a separate limb. Blood covered my face, filled my eye sockets, as soon as I spit out a mouthful of blood, more poured in. I was drowning in it. I couldn't breathe—

I woke up to find Stick Girl kneeling beside me, rhythmically spitting on my face.

Bounmy and Grandma Gerd erred most grievously in approximating their schedule. They were most certainly not back in two days. Nor three days. *Nor four.*

My nerves were fraying. What if something had happened to them on their way down the mountain? What if Grandma Gerd had had a heart attack? What if disgruntled relatives of Mr. Ly had followed them and macheted them to death!?

What if Mr. Ly forces me to participate in the cow sacrifice, the chicken decapitation, and throwing blood in the air!? Complete with metal rattle?

I forced myself to block such thoughts. I couldn't afford to indulge in speculation. My mental well-being was fragile enough as it was.

Having no running water was also taking its toll. Besides the fact I couldn't bathe, the bottles of drinking water were running out. Natural water was difficult to get, and the tribal people drank it sparingly. And even if they did offer me any, I'd be risking my life by drinking it. I might contract giardiasis from the contamination. I was already at risk for malaria, dengue fever—and possibly leprosy. Not to mention cavities. My staggering body odor along with my ever-growing underarm and leg hair did nothing to boost my spirits.

Neither did the fact that Stick Girl had finally managed to get into my daypack by slicing it with her dad's machete. I found her wearing my retainer on a string around her neck and my surgical face mask on her head with the elastic under her chin like a party hat, absorbed in rubbing my Baby Powder Fresh Deodorant Stick all over her legs and feet and face.

I laughed for the first time since I'd been taken hostage. What a character! The deodorant would probably do more for her than it was doing for me.

To pass the time, I wrote up my chapters . . . keeping my notebook with me at all times in case Stick Girl got any ideas.

July 27: I'm freezing. My head itches. I can't remember the last time I had a shower or anything to eat besides sticky rice. This is not how I planned to spend my summer— or end my life. If only we hadn't answered the door that rainy night in May...

And I had another distraction: lice. The entire hut had it, so it was just a matter of time before I did. The itch was unbearable. I watched Stick Girl pinch and pull the lice out of her hair and tried to mimic her. Harder than it looked. After half an hour of watching me attempt to de-louse, Stick Girl took pity on me. She inched over toward me and after giving me a wary I-don't-know-if-I-should-do-this-but-you're-so-pathetic-I-can't-just-sit-here look, began to pick the creatures out one by one with her deft fingers. I felt like a monkey. Once her mission was accomplished, she inched back to her corner and began counting her sticks. I handed her a cinnamon Certs I found in my daypack pocket. She just stared at the round white object in her hand. I motioned for her to pop it in her mouth. After considering me a moment, she tentatively licked it. Then licked it again. She savored that mint, rationing herself to one lick every hour so it lasted for two whole days.

By the sixth day, the Ly family were outright hostile. They had just about given up all hope of their $350. And I was sure that they were contemplating what to do with this overly tall, disrespectful "Western" (make that *Eurasian*!) girl who'd brought curses down upon them. Occasionally, to prevent them from having a corpse on their hands, they allowed me a minuscule bowl of purple sticky rice. My stomach growled painfully, but they showed no mercy. By then, I'd eaten all my cookies, nuts, and Crunkys.

And I had just one bottle of water left.

And I'd run out of Kleenex—and forced to resort to my Latin quotes. Not quite the use my friends had had in mind.

I had to face the fact that something *had* happened to Grandma Gerd and Bounmy—and maybe even Hanks!

My skin shimmied.

No one knows I'm here.

What was I going to do?

CHAPTER THIRTEEN
You Can Plan Your Way
out of Anything

ON THE SEVENTH NIGHT AFTER LY BARRICADED THE door to my sleeping room, my roommate was already sound asleep, her runny nose whistling softly—and still wearing her retainer necklace and face mask party hat. I opened the last of my Latin quotes to use for my pre-bed squat. The paper was wrinkled and smeared, but I could still make out the words:

Carpe Diem.

Seize the day.

Seize. The. Day.

Seize the day!

And why not?

Why stay here? Why not escape? The path is well trod, and I have my Maglite. Why sit around waiting for impending doom? (Or, at the very least, messy retribution.) You have no choice, Vassar. The water supply is almost depleted, and your life's hanging by the proverbial thread. Get going!

I didn't pause to ponder the plausibility of such a plan. The very idea of the Big P gave me an adrenaline injection that sent my heart into palpitations. Empowerment! Action!

Aut viam inveniam aut faciam! Like Hannibal and his elephants, I'd either find a way or make one.

Could I really *plan* myself out of this situation?

My eyes fell on the urine-soaked dirt at the wall's edge—Stick Girl's and my nighttime bedpan. Several bamboo strips attached to the corner of the wall there were severed. I crept over and pushed my hand through. The pliable strips bent backward like a flap, creating a small opening. Did the kids normally enter and exit without the knowledge of their parents?

Stealthily, I laced up my jungle boots (centipede check!) and slipped my Maglight into my pocket. Then I put in my gas-permeable contact lens, wetting it with just a drop of precious water. Only three fourths of a bottle left. Time to think like a camel. Luckily, going down a mountain took far less energy than coming up. I removed my *Savvy Sojourner's Laotian Guidebook* and my *Genteel Traveler's Guide to Laos* from my daypack—then replaced them. *No, Vassar, think light.* I set them next to Stick Girl's head. She could enjoy the photos, at least. I cinched my money belt tightly around my waist with a safety pin.

Then I crept back over to the edge of the wall. Using a squashed, empty water bottle, I furtively dug up the wet earth, simultaneously making a slight snoring sound to cover the scraping. While I did so, I mentally rehearsed my escape: Leave a blanket bunched up so that in the dark, Stick Girl would assume I was still sleeping; bring one blanket in case I had to sleep in the jungle; push my daypack out first, then follow; replace the frayed wall flap carefully after me; and head for the trail. The Angkor Wat-*ch* showed 1:16 a.m. That meant I had at least four hours of darkness to run down the mountain to Vang's village.

I stopped digging. *There. I should be able to squeeze my body through that opening—especially after my starvation diet.*

I turned around. Stick Girl was sitting up, staring straight at me. The hairs on the back of my neck prickled.

I froze—waiting for the bloodcurdling scream that would bring the entire opium-hazed household into this room.

But, no.

She just watched me, clutching her sticks to her chest. She knew what I was doing—*and she was letting me go.*

Now or never. Mr. Ly had already performed his nightly ritual: After checking on the hostage, he smoked opium for fifteen minutes and passed out—a ritual mirrored by the rest of the adults. A mild breeze rustled the fronds on the roof and the papaya trees outside. Stray dogs barked sporadically in the distance. And the snores, snorts, and wheezes all contributed to make white noise. Perfect for muffling any sounds I'd make.

Sure, steady, and slow, Vassar. No abrupt movements to arouse suspicion. A low, continuous rustle of bamboo would be chalked up to the wind, but a crash through said bamboo would be most certainly figured out—even by someone in an opium stupor.

Before I could slide through—Stick Girl got up and held out her hand:

My retainer.

I took it from her. She looked so small and solemn. And sad. I thought a moment. Then I removed my necklace and hung it around her neck. *Nulla dies sine linea.* Was it futile to hope that someday she'd learn to write? The silver Latin medallion hung down to her belly button. She looked down at the glinting metal and touched it tentatively with her finger. Then looked up at me. And smiled. Actually *smiled*.

Then she picked up her bundle of precious sticks. After careful examination, she selected one and handed it to me as if bestowing a wand of gold. The only thing of "value" she owned in the world. I thanked her—the only word I knew in her language—and slipped it into the front pocket of my daypack.

We stared at each other a moment, then exchanged more smiles. I'd miss my little shadow. What would happen to her? Would she be stuck here for life? I had to believe she'd somehow make it out—with her tenacity and determination.

I fought the urge to bring her with me. Unless I could smuggle her out of the country, she would end up right back here. How helpless I felt at the injustice of life.

Good-bye, Stick Girl.

She lay back down on her mat, clutching the medallion in her hand, her bundle of sticks forgotten.

Deep breath. I lay flat on my back and pushed back the bamboo fronds, then slowly slid my head through the opening. I inched my body through. Wiggled my shoulders— tight fit. Too tight.

I was stuck.

Don't panic, don't panic. Think. Use your deductive reasoning and problem-solving skills to solve this mild dilemma. You always pride yourself on your mind—now use it! I tried not to think about my shirt and pants sucking up my very own urine like a sponge. Like it mattered—my stench could already stop a Mack truck.

After pausing to assess the situation, I realized I needed to sever a few more fronds in order to widen the gap enough for the rest of my body to follow. I tried ripping them with my hands, but they were tougher than they looked. It was evident I needed some sort of sharp object to cut the fronds, otherwise I'd be stuck permanently—unable to either return inside or escape outside.

What did I have in my pockets or my buttpack? My flash-light . . . earplugs . . . nothing sharp there . . . Wait! Stick Girl's sharpened stick! It was in the outside pocket of my daypack—which barely grazed the top of my head. If I could only force one arm through the opening, I could remove it. I gritted my teeth and then shoved my right arm through the ragged edge of the bamboo. Not pleasant—like a wedge of cheese shredded by a grater. Ignoring the gashes and the ooz-ing blood, I reached for my daypack. I slowly unzipped the front pocket and then felt around for the stick. *Got it!*

With a surge of strength I punctured the first flattened cane with the stick, then ripped right through five other canes. I froze, listening for any movement from inside. Noth-ing. I quickly slithered the rest of my body out. I was free!

Then something moist touched my face.

CHAPTER FOURTEEN
It Can't Get Any Worse

IT WAS ONLY THROUGH SHEER WILLPOWER THAT I DIDN'T scream. I lay ramrod straight, eyes wide open, pulse drumbeating so loudly, I just knew everyone in the village heard it—my very own Telltale "Disrespectful" Heart!

Slowly, I pivoted my head to see . . . the pot-bellied piglet! His tiny, moist nose inches from my cheek! My limbs went limp with relief as the little fella grunted and prodded me—trying to locate his mother's teat!

I scrambled to my feet, snatched up my pack, climbed over the primitive fence, and walked slowly in the direction of the jungle path. I couldn't risk running—that would arouse suspicion. No one ran around at night in Hmong villages. The moon was full, so I didn't have to turn on my Maglite just yet. I knew I had to make my way around the village until I hit the trail down the mountain. And, once out of sight, I could use it. I noticed, leaning against the fence, a bamboo basket, the kind the Hmong wore on their backs to carry rice, bamboo, vegetables, and babies. I dropped my daypack into the basket and pulled it over my shoulders. I draped my extra shirt over my head like a shawl and wrapped the thin blanket around my waist like a sarong. Up close I couldn't fool anyone, but from a distance at night maybe I could pass for a Hmong woman—albeit a strange, overly tall one.

Grunt, grunt. The sow was following me. Along with her piglets.

A chicken chirped. A stray mutt ran over to investigate the odd sight. The sow and her litter scattered. The mutt's ears folded back as he sniffed my leg. Uh-oh. But after a thorough investigation of my pee-stained pants, he trotted off.

The village slept. I didn't see one soul in my trudge around the perimeter.

That's because they're all animists and fear jungle spirits and don't venture out after dark. Great: perfect thought to have in your head at this moment.

The trail loomed in front of me—I did it! I planned my very own escape!

Don't get all cocky, Vassar. This is just the beginning.

Cocky? I was in the jungle, on a mountain, in a remote tribe, in Communist Laos, and feeling cocky? *Euphoric,* to be exact! I escaped! I'd never felt so self-sufficient in my life! Or so IN THE MOMENT. *Grandma Gerd, I'm LIM-MING!* I wanted to shout.

Wait. What *would* I call her in the future? Something to add to my To Do List.

Then as I began to stumble down the mud-and-rock path, the euphoria dissipated: *I'm alone. In a jungle. Unprotected. Not knowing who or what lurks in the dark foliage that*

*surrounds me. Not knowing when my escape will be noticed and a
bevy of surefooted Hmong tribesmen will be running down the
mountain after me.*

I quickened my pace, still able to see fairly well, thanks to
the slivers of moonlight that shone through the banana
leaves and palm fronds. I stepped in a patch of mud—
skidding! The basket on my back hindered my equilibrium.
I teetered on the edge of the cliff and barely grabbed the
trunk of a giant fern in the nick of time. Okay. Break out
the flashlight. The bobbing spot of light wouldn't be visible
from the village above, but could be noticed by some sleep-
less person in the various huts that dotted the landscape
below. But would they necessarily think it odd or worth investigation? I had to take the chance. It seemed a better risk
than catapulting over the edge of the mountain.

I pointed the flashlight inward toward the mountain and
not out toward the valley. And I kept it low, hoping the
bushes, rocks, and brush would hide most of the light.

I realized I wasn't blinking, so worried I'd miss something. I forced my eyelids closed. Then opened them—*flick!*

My sole remaining gas-permeable contact whizzed
through the air into the darkness.

Uh-oh.

My momentary euphoria seemed like an eternity ago.

Everything was smudged . . . blurred . . . I squinted, trying to make out shapes, but it just caused more blurring.

I am on a treacherous jungle trail, slippery with mud, soon to be chased by an angry tribal mob—*AND I CAN'T SEE A FOOT IN FRONT OF MY FACE!!!!*

Stop hyperventilating . . . calm down, deep breaths, in out, in out. Calm down. LIM . . . that's what I need to be doing: LIM-MING. Live in the moment, Vassar, live in the moment.

Okay.

I inched my way down the trail, using one bamboo stick to make sure I didn't get too close to the edge and another to feel ahead for puddles and rocks and uneven steps. To say it was excruciating would be an understatement. At this rate, it would be dinnertime the next day before I even made it halfway down.

One foot in front of the other. One-two-one-two. On the bright side, I couldn't pretend to see any menacing figures in the jungle. My myopia created a buffer. It seemed so unreal, my fear evaporated. I became just a filthy, tense, squinting mass of sweat hobbling down the mountain.

Luckily, the path was well worn and easy to follow. There would be no getting lost or meandering off on a side trail.

How still it was. I'd anticipated more creepy jungle noises. Instead: eerie calm, broken by an occasional breeze rustling the clusters of bamboo and rippling the banana tree leaves.

What was that stench?

How embarrassing. Just me. Just my ever potent Girl Unwashed in a Humid Climate Body Odor.

I didn't allow myself to think of failure. Of not making

it down. Of getting caught. I couldn't afford to mull over worst-case scenarios. Before I could stop myself, I burst into giddy laughter. For no reason. Was I going insane? Well, it wasn't like I didn't have a reason. Make that *many* reasons.

Squinting gave me a headache. I stopped for a sip of water. Half a bottle left. And who knew how much farther to go? I couldn't see far enough to gauge.

I will never leave the USA ever again. I will plan all my trips within the safety of the continent. I will not venture even into Canada. Never never never again will I get myself into this kind of a predicament. Never never never again will I accompany Grandma Gerd anywhere—not even to Gus's Gas. I don't care if she is my . . . <u>mother</u>.

I tripped over a rock . . . then another. And found myself on my butt. Tears ran down my face, stinging my useless eyes. Salt. It made me even thirstier than I was.

I'll send out thought waves to Grandma Gerd, I thought as I picked myself off the ground: *Come get me, come get me, come get me.*

I realized that this was the first time in my life where there was no certainty of outcome. I could do nothing BUT Live in the Moment. I had no other choice.

As I hobbled down the trail, I realized: Wendy Stupacker will make valedictorian now for sure. How absurd my planning, To Do Lists, and Vassar Spore Life Goals seemed right now. All tasks that focused on the future, never on the current moment. Always "What next?" Achieve, achieve, achieve.

I remembered Wendy Stupacker and me facing off in that regional spelling bee. I knew I was going to win. Tranquility enveloped me like a cloud. I'd studied so hard that every word I spelled was an old friend, not a source of anxiety. I experienced that out-of-body feeling, like I was looking down on myself, delighted at my progress. We were neck and neck until I was spelling "ektexine" and my mind wandered to how my parents and I would celebrate that night—and I accidentally reversed the "k" and the "t." The triumphant look on Wendy's face brought me back to earth with a jolt. How could I have missed such an easy word!?

My problem then was the same as now: worrying about what comes next instead of fully savoring the here and now.

Glad you figured that one out now that you're about to die, Vassar.

Energy. I needed fuel.

I'd tucked a little wad of purple sticky rice into my pocket that I'd managed to save from my last meager meal. Just as I was about to eat it, I had an idea. I rummaged around in the front pocket of my backpack and removed the Polaroid of Hanks and me. Then I spit on the sticky rice to moisten it, shuffled carefully over to the nearest tree, and used it to secure the Polaroid to the trunk—making sure it was only visible to those coming up the mountain and not down.

There. At least my rescuers would know I'd escaped and was somewhere in the vicinity.

My fingers were cramped from gripping the sticks, and

my muscles ached from tensing to prevent slipping. Though it was still cold, sweat glistened on my arms. How far had I gone? The Angkor Wat-*ch* read 3:35 a.m. I'd been walking for almost two hours—and I only had an hour and a half before sunrise.

I paused to give my muscles a rest. Then I heard voices— and *not* in my head. Excited, babbling voices in the distance but definitely moving closer.

From behind me.

CHAPTER FIFTEEN

It Really Can't Get Any Worse

M Y HEART PRACTICALLY RICOCHETED OUT OF MY chest. *Think! Think! What-do-I-do?*

Since I couldn't outrun them, I only had two alternatives: Face them and risk possible dismemberment (or worse)—or hide.

I squinted at the terrain around me. Not much served as a hiding place from what I could see (which wasn't much). I glanced over the edge—nothing but murky blackness. But looking up, the moon illuminated ferns, palms, and chunks of rocks protruding from the side of the mountain. No contest. I shoved my two sticks behind a giant fern growing along the edge of the path. Then I climbed up the side of the mountain like an orangutan. The basket on my back tilted me backward, and my feet, caked with mud, couldn't get a grip on the slippery rocks. I started to teeter. Then totter. Then suddenly I was—

Falling!

Skidding backward across the muddy path!

And free-falling over the edge of the cliff!

My arms flailed wildly as I crashed through a cluster of

bamboo and in the nick of time wrapped around an especially sturdy trunk—aborting my Fall of Death. Before I could catch my breath—the voices rang out loud and clear: *Please don't let my panting and the clanking bamboo be a giveaway.* I jammed my right foot into a crevice and wedged my left foot between a rock and a tree root. And tried not to panic as I felt my throbbing nose to find it was broken. The cartilage clicked.

Just be thankful you're not dead.

They probably wouldn't be able to see me from the path, but could they detect me with their acute sense of smell or intuition or some native "third eye"? My whole body reverberated with fear. My nose stung. Blood trickled into my mouth. My knee throbbed from being whacked against a rock.

Will they or won't they? Will they or won't they?

Was my basket sticking out too far? Would they hear my wheezing?

About ten feet above me, shadowy shapes that I took to be heads abruptly jack-in-the-boxed above the bushes. Would they spot me? Blood from my nose smeared onto the bamboo trunk.

This can't be Vassar Spore clutching for dear life to a bamboo growing out of the side of a mountain while her captors walk right by. . . . It must be a dream.

The low growl of Mr. Ly broke through my "dream." I'd recognize his guttural intonations anywhere. I was indeed awake after all. Unfortunately.

Four other tribesmen were with him and they all were

swiftly making their way down the path. Within seconds they were gone—although it seemed like an *eternity*. Snatches of their conversation cut through the stillness of the jungle. I waited another eternity before I even so much as shifted my weight.

Bloody, scratched, broken, and light-headed from lack of sleep. It would be a relief to get caught. Being held hostage was a cakewalk compared to what I was putting myself through. A faint wash of light began to illuminate the night sky. Dawn. I wiped the sweat out of my eyes with my shirt, ignoring the whiff of rank odor.

Face it, Vassar, you may die up here.

Suddenly it mattered quite a lot to me that I wouldn't be able to turn in my AP/AAP novel. Some perverse part of me was irritated at leaving such a loose end.

Hanks. I didn't want to die before I could finish that kiss.

And, most importantly, not before I could see Mom and Dad—and Grandma Gerd—again. Not to mention Denise, Amber, and Laurel.

If only they could see me now.

4:45 a.m. In fifteen minutes I'd be visible for all the world to see.

What goes up must come down, but in this case it was the reverse. Although they were heading down the mountain—away from me—when they didn't find me, they'd be heading right back up: toward me. *So what do I do now? Stay here clinging like a monkey to this bamboo, or risk the trail?*

I calculated the odds of discovery and decided to take

the gamble. Though queasy thanks to my broken nose, I mustered the strength to pull myself vertically up the muddy cliff. I was tempted to rip off the basket and toss both it and my daypack over the side, but who knew how long I'd have to hide out in the jungle in survival mode. My entire body trembled as I strained to hoist myself up. The veins in my neck pumped like little fire hoses. Fresh sweat gushed out of me. My fingers released their grip on the bamboo of their own accord. And I slid right back down to my starting position.

Now I was really stuck.

CHAPTER SIXTEEN

Miracle?

CLINGING TO THE SIDE OF THE CLIFF, MY BREATH COMING
in jagged spurts, I got tunnel vision because of my
locked knees. Since it was impossible to put my head between my legs—much less move—I knew I was about to
black out. Which meant I would loosen my hold on the
bamboo. Which meant . . .

*This is it. If I pass out, I pass into the next life. IF there is a
next life.*

Since I had nothing to lose:

"Help! Help me!"

Was that my voice croaking feebly? No one would be
able to hear that.

Blackness clouded my eyes. My ears rang.

"Heeelllppp!" Barely a warble.

My grip weakened.

"God—if indeed you're NOT dead and DO exist—now
would be a REALLY good time for a miracle! That is, if
you still do them in the twenty-first century?"

Sliding!

"Okay, God. You've forced it out of me: I *can't* plan my

life. Isn't that right? Isn't that what you're waiting for me to admit? Fine, okay, you win. Hear me? YOU WIN!"

Then I realized: I was not wearing my bra. My bra was missing. My bra was not on my person. My bra was AWOL. I could still feel the wet fabric of my money belt around my waist, but my bra was *gone*.

Where was it?

WHERE WAS MY BRA!?!

That's it. I'm hallucinating. I'm in a surreal world where undergarments evaporate right off the body.

Slipping!

This is it, God! Are you ready to welcome me with open arms up there in the sky or—

Thwack! Something long and skinny hit me in the face.

"Aaaahhh! Snake!"

"It's not a snake, it's a lasso," came a familiar voice.

"Hanks!?!"

"Put it over your head and secure it around one shoulder and under the other armpit."

"I can't . . . I'm blacking . . . out. . . ."

"No, you're not. Just let go of the bamboo and grab the rope."

"I'll fall!"

"You've got to let go before you can be saved—now let go!"

"Let go, Frangi!" Grandma?

"Let go, miss!" Bounmy?

"Come on, Spore, you can do it. You can let go."

*Let go, let go, LET IT GO. That's LIG instead of LIM . . .
or LITM.*

My whole body shook, reverberating the cluster of bamboo surrounding me and sending them clanking. *If you're going to do it, do it fast! Don't think, just act. Re-act.* I pried my right hand off the stalk of bamboo, then snatched the rope dangling in front of my face.

"Atta girl! Now the other one."

"But—"

"No buts, Frangipani! Get a move on!" Grandma Gerd couldn't hide the fright in her voice.

I held my breath and peeled my shaking, sweaty left hand—

Really sliding!

Somehow I managed to get the lasso around my slippery-sweat-soaked body and cinched it tight across my braless chest. Within seconds I was hanging in the air—then slowly I was dragged up the cliff, whipped by ferns, gouged by stumps, scraped by rocks. The assault on my body before was nothing compared to being rescued.

Firm arms encircled my shoulders.

"And you thought my lassoin' skills were good for nothin'," came Hanks's twang in my ear.

I found myself sprawled on the muddy trail, surrounded by blurry blobs.

Was that Vang grinning at me?

And Grandma Gerd's fuzzy face loomed above me. Her ringed fingers grabbed my legs. "Frangi!" She was crying.

"They beat her up! Look what they did to her nose—those bastards!"

A water bottle appeared, and I almost downed the whole thing before someone pulled it away. Then I was chewing a slice of mango. Someone wiped my face with a cloth—a red bandanna.

"Was . . . was it the Polaroid?" I asked in a feeble voice.

"Polaroid?"

"She's probably delusional. . . ."

"She stink like Vang wife's breath," said Bounmy.

I squinted at the trees around me, trying to locate the one with the sticky rice Polaroid—then froze. For there, hanging off a stalk of bamboo growing at the edge of the cliff, was my bra.

My missing bra! My grimy, white, sweat-stained bra! Unmistakable (even with my bad eyesight) against the dark green of the jungle. And positioned in such a way that only those coming *up* the mountain could see it, not those going down. So *that's* what had notified my rescuers of my presence!

"Mighty clever usin' underwear. Better than a flare. . . ." Hanks's voice faded into the distance.

How on earth? Did it somehow get snagged while I was falling? Did it slip out? No. It simply was not feasible. There was no way a bra, underneath my shirt, could have been pulled out without said shirt coming off, or ripping. That was neither reasonable nor logical. And even if it did somehow come off, how on earth had it gotten up on that stalk of bamboo? Could a monkey . . . ? Or an especially gusty wind . . . ?

No.

No monkeys. No winds.

Face, it, Frangi: It's your very own miracle—the Miracle of the Bra!

Then I passed out.

PART FIVE

Where Do I Go from Here?

CHAPTER ONE

Am I the Same Vassar Spore?

ALL I REMEMBER AFTER THAT WAS BEING CARRIED DOWN
the mountain on a bamboo stretcher. And Hanks picking up the Polaroid—which he found facedown in the mud.

"Sticky rice isn't a good adhesive," he said. "Especially when you got hungry jungle ants."

And Grandma Gerd's strained face hovering above mine as if she didn't dare take her eyes off me. *And* her faint whisper: "I thought I'd lost you."

It turned out that Bounmy had absolutely no idea how he'd gotten to the opium den village in the first place. So he and Grandma Gerd got lost on the way down the mountain and couldn't even find Vang's village for two days. By then, they were exhausted and had to rest up before heading farther down the mountain into Luang Prabang. After Grandma Gerd withdrew the $350 in cash, she, Bounmy, Hanks (whose foot was almost back to normal), Vang, and three No Road Travel guides trekked back up the mountain. But Bounmy simply could not remember which way he'd gone. Apparently there were numerous villages scattered throughout the mountains, their exact whereabouts unknown to the folks from town. And the village where I was being held hostage was one of them.

They were at the point of returning to Luang Prabang to seek help from the Communist government or even the Laotian mafia—since the American embassies were usually little help in these cases. But Vang encouraged them to keep going, to keep the faith.

"Miracle. Vang say to expect miracle," Bounmy had interpreted.

So to appease him, they headed up the path one last time.

And an hour later, Grandma Gerd spotted my bra: that grimy, ignoble, *miraculous* garment.

So it wasn't Hanks who had rescued me a fifth time. It was someone a whole lot more *divine*—who didn't make a habit of wearing chops (as far as I know . . .).

When Grandma Gerd reported the opium den village to the authorities, they found our adventures highly amusing and said that's what we got for "sleeping wrong" in an animist village during the August Full Moon Festival.

For the next week I simply existed: ate, drank, took medicine, and slept twelve hours at a stretch in the Ever Charming Guesthouse. Hanks brought me water, fruit, and clusters of frangipani. And read aloud to me from *Dustup at the Double D*. Not as bad as I'd expected, although a few too many "Let's round up them doggies!" for my taste.

When I told him The Big Secret, he said:

"So that makes two Asians in Port Ann."

My cuts and bruises were healing—except for my nose. The cartilage still clicked. A solemn, balding Laotian doctor had intoned, "Your nose will make 'clicking' until cartilage fuse back together."

"How long will that take?"

"Months. Years. Decades. Perhaps never."

So I would be reminded of my close encounter with death every time I rubbed or blew my nose. And now that the stitches were out, there was a scar on the bridge.

"Your old nose was too perfect. This one's more whimsical," said Grandma Gerd. "Much more interesting."

"I know, I know: Nothing perfect is ever interesting."

A few days later, Hanks helped me down the street to an Internet café. I had a hundred emails. . . .

Laurel: *We think Sarah and Wayne need to kiss again before the end of the book.*

("Well, now, we'll just have to work on that," said Hanks, reading over my shoulder.)

Amber: *Speaking of kissing—Laurel and Garrett are officially girl-friend and boyfriend. We're expecting them to kiss ANYTIME now. (Outside the Mini-Mart, perhaps? :))*

Laurel: *Denise managed to attend her ballroom dance class without breaking into hives. She's even able to make minor small talk now.*

Denise: *As long as it's scientific, mathematic, or logistic in nature.*

Laurel: *Guess who turned up at Amber's last chess tournament? Her mom!*

Amber: *Although she totally got BANNED and escorted outside within ten minutes for painting her face in the school colors, blasting her foghorn every time I made a move, and heckling my opponent. (And I thought her taunts at my brothers' basketball games were mean-spirited.)*

Laurel: *It's the thought that counts!*

Amber: *And get this: Mom actually WANTS to attend my next tourney. I'm sure it's just an outlet for her MASSIVELY competitive ego—but, hey, it's something. Now I'll have to start working on Dad—which will be a tough sell until the day chess tournaments include goal posts, helmets, and ballpark franks.*

The recent emails became more and more insistent:

Denise: *So? What happens next?*

Amber: *Come on, tell us!*

Denise: *I shouldn't have to say this, it's around your neck: <u>Nulla dies sine linea!</u>*

Laurel: *Ahem, waiting for your chapters.*

Amber: *STILL waiting for your chapters!*

Denise: *WHERE the *#%@ ARE YOUR CHAPTERS!?!?!*

I emailed them the chapters I wrote in my jungle prison.

Mom: *I'm so proud of the progress you've made on your book. I can't wait to read it!*

(Oh, believe me, you can . . .)

And I can't wait to have my Vassar home again. I've missed you so much! Luckily I've been able to fill the time working with Amber. I must have done her some good as she's referred me to three other students at your school—not to mention two sets of parents and a standard poodle (who requires a comprehensive plan for winning the Westminster Dog Show). I must admit, I've missed life coaching. But don't worry, Vassar, I told them I certainly wasn't going to work outside the home until my daughter has completed her PhD. . . .

(Hmmm . . .)

Dad: *Where are you? According to my calculations, you should have returned from your trek seven days ago. I'm allowing your mom to assume I've heard from you. (We certainly don't need a relapse.) Please reply as promptly as possible and mark your email "priority" so I'll be sure to read it first thing. (Oh, and we've yet to receive your luggage. How did Gertrude send it? By water buffalo?) Don't forget to call us the day before you depart, to confirm your flight. I need time to plan the most efficient route to the airport since once again there's construction on the I-5. . . .*

I sent Dad a brief yet reassuring email saying I was alive and kicking. But I wasn't going to elaborate until I had talked to Grandma Gerd. *In depth.*

Once I was able to walk without assistance, Grandma Gerd and I took a slow stroll along the Mekong. It was our first chance to really talk since I'd found out The Big Secret. There were so many questions I'd been dying to ask her for so long, I jumped right in.

"Why did you give me to Mom and Dad?"

"I knew I couldn't raise a kid. Emotionally, I was in a dark place—just couldn't hack it. After all, I'd always thought I was barren. Although it turns out your grandpa was the infertile one all along. In those days, it was hard to tell. That's why we'd adopted Leonardo. Conceiving you was the shock of a lifetime—I was forty-three! Forty-four when you were born. Talk about a miracle. And the timing. Althea always knew she couldn't conceive, so she and Leonardo had been looking into adoption. And when you happened, well, I felt I was supposed to give you to them—as a gift."

Me, a gift.

We sat down on the same stone bench where we'd waited for Bounmy. The trek seemed eons ago.

"So when you called us in May . . ."

"I intended to blackmail your parents into letting you come on this trip." Grandma Gerd ran her hands through her silver hair, making it stick up all over. She looked like a concerned chrysanthemum. "See, at the time, I felt I couldn't just stand back and watch them turn you into a smug teen superachiever. Talk about arrogant—trying to change someone I didn't even know. And I had no right after 'abandoning' you. But I kept my distance all those years because Althea thought it was best: 'Having her birth mother around will be confusing. Too many variables,' she said. At the time, I agreed. I didn't want you to have—what's it called? Oh, 'conflicting loyalties.' Until I got that doozy of a thank-you note for my rubber ball birthday collage. I couldn't stomach who you were turning into. It hit me: You can't cut the cord completely. No matter how sharp the scissors, a tiny bit of fiber still connects the two."

Grandma Gerd reached down and picked up something off the ground, setting her silver bracelets clinking. A Laos Ale label. She smoothed out the wrinkles as she continued:

"I told them I'd spill the beans if they refused to let you come on this trip. Part of the deal was that I'd let them tell you *after* you got your PhD—when you were 'mature' enough to handle the truth. They didn't want anything to 'impede your scholastic achievement.'" She smiled. "Ooops."

I pulled my notebook out of a woven bag like Grandma Gerd's I'd bought at a shop in Luang Prabang. With a felt-tip pen, I wrote:

bubble, birth, too young, rubber ball, dying, egg.

Then I handed her the notebook and pen.

"This is what I overheard you say that night. Can you fill in the blanks of the rest of the conversation? Kind of like

Mad Libs, but in reverse. It's been driving me crazy. I've got to know or I'll never get these words out of my head."

"Mad Libs? Let's see if I can remember. . . ." She started to write, then paused. "It won't be a hundred percent accurate, but you just want the gist, right?"

"The gist will do just fine."

Ten minutes later, this is what she had:

*Me: "Face it, you two: Vassar's in a **bubble**. I think it would be good for her to come to Southeast Asia. Of course I won't tell her the truth about her **birth**. I'll leave that to you. . . . No, I don't think she's **too young**. She's sixteen. It's better to tell her sooner rather than later—a PhD won't help her process it any faster. . . . The thank-you note for last year's **rubber ball** birthday collage was obviously a cry for help. You know she's **dying** to get out of the stuffy world of academics and into the real world for a change. . . . Come on, you owe me. After all, she was conceived from my **egg**, Althea. Maybe Vassar would be interested in knowing that little fact—"*

Leonardo: "That's blackmail and you know it!"

"Finally!" I said. Now my intellectual curiosity was satiated. My unknown birth father would always be a loose end (which, to be honest, unsettled me), but at least one mystery was solved.

And now that I thought about it, Mom's doodle in her journal wasn't of a pear—but of a womb!

Grandma Gerd cleared her throat. Looking out at the

Mekong, she said, "I hope you're not too disappointed that Althea and Leon aren't your birth parents." Before I could answer, she hurried on: "Can you forgive me for deserting you—even if it really was for your own good?"

"Yes." And I meant it. "I don't know if it's because it hasn't sunk in yet or what, but I actually don't mind."

Relief flooded her face.

As I watched a yellow long-tail boat glide down the river, I thought:

I'm not who I thought I was, and I can't understand why I feel so relieved.

My identity had been turned completely inside out—I should have felt lost. Betrayed. Angry. But, instead, I felt *free*. Like a heavy backpack full of Latin textbooks had been lifted from my shoulders.

"Time to get you back. Don't want to overdo it." Grandma Gerd stood up.

I slung my woven bag over my shoulder. "So what should I call you?"

"Why don't you just call me what you've been calling me. 'Less variables' that way. And it'll be a whole lot easier on Althea. After all, she's still your mom, and Leonardo's still your dad. And you can go back to being Vassar. You've been a good sport."

"Oh, I don't know," I said. "I kinda like Frangipani. It's 'lyrical and musical and a fairy tale rolled all in one.' "

She laughed and put an arm around my shoulders. "Oh, why the heck didn't I blackmail your parents sooner?"

Returning to Melaka was like coming home, in a strange way. The familiar sights and sounds relaxed me. When I limped into The Golden Lotus Guesthouse lobby, Azizah had given me one look and said, "*Selamat Pagi!* Welcome to The Golden Lotus Guesthouse. Do you have a reservation?"

"It's me: Frangi—Vassar—Spore. Gertrude's daughter—granddaughter."

"Who is this girl? And why is she drunk so early in the morning hours?" she asked rhetorically, gesturing wildly with her turquoise nails—which of course matched her turquoise headband, blouse, and eye shadow.

Only when Grandma Gerd finally appeared with our backpacks did Azizah finally believe me. "What happen to her? Bandits? Full-moon party?"

"You could say that," said Grandma Gerd.

"So want bags now?" asked Azizah. She unlocked the door behind the counter to reveal a closet jam-packed with—

My ten monogrammed suitcases!

Grandma Gerd shrugged and smiled sheepishly. "Hey, I had to do what I had to do."

But I wasn't fazed in the least.

After removing my laptop from Bag #1, I turned to Azizah and gestured towards my luggage. "It's all yours."

Then I headed across the street for my last trip to a Southeast Asian Internet café.

ふ   ふ   ふ   ふ   ふ   ふ   ふ

Amber: *WOW! STELLAR! WAY TO GO! LOOOOOOOVE IT!*

Laurel: *We're all shouting, "Euge!" Can you hear us?*

Denise: *Overall, excellent execution. However, the whole hostage sit-uation is clichéd and politically incorrect. Opium dens in this day and age? And we think your twist about the birth mother—albeit clever—is highly unbelievable. Would never happen. Ovaries are—for all intents and purposes—dead after forty. But you do write convincingly, and it kept us turning the pages, so to speak. . . .*

Laurel: *Well done! But perhaps you could make The Big Secret a bit more realistic. Make the aunt an undercover agent or a mem-ber of Interpol. Then again, I did like the whole Eurasian reveal and I believed <u>everything</u> as it was happening, even when it went against my common sense. . . .*

Amber: *KISS! KISS! KISS! Give us another one, would ya!?*

Laurel: *If she were real, I'd adopt Stick Girl in a second!*

Denise: *Oh, and the whole Miracle Bra thing—come on.*

Amber: *We all like Sarah MUCH better now that she's been banged around a bit. And think she deserves Wayne after all.*

Denise: *By the way, what was the <u>real</u> Big Secret? Did your grandma tell you? Did you figure it out?*

Laurel: *You have quite the imagination! Making this all up out of your head—and on such short notice. P.S. Spoons?*

Denise, Amber, Laurel: *HOW DOES IT END??????????*

Just wait till they found out it was all *true.*

But how could I email them the ending when I didn't even know it myself?

CHAPTER TWO

The Collage

ON MY LAST NIGHT IN SOUTHEAST ASIA, GRANDMA Gerd barged through the door of our guesthouse room wearing her green rice bag skirt and carrying a large, flat package wrapped in brown paper. Her silver-grey hair was even more disheveled than ever and sprinkled with wood shavings. When she saw me, her eyes lit up.

"That's my girl!"

Though it itched and definitely did not flatter, I was wearing the blue rice bag skirt with the pink lotus. As a sort of . . . tribute.

"Here. I wanted to give you this now so you can pack it." She handed me the flat package.

I ripped off the brown paper to reveal:

A collage made entirely out of all the litter, mementos, clues, and Polaroids from the summer that pertained to me. *Everything* was layered on the canvas: the D-A-D-E-T-P-O letters, dried frangipani blossoms, Pepto-Bismol tablets, Crunky wrappers, airplane and bullet boat tickets, Fanta bottle caps, the Lotus cigarette pack, Stick Girl's stick, the wrapper from my pee bottle, my orange earplugs, the

Angkor Wat-*ch,* the sketch of the Ear Nibbler, a ball of sticky rice—and even one of Hanks's chops! (How had she managed that?) And the Polaroids of: me with bug-bite solar system, me stuck in the bullet boat, my bare ankles, Grandma and me with pizza sauce on our faces, the Paint by Numbers Jesus, Hanks and me in the café, the *apsara,* my blouse with the putrid "platypus" stain, the Vang family, Bounmy lighting up, Hanks wearing his Godings—and the one of a younger Grandma in her pouffy A-line dress from her Everything Book.

"Pregnant with me," I said, touching it.

"Pregnant with you."

The disparate elements somehow congealed to form a colorful map of Southeast Asia. It sounds bizarre, but in Grandma Gerd terms: It was sensational. Absolutely *sensational.*

Whereas before I'd want to destroy any photo or memory of me that wasn't perfect, I was now glad that all the parts of my journey were represented, both good and bad. Full Moon in Full Squat keister and all.

"I'm hanging this above my bed." I leaned it against the wall and blew my nose.

"I thought my rubber ball collage was hanging above your bed," said Grandma Gerd slyly.

"Okay, okay. I threw that away the day I got it. That was the old Vassar. But the new Frangipani will keep this *forever.*"

"Sure you will," she said. But I could tell she was pleased.

"Is the point of the collage to remind me of how life

doesn't always make sense at the time but in retrospect, all the pieces come together to form a coherent pattern?"

"Yeah, that." She laughed and gave me a hug. A cloud of sandalwood enveloped me. "So, Hanks is taking you on a date? Where?"

"I have no idea. And you know what? I don't care. Because—I'm LIMMING."

"Atta girl! At least my one good quality rubbed off on you. Maybe your planning quality will rub off on me—*right.*" She chuckled. "Well, I'm off to check in with Renjiro. I'm sure he's freaking out about all the packages piling up at MCT. Especially the one containing an entire dismantled Hmong hut. The piece is turning out more art installation than collage. Might just take up half the lobby. Well, at least he's getting his money's worth."

"But what about your focal point? Since you don't have the Iridescent Ruffled Beetle—"

"Or the *apsara.*" She grinned. "You know, Frangi, you were right about that. Sometimes in my quest for creative fulfillment, certain values just—*fffweet!*—fly right out the window. If it wasn't for you, I'd probably be in a cell in Phnom Penh as we speak."

"But what about your focal point?"

"You know, I'm not going to worry about it. I'm going to—"

"LIM!" we said in unison.

"I wish I could stay until you finish it."

"Oh, it'll take me months to complete. Don't worry, I'll take photos. But after that, I'm thinking of another trek—"

"Are you crazy?"

"—through the wilds of the Pacific Northwest."

"You're coming to Port Ann?" I asked, unable to contain my excitement. And I'd thought I wouldn't be seeing her for months—or even years.

"Think your parents would mind a visitor?"

"There aren't enough Tums and Valium in the world! But come, anyway."

"Nothing could stop me." Then, just as she was closing the door behind her, Grandma Gerd said, "Have fun tonight, Frangi. And tell Hanks he's one lucky guy."

Right. But first things first: I had a call to make.

CHAPTER THREE
Everything or Nothing?

"SO WE'LL BE AT THE AIRPORT ON SATURDAY AT 12:35 P.M.," said Dad, his chipper voice crackling thanks to the bad phone connection.

"Don't forget you'll only need one Volvo this time," I said.

He chuckled. "Then I take it you haven't purchased many souvenirs?"

"Nope. I've adopted Grandma Gerd's philosophy on those. Oh, and I'd give up all hope of my luggage arriving, if I were you."

Then I said casually: "By the way, Mom, I don't mind if you go back to life coaching."

"What's that?"

I'd definitely caught her off guard.

"I just couldn't wait until I got home to tell you how proud I am of all you've done for Amber—especially helping her with her pushy parents. *So* proud that I can't selfishly keep you all to myself. I want to share you with those less fortunate, goal-challenged souls who desperately need your expertise."

Was I laying it on too thick?

"You honestly feel that way about it?" she asked, voice quavering.

Guess not.

"Yes, yes, I do," I said firmly.

She cleared her throat. "Speaking of 'pushy parents,' I know it probably sounds completely outlandish, but it's struck me that perhaps at times I've been—"

"Althea, this sounds like a conversation for our next Hour of Reflection," said Dad hurriedly. "It would be much better in person—and much cheaper. It's been twelve minutes and thirty seconds already. And you know how pricey overseas rates are. Besides, Vassar will be home in less than forty-eight hours."

Just when it was getting juicy!

"You're right, Leon, much better to discuss it in person."

But before I got off the phone, I just *had* to test the waters:

"Would you two mind if I decided to go by a different name?"

"And why would you want to do that? 'Spore' is a perfectly sturdy, robust suffix. And conveniently easy to spell," Dad said.

"No, not Spore. My first name. Lately, I've become partial to—*Frangipani*."

Simultaneous intake of breath.

Then silence.

"Hello?"

"What has Gertrude told you?" Dad asked warily.

I told them the story of how I learned my real middle name.

"It's true, isn't it?" I asked.

I could hear them murmuring in hushed tones. Then Dad said, "Yes, it's true. And Gertrude is absolutely correct: It wasn't fair of us to legally drop your middle name and not tell her."

Mom's unsteady voice added: "Did she . . . did she tell you anything else?"

Do I tell them? Or wait until I get back? Or keep the truth from them like they've kept it from me?

Grandma Gerd had left it entirely up to me whether to tell Mom and Dad everything or nothing.

"You're right, Dad. This is one expensive call. And like you said, I'll be seeing you in less than forty-eight hours."

"But—"

"Wait—"

"I love you both—*no matter what.*"

And I hung up.

For the first time in my life, I wasn't going to plan everything out. I'd play it by ear and see what happened.

I would LIM.

CHAPTER FOUR
My Very First Last Date

T HE IRONY: I FINALLY RECOVER ENOUGH TO GO OUT ON a real date with Hanks—and my flight leaves the next day.

Get yer keister movin', Frangipani, he'll be here any minute.

Using some recently purchased cosmetics (Most Lovely brand) from the *kedai* next door, I made up my eyes and also applied brownish-red lipstick. But I didn't bother with foundation in this humidity—I'd learned my lesson.

Through the open window came the sounds of motorbikes, trishaws, and taxis intermingled with snatches of Malay and strains of whining music. A cacophony of honks. The smell of fried noodles wafted in, competing with the sweet fragrance of the frangipani on my dresser. The ceiling fan swished the warm air from one part of the room to the other.

I missed Southeast Asia already—and I hadn't even left.

I stepped back and consulted the mirror. Not bad. I no longer looked like a mugging victim. All that remained of my war wounds were a couple fading scratches on my cheek and the small scar on my nose. And all those bug bites had completely faded. Mom and Dad wouldn't even recognize me with my Most Lovely makeup, hair in a French roll, dark tan, and overall gauntness. If only I didn't have to wear my spare glasses and the rice bag skirt, the effect would be a whole lot more exotic. Although the skirt hung in a stiff tube around my legs, maybe with my new white silk blouse it didn't look half-bad—

"You look like a giant tube of toothpaste."

Maybe not.

Hanks stood in the doorway dressed in a dark blue mod 1960s suit with a skinny burgundy tie and black wingtip shoes—and his cowboy hat.

"Anything to promote good oral hygiene. New suit?"

"One of Renjiro's."

"What's going on there?" I pointed to his chops. They were a whole lot sparser than the usual ones.

"The old ones were startin' to chafe, so I'm growin' my own. They suck right now, but—"

"I like them. Very organic. And that suit—very slick. Like it, too."

He threw his hat onto my bed, ran a hand over his shiny black pomp, straightened his tie, then sauntered over to me.

"And *I* like noses that click on girls named after flowers." He gently wiggled my nose with his finger—*click, click*. And then we were kissing.

This time was much more romantic. No holding my breath—and no holding urine.

Old Spice.

Flip-flop flip-flop flip-flop flip-flop flip-flop flip-flop flip-flop flip-flop flip-flop!

Why, oh why, couldn't he live in Washington? Or why couldn't I live here? Figures when I find the perfect guy, he's located halfway across the globe.

"What do your folks think about you havin' visitors?" he asked after we finally broke apart.

"Grandma Gerd already asked me that." I untangled my fingers from his hair and smoothed it back—but left a few decorative strands hanging over his left eye.

"I'm talkin' about me. I'll only be a couple states away. Wyoming. Dad's lettin' me go to Little Creek Community College after all. I guess Gerd and Renjiro brainwashed him into thinkin' I'd single-handedly saved your life or somethin'. And deserved some sort of 'positive reinforcement.' Whatever works." He attempted to play it casual, but he was obviously excited.

Hanks would be merely a state or two away? I had to sit down. The room was spinning.

"Wow," I said, once I could think clearly. "I can't believe it!"

"I take it you're not too disappointed—"

The kiss I gave almost toppled him.

"Hold yer horses," he gasped. "Save some for later."

Wait until Denise, Amber, and Laurel met my genuine Malaysian Cowboy in the flesh! Then: "Do you realize this is our first official date?"

"You mean *your* first official date ever. What would John Pepper say?"

"Shut up, cowboy."

"Yes, ma'am."

"And give me a kiss."

"Yes, ma'am."

This one was the best yet. Spinning. More *flips,* more *flops.*

We pulled apart and just stood there staring at each other. Not quite believing that this was really happening to us. To *us.*

He smiled and grabbed my hand. His silver horseshoe ring felt cool on my skin.

"Ready, little lady?"

"Wait." Without releasing him, I pulled him over to the dresser and picked up a frangipani blossom. I inhaled the creamy petals, then tucked it into my hair. Then I led him over to the bed, scooped up his cowboy hat, and plopped it back on his head.

"Ready."

And still holding hands, Sarah and Wayne headed downstairs, past Azizah and her soaps, out the door, and into the street.

CHAPTER FIVE

Frangipani's Revised Life Goals

Non scholae sed vitae discimus.
We do not learn for school, but for life.
—Seneca

1. LIM 24/7.

2. Travel light.

3. Legally make Frangipani my middle name (again) and go by that instead of Vassar.

4. Plans and goals = guides, not absolutes.

5. Live my life, not my parents'.

6. Learn for learning's sake.

7. Consider ALL colleges, not just Vassar (with special attention to colleges in the vicinity of Wyoming).

8. Spend summers with Grandma Gerd.

9. Get soft contact lenses.

10. Send nicotine patches to Bounmy, Polo cologne to Vang, and somehow get a care package to Stick Girl.

11. Research Thailand.

12. Find more Godings.

13. Research God, spirituality, miracles, trick bras, etc.

14. Marry a 5'8", chops-wearing Malaysian cowboy for love.

15. Complete my novel for AP and AAP English credit. ~~And make Valedictorian. Accolades and Pulitzer to follow.~~ (LIM, Frangi, LIM!)

16. Buy Laurel a spoon in the airport or she'll kill me!

17. AND NEVER, EVER TAKE THE TOILET FOR GRANTED AGAIN.

Epilogue

"*L*ET EACH OF US EXAMINE HIS THOUGHTS; HE WILL FIND them wholly concerned with the past or the future. We almost never think of the present, and if we do think of it, it is only to see what light it throws on our plans for the future. The present is never without end. The past and the present are our means, the future alone our end. Thus we never actually live, but hope to live, and since we are always planning how to be happy, it is inevitable that we should never be so."—Pascal's *Pensées*

AUTUMN CORNWELL'S LIST OF ACKNOWLEDGMENTS

In the spirit of Vassar Spore, I'd like to list all those who helped catapult *Carpe Diem* into the world:

1. My parents, William and Patricia Erickson, for jumpstarting my love of Southeast Asian culture as an MK in New Papua, and my love of reading by refusing to own a TV—thus forcing my sister and me to check out stacks of library books every week out of sheer desperation.

2. My sister, Danica Childs, fan of textured, virtually unlikable heroines adventuring in exotic locales, who wanted me to write the book we'd always wanted to read.

3. My supportive in-laws and extended family, who never suggested alternate employment to the unpublished writer in their midst.

4. Friend and fellow writer Ruth Campbell, for her absolutely *insane* level of encouragement.

5. Artist Helen Homer, who taught me how to see the extraordinary in the ordinary—and who really did "sleep wrong!"

6. All the friends I made in my travels and treks through Malaysia, Vietnam, Cambodia, Thailand, Laos, and Burma—from tour guides to engineers to refugees to entire hill tribes. Especially those living in countries under oppression.

7. Author April Young Fritz who, through SCBWI, was the first person outside of family to read my manuscript and whose enthusiasm propelled me to send it to . . .

8. My enthusiastic agent Rosemary Stimola, who in her infinite wisdom sent it to . . .

9. My enthusiastic editor Liz Szabla, who embraced Vassar, Hanks, and Grandma Gerd wholeheartedly enough to put their adventures in print.

10. And finally, my husband J.C., to whom this book is dedicated: Best Friend, Sugar Daddy, Constructive Critic, Patron, Cheerleader, Soulmate, Big Cheese—who, in the spirit of Hanks, will no doubt say to "cut the sap and end this already."

GO FISH

AUTUMN CORNWELL

Where do you find inspiration for your writing?
Everything that happens to me, *every* place I go, and *everyone* I meet is material for my books. (So beware!)

What would your readers be most surprised to learn about you?
That eighty percent of the situations and adventures in *Carpe Diem really* happened to me (in one form or another, and allowing for artistic embellishment, of course!). *SPOILERS!* Including: trying to pee in a bottle in the middle of the night in a jungle hut (my husband was the one holding the blanket!); using the Bullet Boat facilities; the Nibbler sampling my ear; having the runs at Angkor Wat; shooting an M16 (research!); meeting Stick Girl; sleeping in the opium den; and even getting held hostage—although it was much briefer than in the book and included a run-in with the Laos Mafia, which I didn't write up because then it would seem *way* over the top. (Truth is *always* stranger than fiction! At least in *my* life!)

Which of your characters is most like you?
Like Dr. Jekyll and Mr. Hyde, I'm half Vassar, half Grandma Gerd. I find myself channeling them alternately throughout the day.

I've always been a planner, whether it has to do with my career, a vacation, a reading list, or life in its entirety. Yet I'm also creative, right-brained, an adventurer—and I embrace the unexpected. (And often use it for material!) I do find it tough to continually LIM (Live in the Moment) like Grandma Gerd—my brain is always whirling: "Sure, this is a fun picnic—but what are we doing *next*?" Or wondering if I should be doing something else instead of what I *am* doing. Grandma Gerd was always present in whatever activity she was doing—didn't concern herself about the past or the future, only that particular moment. There is something very freeing about that.

What do you want readers to remember about your books?

The idea that they can live their life as an adventure—whether they're in Angkor Wat or in homeroom. And I'd like my readers to practicing *limming*. To Live in the Moment and appreciate where they are in life right now. Not to throw planning out the window—just not allow it to inhibit the enjoyment of each individual moment *while* it happens. To strike the right balance between planning and limming. Basically, to apply the Pascal quote at the end of the book to their lives.

What's your favorite childhood memory?

My *entire* time as a missionary kid in Irian Jaya: I ate guavas from our own trees, played in waist high mud on river banks, visited tribes of reformed headhunters and cannibals, lived through an 8.0 earthquake, cavorted outside during monsoons, almost drowned three times, watched my sister fall into an open sewer in Jakarta, kept my own pet fruit bat—and loved (almost) every single minute of it.

What do you wish you could do better?

I wish I could master the art of getting up in the morning! Oh, to be a morning person and bound out of bed the minute the sun's rays hit your pillow. Instead, I'd rather burrow deeper into my duvet and sleep a minimum of ten hours. (No maximum). My dad used to have to squirt me with a spray bottle to get me up on time for school and church—that's how bad I was (am)! (Seriously, until I had my son, Dexter, my schedule would be to write until 4AM and get up at noon.)

What do you like best about yourself?

The ability to live my life as an adventure at all times—whether trekking in the jungles of Burma or changing my son's diapers at home.

What's your idea of the best meal ever?

Anything Asian: Thai *thom kha kai*, Korean *bee bim bop*, Indonesian *lumpia,* Laotian sticky rice and *larb*. Yum! (But for a writing break pick-me-up, I swear by a pot of hearty English tea—like PG Tips—and peanut butter and honey toast peppered with raisins.)

What makes you laugh out loud?

My husband J.C. totally cracks me up with his one-liners. Like, there's nothing that bugs him more than when I'm writing, I ask him for his opinion and *never* take his advice. Which happens a lot. The other day, we were sitting in the living room and I asked him: "Which is funnier: 'hindquarters' or 'buttocks'?" And he turned to me and said, "Pretend I'm at work."

Ha! Maybe it's just me. Or you had to be there. In any case, it's good *I* think he's funny since I'm stuck with him!

Where do you write your books?

My favorite place to write is at our 1960s Airstream trailer on the Central Coast of California. We bought it with some of my advance money and restored it in a "retro" style—think tiki and bamboo. Thanks to my saint of a husband and angelic in-laws, I'm able to get away periodically to this hide-a-way to write while they watch my son Dexter. I play Henry Mancini tunes and write for hours at a time—interrupted only by making pots of tea and counting jellyfish on the beach.

What was your first job?

One of my first jobs after graduating from college was working as a tour guide for the historic Hearst Castle in San Simeon, California. After a couple months of instruction, I regaled visitors from around the world with the history of William Randolph Hearst, architecture, art, botany, and the Golden Age of Hollywood. I had to wear a uniform and relay humorous anecdotes about movie stars cavorting across the lawns. A fun gig. Unfortunately, you couldn't accept tips—which was a bummer, since it would have helped me pay off my student loans!